THE **FINE** LINE

ALICIA KOBISHOP

For Amy,
Here's to living life
with no regrets. ♡

A. Kob

This book is a work of fiction. Names, characters, places, and incidents either are products of the author's imagination or are used fictitiously. Any resemblance to actual events or locales or persons, living or dead, is entirely coincidental.

Published by
Alicia Kobishop
PO Box 510183
New Berlin, WI 53151

Cover by Mayhem Cover Creations
Edited by Angela Barber Farley

ISBN-13: 978-1494232061
ISBN-10: 1494232065

For Don
My best friend…and so much more.

Prologue

Some people wear their hearts on their sleeves. I learned a long time ago that preserving one's heart means keeping it protected. Sheltered. My heart is hidden deep within the secure layers of my soul, where it rests easy with the knowledge that nothing can penetrate its everlasting impervious shell.

<u>Twelve Years Ago</u>

Yelling. Always yelling. The hardwood floor in my bedroom chilled my toes as I slid out of my bed to see what was going on. I wouldn't dare leave my room, though. I knew better. As I tip-toed to the bright crack in the door, something crashed to pieces, and I squeezed Mama Bear tight.

Is Mommy crying?

My hand found a place on the cool metal door knob as I peeked through the crack. I brought Mama Bear up to my chin so she could see too. Her soft, fuzzy fur tickled me. Mommy sat on the floor with her back against the hallway wall, her head in her hands while Daddy stood tall above her. Her shoulders lifted up and down as she wept.

No, Mommy, don't cry!

"I want a divorce," she whispered.

What was a divorce? Whatever it was, Daddy didn't seem too happy about it. He crouched down so that his eyes were across from hers. Fisting her t-shirt, he yanked her close to him.

1

With the other hand, he pointed his finger at her, jabbing her as he spoke. His voice stayed quiet, and I couldn't hear what he said, but I knew it was something scary.

The door knob clinked as I lost my grip on it, and both of their heads turned to look at me. My eyes widened, and I gasped. I ran back to bed as fast as I could, quickly covering myself in my blankie. *Oh no, I dropped Mama Bear!* My door creaked open, and light came through the seams of my blankie.

"Olivia?" Daddy said softly.

I didn't answer. Mommy was always telling me to make smart choices. I chose to stay perfectly still and not to breathe too loudly, but it wasn't easy because my heart was pounding hard. It was a smart choice, though, because after a few seconds, the door creaked closed. I was safe. Mommy would be very proud of me.

I peered at the floor, searching for Mama Bear, but she was nowhere to be seen. Daddy must've taken her. *Who's gonna sleep with me?* I pulled my knees to my chest and held onto them tightly. Mommy says I'm brave. Brave girls don't need silly toys. Brave girls sleep by themselves.

Eight Years Ago

It's been a year since Dad told me I wouldn't be able to spend time at his house anymore. He said he was leaving to get a new start. At first, his emails came daily and postcards came weekly, but I haven't gotten either for at least a month. Mom says he's moved on, with his new wife and baby, and that it's the best thing for all of us.

I was glad to have Kevin. He loved me and Mom. Happiness didn't even begin to describe how I felt when Mom told me he was moving in with us. If he lived with us, it would mean I would get to see magic tricks and laugh at his stories every day.

Mom told me about the accident last week. Kevin got hit by a drunk driver. I knew something was wrong when she dropped the phone on the floor and began sobbing. I had seen her cry before—but never like that.

I stayed with Nana for five days after that call, and when I returned home, Mom took me into my room, sat me down on my bed, and broke the news. The funeral service had been the prior day. Mom thought it would be best if I didn't attend because it would be too difficult for me. I cried myself to sleep that night. I couldn't get the thought of Kevin, being buried deep in the ground, out of my mind.

The next morning, I thought a lot about the way things work, and I figured out that nothing's forever. Nothing. I had to be strong. Brave. I hated being sad. I hated crying. I vowed to find a way to make sure I never felt this horrendous feeling ever again.

Three Years Ago

I glanced around our heated garage as Adam poured the amber liquid into our little glasses. All the tool chests and auto supplies had been packed up and hauled out. He filled his glass to the brim while mine was only filled a quarter of the way. He said I couldn't have a full glass because I was only fourteen.

Hanging out with Adam came naturally. It was easy. He was much younger than Mom, but I was under the misguided impression that they were in love, regardless of his age.

Normally, the whiskey we shared was in celebration of an accomplishment. A new paint job, installing the new engine, fixing the interior. I had spent most of my evenings and weekends for the last three years watching Adam restore his 1968 Pontiac GTO. He bragged to people about how much I helped him, but really, I just watched him work and handed him tools as we talked.

Today, we toasted goodbye. It would be the last time I'd ever see him. My throat burned as the liquor flowed down it, but I welcomed the feeling. It reminded me of good times.

"I'm gonna miss you, Sweetie," he said with tears in his eyes. "I asked her to marry me, you know. She said no."

Anger quickly flooded my system, washing away the heartbreak. How could she say no? It had taken me over two years to let my guard down around him. Two years to break the vow that I had kept for so long and let myself feel again. *She* was making him go away. This was *her* fault.

I watched as Adam rolled his refurbished car down the driveway and out of my life. Without thought, my body stormed into the house in search of my mother. I found her staring blankly out the living room window.

"How could you say no?" I screamed.

"Livie, what are you talking about?"

"He told me, Mom! He told me he asked you to marry him!"

Her shoulders sunk as she let out a sigh. Then, her expression turned angry. "Did he tell you he was seeing another woman? Did he tell you that he asked me to marry him only after I found out?"

My heart stopped. My mind barely comprehended what my mother had just told me. It couldn't be true. Adam loved us. With regret in her eyes, she rushed toward me with open arms.

"No." I held out my hand. "NO!" Tears spilled out of my eyes as I ran to my bedroom, locked my door, and flopped belly down onto my bed, sobbing uncontrollably into my pillow.

Why does everyone I love have to leave?

Never again. I'm done. This is the last time I will ever have this feeling.

Chapter One

"Olivia, do you know those people in the parking lot?" My manager approached me, brows furrowed in worry.

I had just finished facing the aisles at Frank's Drugstore, my employer for the last nine months. I had gotten the job just after my seventeenth birthday.

The night had been slow. Monotonous. And I couldn't wait to get off work. I walked to the glass front doors and peeked outside where I saw a familiar silver Chevy Impala parked in the back of the small lot. It was an older model, about six years old, but still in mint condition.

My best friend, Melody, leaned against it, cigarette in hand, as she laughed at something one of the boys must've said. Her boyfriend Nate was with her, along with our good friend Isaac. I wondered if it was the fact that they were all smoking that caused my manager's nervousness.

"They're here for me, Stacy," I reassured her.

"Should've known," she smiled. "Have a fun night."

It felt refreshing to take an outdoor breath. The fluorescent lights and stale, air-conditioned air had suffocated me. I approached the car and smiled as Melody ran up to me and wrapped her arms around me.

"Hey, Liv," she said, as she squeezed the air out of me. "It's about time. We're going to River Fest. Hop in."

Melody and I scooted into the backseat while the boys stayed up front. Nate started his car and cranked up the volume on a Rihanna song as he pulled out of the parking lot and onto "the strip," a highway where teenage boys and girls drove fast and cranked their music.

"Jesus, Nate! Turn that down! I wanna to talk to Liv!" shouted Melody.

Nate turned around, but only half-way, and put his hand to his ear as if to say, *"What? I can't hear you."*

"I said, TURN IT DOWN!" Melody yelled.

Nate shrugged as if he had no clue what Melody was saying and continued driving, leaving the volume right where it was. He smiled as he turned to Isaac, and although I couldn't hear them due to the incredibly loud stereo, I could see that they were both getting a kick out of Nate's little joke.

Melody and I looked at each other briefly, then broke out into laughter. Clearly, we weren't going to be having any meaningful conversations during this drive, so we enjoyed the music, singing along and "seat-dancing" to the music of Drake and Imagine Dragons.

Even though Melody and I were polar opposites, we accented each other. The introvert in me loved her outgoing nature. Not to say I couldn't have fun…It just took me a little longer to open up to people. Guys died for Melody's long dark brown hair, amber eyes, curvy figure. I thought of myself as a little more ordinary…tall and thin with blue eyes and long, wavy, strawberry blond hair. Despite our differences, we clicked from the moment we met, and quickly became best friends. I knew I could count on her for anything.

We arrived at River Fest ten minutes later. As we drove around, trying to find a parking spot, Isaac turned the volume down and pulled his cell phone out of his pocket, bringing it to his ear.

"Hey, man...Yeah, we're here," Isaac said into the phone. "I know. Sorry, we had to wait for Liv to get off work...She's Mel's friend...Ok, see you in a few."

Apparently, we were late. I didn't feel good about being the reason we were late. Hell, I didn't even know I was coming here tonight.

"Who are we meeting here?" I asked.

"Just some friends. Logan and Carter. They're cool," Isaac replied as we got out of the car and began walking toward the festival. I could hear a mixture of laughter and screams from the people on the rides and the low pound of the music in the distance.

"You'll *love* Logan," Melody chimed in. "He's..." She looked at her boyfriend, then back at me and grinned, "Cute." Nate rolled his eyes. She may as well have winked and given me a thumbs up for God's sake. That girl was not subtle.

Mel constantly tried to set me up with boys, and it never failed to be incredibly awkward. She knew how I felt about relationships—that they're a waste of time–but that never stopped her from trying. I hoped this Logan person didn't think this was some kind of set-up.

She tried with Isaac a few months ago, and although he's a great guy and extremely attractive in a punk rocker sort of way, there were never any romantic sparks. After hanging out together a few times, we came to the mutual conclusion that we had fun together—but it was a platonic kind of fun and nothing more.

We didn't have to walk far before we got to the tent where we were meeting the other guys. There was a rock band playing, and it looked like people were getting carded as they entered the tent.

I turned to Isaac, concerned. "They're not going to let me in there. I don't have a fake ID."

Pretending that I hurt his feelings, he brought his hands to his heart and leaned back as he grinned. "Have you no faith, Liv?"

"Faith that they'll let a seventeen-year-old into a beer tent?" I smiled. "No. No, I don't." Pointing back and forth between Nate and Isaac, I continued, "At least you two probably pass for twenty-one. Especially Nate with his scruff. Mel and I are kinda screwed here."

Nate and Isaac, both nineteen, had completed their freshman year of college. Nate was a fan of the "five-day shadow," as opposed to the "five o'clock shadow," but it looked good on him, and Mel thought it was hot. Melody met Nate a year ago on the strip and they've been inseparable ever since.

When we got to the tent, the bouncer held up his thumb and pointer finger with a blank, *"I don't care"* look on his face, motioning that he wanted to see our IDs. Just as I was about to say *"told you so"* to Isaac, a guy with dark chocolate, medium-length hair and the most unique eyes I'd ever seen walked up behind the bouncer, nodded at Isaac, and placed his hand on the bouncer's shoulder.

Then his eyes, a bright mixture of gray and green with a little bit of amber in the middle—which I suppose is called hazel—locked with mine and it was like being in some kind of bizarre, yet strangely enticing, time warp. I'd heard about moments like this in movies and books, where time slows down or stops all together, but I never thought they were actually real. I couldn't seem to look away, and neither did he. His head cocked to the side as a barely noticeable grin formed on his lips which in turn caused my heart to pound furiously in my ears, over the loud music inside the tent.

What the hell was happening? And why was I suddenly nervous? My initial thought was that it could be the fact that he looked like an *American Eagle* model, but then again, I had been around good looking guys before and never had this reaction.

"They're with me, Matt," he said, not once taking his eyes off me.

Completely unsettled by my unusual reaction to him, I forced myself to break his stare and began focusing on the bouncer instead, a brawny guy with a shaved head and tattooed arm. I could see a vein bulging out of his neck, right above the collar of his tight black t-shirt.

"This is *it*, man," Matt the bouncer grumbled, attempting to control his irritation. "No one else comes in after this, who shouldn't be here."

My hand grasped Isaac's arm as we quickly passed by him. Nate and Melody trailed behind us, hand in hand. The tent was more crowded than I thought it would be. Smoke mixed with the smell of beer, and greasy food drenched the air. The band had the crowd going and sounded awesome, but I didn't recognize any of the music they were playing. I wondered if they wrote their own stuff.

"Liv, Logan. Logan, Liv," Isaac introduced me to the guy with the eyes.

The corners of Logan's mouth turned up as he studied me and with a gleam in his eyes. He cocked his head to the side. "So *you're* the one we've been waiting for."

My cheeks began to burn. I hated being late. And I hated that my cheeks were burning.

"I didn't ask them to wait for me." I tried to defend myself. "I didn't even know we were coming here tonight."

He seemed intrigued. "Don't worry about it, sweetheart. You're worth the wait." With a slight grin, he turned to walk toward the bar.

I rolled my eyes, "Sweetheart? Oh, that's smooth."

He looked back at me, still amused but clearly taken aback that I had just called out his poor attempt at sweet talk. He must not get that too often. I wouldn't imagine girls are much of a challenge for someone who looks like him. After a moment, his eyes softened.

"Really, it's no big deal. We weren't waiting long," he assured me. "C'mon, let's get a drink."

Melody grabbed my hand instead.

"We'd rather dance!" she shouted and pulled me to the dance floor. Melody and I never had a problem letting loose on a dance floor, and this time would be no different. It had been a while since we'd been out to see a band, and this one currently performed an upbeat song with pounding bass.

We enjoyed the moment fully, swinging our hips and whipping our hair around, and before we knew it, Nate and Isaac were dancing with us. Nate and Mel, being extremely comfortable with each other, began grinding to the beat in a more provocative way while Isaac and I kept our dancing fun and innocent.

As the beat of the drum pounded and the strum of the electric guitar sang, Isaac took my hand and twirled me so that my back was against his chest. In that moment, as we moved against each other, I glanced at the bar and spotted Logan, with whom I assumed was Carter. Carter seemed to be in a deep…flirtation…with the pretty red-headed bartender, but

Logan didn't seem quite as interested in their conversation. His eyes were on us.

Isaac twirled me back to face him, and we continued to dance. A few songs later, after exhausting our energy, we headed to the bar to join Logan and Carter. After getting our drinks, I noticed Logan pull his cell phone out from his pocket and answered it. His eyes intensified, but only slightly, as he listened.

"I'll be there in an hour," he said into his phone, just before returning it to his pocket.

He turned to me with a minor look of distress in his eyes.

"Liv, it was a pleasure meeting you," he said as he reached out his hand. When I placed my hand in his, one corner of his mouth turned up, and his eyes seemed to glow. He lifted one eyebrow up and continued, "Maybe next time won't be so brief."

I nodded, saying something along the lines of "nice meeting you too" and watched as he said his goodbyes to the rest of us and left with Carter. A strange pang of disappointment fluttered in my chest as he walked away, and I found myself wondering if I would ever see him again. I shook my head to snap myself out of the weird, unfamiliar trance I was in, remembering that I would not allow myself to be flustered by a boy. Even if he did have the most incredible eyes I had ever seen.

We enjoyed the rest of our night, playing carnival games and going on the rides. Nate even won a ginormous stuffed unicorn for Mel, and Isaac was thrilled when he scored a girl's phone number. After stuffing ourselves with funnel cakes and cotton candy, we called it a night. They dropped me off at Frank's Drugstore so I could pick up my Ford Focus and drive myself home.

I made it home at 12:25pm...five minutes before curfew. The fact that I even had a curfew made no sense to me since there was rarely anyone home to enforce it. My mother and stepfather had opened a small pub, making it extremely rare for them to be home before me on a weekend night. Per the "arrangement" I had with them, however, I was supposed to call the pub when I arrived home each night so they could verify I was home on time.

Technically, I could call from anywhere and they wouldn't have a clue about it, but I followed their rules anyway. They didn't want me to text because they preferred to actually hear my voice, and they didn't want me to call their cell phones because they were too preoccupied to notice their cells when they were bartending. I grabbed my phone and dialed the number to the pub as I walked to my room.

"American Pub!" a man answered.

"Can I talk to Grace please?" I replied.

"What?!" he yelled, trying to shout above the pounding background music.

"Grace! Is Grace there?!" I hollered, with my voice echoing through the quiet house.

"Hang on!"

Geez, this wasn't going well already. It must've been a busy night at the pub. I waited for a moment, listening to the laughter and fun that the pub patrons were having. Finally, my mother was on the line.

"Hello?"

"Hi, Mom. I'm home."

"What?! Who is this?!"

"Mom, it's me! I'm home!"

"What?! I can't hear you!!!"

Oh Lord, here we go, "I...AM...HOME!!!"

There was a short pause.

"Livie, I can barely hear you, but thanks for calling, sweetheart," she said in a quieter, more relaxed tone. She must've looked at the time. "I'll see you in the morning," she finished.

She hung up, and it was suddenly very dark and quiet in the house. The exhaustion from my full day hit me hard in that moment. I slipped off my sandals, flopped onto my bed, and closed my eyes, making a mental note to sit down with my mother in the morning to revisit the texting-when-I-get-home-instead-of-calling conversation. A simple text would be so much easier.

Chapter Two

The sweet, buttery aroma of bacon and eggs mixed with coffee, stirred me awake the next morning. My eyes cracked open as I glanced at my alarm clock to see a blurry, green "9:07AM." Crap, it was already late, and I had a full day of work ahead of me. I sprung out of bed, causing a blinding head-rush. Once I felt normal, I dressed and went to the kitchen.

"Morning, Livie," my mother chirped.

She was the "mother" of all morning people. It baffled me the way she could go to sleep later than me, yet wake up before me. She seemed to only get about six hours of sleep per night, yet she was always so energetic in the morning. I wished I had that problem.

"Morning," I mumbled.

"Hey, will you bring home my cellphone from the pub? I left it there last night."

"Aren't you going there later?"

"No," she glanced over at my stepdad who was reading the paper at the kitchen table. "Jeff and I are taking the night off to go to dinner and a movie."

Mom met Jeff two years ago and married him a year later. He was a nice enough guy, and treated us well…the way they all do at first. As much as my mom wanted me to form a strong bond with him, the way I did with the others, I couldn't bring myself to get close to him. We were cordial and friendly with each other, but really…what would be the point of anything more than that? Especially considering there was absolutely no doubt in my mind that, at some point, he'd be gone.

Shortly after Mom and Jeff took a lease out on the pub, they had offered to pay me to clean it on the weekends, and I enthusiastically accepted when I found out how much they would compensate me to do it. It was a dirty job, but it only took me about three hours, and I couldn't pass up the pay. I made it more enjoyable by cranking up the music and taking time to practice my pool game.

The pub opened at 2:00PM on Saturdays, which was the same time I was scheduled to work at Frank's today. I had to get going so that I would have time to shower before Frank's. I quickly shoveled down breakfast and headed out the door.

*

Mel was the only one waiting for me in the parking lot when I left Frank's that night. It had been a while since we had even a little bit of one-on-one time together, so I was glad to see her alone. Leaning on the hood of her white Pontiac Grand Prix, she texted on her cell as I approached. Hearing my heels click on the cement, she looked up with a gleam in her eyes and gave me a grin.

"There's going to be people at Gavin's tonight. You wanna go?" she asked.

I shrugged. "Sure. I've had a long day. I could use a little fun."

Gavin, a friend of Nate's, was a soon-to-be college sophomore who met Nate in a study group last year. Between his job, classes, and frequent parties at his place, the kid worked hard and played even harder. His modest ranch-style house—

which was the gathering place for the group of friends Mel and I had adopted when she started dating Nate—had a partially finished basement with a pool table, wet bar, and a few old mismatched couches and chairs arranged in a half-circle in front of a TV. We could either get crazy or just kick back there.

One kick-back night, a few months ago, Gavin and I got into a deep conversation about how he managed to buy the house just before his nineteenth birthday. He majored in real-estate and while interning part-time in a local real-estate office, he had heard about this foreclosed house, just before it actually went on the market. He'd get an incredibly sweet deal on it, with his mortgage being equal to what he had currently been paying in rent at his apartment, but apparently, he had to practically beg his parents to co-sign the mortgage so that his loan would be approved. They agreed to co-sign after he had convinced them of the one-of-a-kind investment opportunity, and promised that he'd be solely responsible for paying the mortgage on time every month. The loan was approved, and he got the house.

Melody and I approached his place and spotted Nate and Gavin just outside the garage, standing around a flawless canary yellow muscle car with the hood up. Nate walked toward us as we stepped out of Mel's car.

"Do you know what that is, baby?" He grinned at Melody with a twinkle in his eyes as he laced his fingers in hers and pulled her toward the car. I followed behind them.

"A car?" she responded, sarcastically.

"*That*…is a 1969 Ford Mustang." Then he rattled off some information about the engine.

"Okay?" she said, clearly not as enthusiastically as Nate had hoped. Noticing his disapproval, she continued with a little more encouragement, "It's a pretty car, baby."

17

"Whose is it?" I asked

The car-hood slammed shut and there stood my answer, all six foot three of him, stopping me in my tracks.

The first thing that caught my attention? Abs. Perfectly tanned, contoured ones that led down to an equally defined V-line. *Damn.*

Next? A strong, muscular chest and solidly shaped shoulders that were attached to a smooth as sin neck that I could easily see myself kissing. Yep, I was already fantasizing about it.

When my gaze wandered up to a warm grin and inviting hazel eyes that had a million and one emotions behind them, I became thoroughly fixed on the man in front of me. I'm not sure how long I had been standing there, staring, but it must've been longer than socially acceptable.

"You like what you see, Liv?" a shirtless Logan whispered softly with an amused smirk, as I finally snapped out of it.

Shit! Did he just say that? Was I that obvious?

I could feel my cheeks getting red and my heart began to skip beats as I began to approach him. Of course he would notice me staring at him. The others were already walking into the house, so thankfully I don't think they had heard him.

"Shut up." I inwardly cringed right after my response came out. *Oh yeah, real nice comeback, Liv.*

His eyes sparkled as he let out a chuckle. My gaze searched for something to focus on, anywhere but his eyes, as I desperately tried to come up with something witty and clever to say, but nothing came to me.

What the hell was going on with me? I didn't usually get so flustered around boys—even exceptionally attractive ones. I had a lot of fun with some of them, but there were never any expectations, or God forbid…feelings…and that's how I liked it. There was something about Logan, however, that gave me….butterflies. This was not a sensation I was fond of.

"I was talking about the car." he replied, lifting a brow. Still smiling, he grabbed his t-shirt out of the back of his shorts and put it on. "Better?" he teased.

I rolled my eyes, knowing full well he was not talking about the car. Clearly, he was not lacking in confidence. In an effort to change the subject, I asked, "So, where did you get it anyway? The car, I mean."

I'm not sure why I felt I had to clarify that. I mean, what did he think I meant…where did he get his abs?

His smile toned down a bit, but not all the way, and his eyes became distant. "My dad and I spent five years restoring it. He left it to me when he passed away last year."

"Oh my God, I'm so sorry." I was floored. Could this conversation have gotten any worse?

He must've noticed my panic, and his eyes softened. He hooked his arm around my neck and began to walk me toward the house where the others had already migrated. "Don't worry about it, Liv. I'm okay."

My heart hurt for him, and as we entered the house, I found myself wondering about his life.

In the basement, the party was already starting. I could tell it was going to be more of a "get crazy" night than a "kick back" night. School starting on Monday for Mel and me meant this would be our last party of the summer.

Rock music blared. Nate and Mel were at the pool table starting a game of doubles with Isaac and the girl he met at River Fest, while Gavin poured himself a drink at the bar. Several people lingered around the couches that I didn't recognize.

I caught Gavin's eye as we approached the bar.

"Liv!" He pointed at me. "You want the usual?"

I smiled and nodded, delighted that he remembered my drink of choice.

"Hi Logan." A girl with a slim but voluptuous figure, in a form-fitting halter dress, ran up to Logan and wrapped her arms around him. Bright pink streaks and the ends embellished her long, straight, bleach-blond hair.

"What's up Chloe." Logan simply stated, as if he weren't expecting an answer from her. Unfazed by her affection, he continued around to the other side of the bar, where he and Gavin knocked knuckles, leaving her behind looking disappointed. While she walked away, he helped himself to a beer from the mini-fridge, then stayed behind the bar with Gavin and started some car talk. Clearly the guys were friends...why had I never seen him here before?

As Gavin handed me my drink, his phone lit up, interrupting their conversation, and when Logan's attention moved from Gavin to me, and he *winked* at me, I realized that yet again, I had been lingering with my eyes on him like the Logan groupie that I had obviously just become. My face scrunched up in disgust partially from the wink, and partially because of the way I turned into a heart-palpitating gawker around him.

Let's be real, I liked the wink. And by the enormous smile that just appeared on his face, he liked my weird reaction to it. On the other hand, I didn't enjoy the way my palms had just gotten all sweaty, so instead of prolonging my discomfort, I walked over to join Mel by the pool table.

"Hey, girl. I was wondering when you'd finally get down here." Melody actually winked this time. Seriously...what was with all the winking? Then she leaned closer and joked, "I was hoping it would've taken longer. Ugh, you need to work on your game if you want to land a guy like Logan."

My hand instinctively smacked her in the arm, while I almost choked on my drink, "Melody! You know me better than that. I'm not trying to *land* anybody."

She laughed, "Well, that doesn't mean you can't have some fun. I see the way you've been looking at him. You like him. So...have *fun* with him. Live a little...Liv."

I rolled my eyes at her pun and glanced over to the bar where Gavin and Logan seemed to be having a heated talk.

I grabbed Mel's arm, "Come with me."

"Aw yeah, that's what I'm talking about," she proclaimed, "Work it, baby, I'll be your wing-woman."

Oh, Melody...I loved her and her humor. Through my laugh, I shushed her.

Out of pure curiosity, and not because I liked him, I returned to the bar, dragging Mel with me, and took a seat on a stool. Maybe it wouldn't hurt to explore what I was feeling at the moment.

"Dude, I don't need to. I just raced last night," Logan said, annoyed.

"He wants a rematch, man. You could take double what you brought in last night," Gavin persisted.

Logan turned to me as he realized that I was listening. He seemed to be contemplating something as his eyes met mine. After studying me for a moment, a spark lit in his eyes as if he just had the best idea of his life. Still looking at me, he grinned and said, "Ok, I'll do it...But only if Liv comes."

Gavin turned to me with an unsure look on his face.

"Liv...have you ever been to a race before?" Gavin asked.

Chapter Three

It wasn't my first time in a muscle car. Logan held the door for me as I lowered myself into the passenger seat, closing it gently once inside. The car was very well cared for. The vinyl bucket seats were unblemished, and not a speck of dirt or dust could be found anywhere inside the car. The smell of Armor All and vinyl immediately took me back to my pre-adolescent years, and I thought about Adam.

My mind drifted to what he might be doing these days. Did he still restore cars? Had he returned to the woman he cheated on my mom with? Did he marry her? Or did he cheat on her, too? Did we ever cross his mind?

Logan slid into the driver's seat and put the keys in the ignition. As I watched him turn the key, my eyes caught a little blue button on the steering wheel, but before I could ask what it was, I heard the high-pitched sound of the starter wheeling, followed by a loud, heavy roar and low rumble. As the car shook to life, I felt a burst of adrenaline rush through my body. If just starting the car was this thrilling, I wondered what it would be like to drive it.

The dashboard lit up along with what appeared to be a small touch-screen computer monitor in the middle of the dash. I looked over at Logan. His eyes were on me, and he had a small mischievous grin on his face. I wondered if he was getting an adrenaline rush from this as well.

"You might want to put your seatbelt on," he said with a smile and that one eyebrow raised up again. I laughed and politely obliged.

He backed slowly out of the driveway. It felt intimate being in such a tight, confined space with him, the shifter in the middle of the seats being the only thing separating us. Once we were on the road, he hit the throttle. The car lifted to the right, my head jerked back, and I could feel the rumble in the floorboards from the exhaust. He was going fast. I wanted to tell him to slow down but it didn't come out because of the exhilaration I felt.

Everyone but Gavin stayed behind. He followed us in his own car. I chuckled as I thought about how ironic it was that everyone but Gavin was partying at Gavin's house. Chloe had been incredibly disappointed when Logan left so quickly after he had arrived, giving him a pouty face as he left. I wondered what their relationship was, but then quickly brushed the thought aside, telling myself that it didn't matter and that I shouldn't care.

We approached a gas station packed with what seemed to be twenty different compact cars in the lot, some with their hoods up, many of them looking incredibly flashy. A group of people surrounded the cars, and as we drove by, a girl pointed to us and shouted something, causing the people to scatter back to their cars and disperse from the gas station, following us to our destination.

We arrived at an industrial park a few minutes later. The people got out of their cars as they parked, some staying close to us, others going up the road further.

"Stay in the car for a minute. I'll be right back," Logan instructed me as he got out of the car.

Clearly, he wasn't aware that I didn't take orders from anyone, and I followed him out, causing him to stop at the sound of my door closing.

"What the hell?" he exclaimed, as he looked at me, confused.

"What?! You're not the boss of me," I so eloquently replied, causing his confusion to melt into delight. I laughed at my childish remark. Didn't he know I've never been to anything like this before? I wasn't about to sit, waiting around in a car while there was all this activity. How boring would *that* have been?

"Alright then," he replied as he extended his hand out to me.

I placed my hand in his, and we walked over to where Gavin had already started a negotiation with another guy, who looked older, mid-twenties maybe. The intense, anxious look in the guy's eyes, along with his constant rocking and fidgeting, hinted to the fact that he was not here for fun. They seemed to finish their negotiation just as we approached.

"Are we all set, Derrick" Logan asked his competitor.

"Yeah, we're good, man," he replied.

Logan turned to Gavin for confirmation.

Gavin nodded. "Let's do it, man."

Logan shook hands with Derrick then began to walk back to his car, pulling me with him.

Geez, that was quick. They must mean business.

Logan looked at me for a moment, contemplating something, then smirked and turned around, looking back at Gavin and the man.

"Oh, and Liv's gonna be the flagger," he announced with a gigantic grin.

"What?!" My eyes widened and my heart started pounding. "What the hell does that mean? What does a flagger do?"

"Don't worry, it'll be fun," he encouraged. "You're going to tell us when to go. All you have to do is stand between the cars, lift your hands up above your head, and when you want us to go, drop them down to your sides." His reassurance settled me slightly, and my panic dissolved into excitement.

"Ok, fine. I'll do it." I replied with only a slight hesitation.

He pointed to a spot in the road. "That's where you'll stand," he said, then he and Derrick got into their cars.

I stepped into place, facing Logan's Mustang on my left, and the man's royal blue Honda Civic on my right. The drivers revved their engines. Looking over to my right, the man with his brows deeply furrowed, and a focused, troubled expression, nodded that he was ready to go.

I looked to my left, seeing the corner of Logan's mouth turned up as his eyes met mine, and with an expression exuding calmness with a twinge of anticipation, he nodded, indicating that he was ready. Looking away from me and towards the road in front of him, he became more focused but still seemed to be having fun.

Adrenaline began to course through my veins. All eyes were on me as I lifted my hands in the air and held them up for a few seconds. Engines revved. Then, the very moment that I abruptly forced my hands down to my sides, the engines roared like lions, tires squealed, and the hot wind from the cars as they quickly flew by, gave me an incredible rush.

Smoke and the burning rubber from the tires, combined with exhaust, filled the air as I turned around to observe the race. But I couldn't tell who was winning from where I was standing. Cheering sounds from the crowd up the road alerted me to the

26

fact that the race was already finished, and before I knew it, the cars turned around and headed back.

The Honda Civic sped towards me. Derrick slammed on his brakes five feet in front of me and immediately jumped out of his car.

"Fuck!" he shouted as he slammed the door violently. He must've lost the race. He stomped over to a group of women and grabbed one of them by the arm. "We're leaving...Now!" he demanded.

"What the hell, Derrick?!" the woman argued, ripping her arm away from his grasp.

His rage toned down but only slightly. "Let's go," he said with both hands raised in the air as if to tell her he knew he shouldn't have grabbed her. She sighed, seeming to feel sorry for him, as she took his hand and waved goodbye to her friends while getting into his car.

"So, how did it feel?" Logan's voice came from behind me.

I quickly turned around, unable to hold back the enormous smile on my face, and before I could control myself, I wrapped my arms around his neck and kissed his cheek.

"That was incredible!" I gleamed as I stepped back, trying my best to cover up the embarrassment I felt from my impulsive display of affection. "Congratulations! You won!"

He let out a laugh, then still smiling and with a curious expression, as if he was trying to figure me out, he shook his head slightly and said, "C'mon, let's get out of here."

"What? Already?" I asked as we started walking back to his car. "All these people seem to be here for you. Don't you want to hang around for a while?"

"I'm not here for them. I wasn't even going to do this tonight, until..."

"Until what?" I stopped and looked directly at him, meeting his eyes.

He appeared to be searching for the right thing to say. "Until I caught you eavesdropping on my conversation with Gavin," he teased with a smirk. "I thought you might have fun with it...and it looks like you did, so my job here is complete."

"Oh, right, you did this for me..." I contested sarcastically, remembering the look of excitement on his face just before the race. "I'm pretty sure you had just as much fun as I did. And I wasn't eavesdropping! I just happened to be in ear-range."

He shook his head and chuckled. "If I stick around here, other people are going to want to race, and I'm done racing for the night. Let's go back to Gavin's and have some fun."

I agreed and after saying goodbye to Gavin, who was with a group of men looking under the hood of a red Toyota Celica, we hopped in the Mustang and headed back to Gavin's house...Without Gavin.

Chapter Four

The party had died down by the time we got back. Mellow reggae music was playing and only a few people were left sitting in the circle of couches and chairs. Chloe was gone. Melody, who had always been somewhat of a lightweight, was already asleep with her head on Nate's shoulder.

I wasn't ready to slow down. The rush from earlier was still in my blood, and I was incredibly disappointed when I saw everyone already kicking back.

I let out a sigh and leaned back against the bar. Logan looked at me, then the pool table. Then he walked over and grabbed a pool cue, "Rack or break?"

"Break," I replied with a grin, delighted that we'd be doing something other than sitting around.

"Oh, really now," he replied as he eyed me and handed me the pool cue. "Do you play?"

I shook my head and shrugged with a smile.

I watched him closely as he racked the pool balls. Attractive would be an understatement. This man was beautiful and could give any A-list actor a run for his money. He looked up at me a few times while he racked, his eyes lighting up every time they locked with mine. Or maybe it was my eyes lighting up. But whatever it was, it sent a small shiver down my spine each time.

"Alright, Liv. Let's see what you've got," he challenged.

I took the cue ball and placed it just right of the center mark. After eying my shot, I leaned down, aimed, and made my move. Two solids and a stripe went in the pockets from my break. All that practice at the pub had improved my pool game incredibly. Knowing Logan was watching me gave me butterflies, but I managed to keep calm enough to sink two more solids before missing a shot.

"Impressive," he smiled. "Where did you learn to play?"

I told him all about my parents' pub, and how I cleaned it on the weekends, as he sunk three stripes, making us even. The game was close until the very end when there was only the eight ball left. I leaned down to take the shot, trying to block out the fact that Logan was clearly checking me out, and after a moment of calculating, I sunk the eight ball in the corner pocket.

Applause emanated from the couch area, and I looked over, surprised to see that we had spectators. Then I turned to Logan, who was shaking his head with a grin, and an expression that was almost…proud.

"Shit! Liv, we have to go, we're late!" Melody shouted as she looked at the time on her phone. The applause had woken her.

"You're not driving," announced Nate as he raised his arm, pointer finger up. "I'll take you home."

Mel looked thoughtful. "Oh, that means Liv will need a ride home, too." She was smiling from ear to ear as she looked and me, then at Logan, and I wondered if she had planned this. "Logan, you'll take her home, right?"

Sending Mel my disapproving vibes I replied, "He doesn't need to do that, Mel. I'll just…"

"I'd be happy to take you, Liv," Logan interrupted.

I glanced at him, trying to gauge his intentions. The truth was I enjoyed his company and the thought of spending more time with him made my heart flutter. It was obvious that I felt drawn to him.

Another part of me, however, felt apprehensive from the unfamiliar effect he had on me. My tightly sealed guard already had a tendency of wavering around him. And I knew what would happen if I let my guard down.

The bottom line was that in the end, he'd leave.

That very reminder eliminated my reservations and brought me back to my senses. I would be in control of my own fate. A little bit of fun, though temporary, wouldn't hurt anyone. And knowing that I'd need to get a ride home from *someone*, I accepted the offer. "Ok, thanks."

We followed Mel and Nate out and saw Gavin walking toward the house.

"Nice party, man. Maybe next time you'll join us." Nate said as Gavin walked past us.

Gavin chuckled as he opened the screen door. "Later guys."

As I waited for Logan to unlock the car door, Mel hooked her arm in mine and pulled my ear to her face. "Call me tomorrow, okay? I'll want details."

There would be no details to share, but I smiled at her one track mind. "You know I will, Mel."

Logan and I said our goodbyes to Nate and Mel and hopped into the Mustang. He turned the key, bringing the engine to life with a low powerful growl. The faint smell of exhaust mixed with the heavy rumble made me feel oddly at home and I felt the corners of my mouth lift up. I turned to face him as he backed the car out of the driveway and pulled onto the road.

His right hand held the top of the steering wheel as he looked ahead at the road. Each time a streetlight lit up his face, I noticed a new incredible feature. His chocolate hair was lifted up at the top but was just messy enough to tell the world he didn't care about things like hair. His full lips were completely closed with his top lip being slightly larger than the bottom. His maroon colored t-shirt was worn, but not holey, and was just the right size to say he had a body, but didn't need to show it off.

"You're doing it again." He said as a grin took over those lips and his amused eyes turned to me.

Shit! I'm staring.

I quickly turned to face the road. "Doing what?" Playing dumb was the first thing I thought of, but I suddenly became nervous that he would call out that move.

He let out a short laugh, "Nothing." Out of the corner of my eye, I notice him turn to face me again, just before returning his gaze to the road and he tapped his thumb on the steering wheel. "I've been friends with Gavin for a while, and I've never seen you at his place before. Where have you been hiding?"

I shrugged. "I'm not hiding anywhere. I've been to Gavin's a few times."

He responded by turning to me while raising a brow, signaling that he was looking for more details.

"I've just been busy with work, I guess. I plan on moving out once I'm done with school, and I want to make sure I can support myself."

"No college?"

"I don't know, maybe. We'll see," I replied. I didn't like to talk about myself, and most people were put off by the fact that I didn't want to go to college. I learned to keep that piece of information to myself. Honestly, I had no clue what I wanted to

32

do with my life yet and I couldn't see paying for college when I didn't know if it would benefit me. "What about you? Are you in school?"

"Nah, I graduated high school last year and after my dad passed, I decided to take a year off before starting college right away. I'm fine the way things are. College isn't for me right now."

I found it interesting that he was so openly candid about his father. "Do you work?" I asked, wondering what he did all day if he didn't go to school.

"I guess you could say that," he smiled, with his eyes on the road.

What kind of answer is that? Following his lead from before, I playfully eyed him, letting him know that I wanted him to elaborate. When he saw me staring *again*, and on purpose, he laughed.

"My work is keeping my car in top condition and keeping up on the latest technology," he continued. "Most of the cars I race against are compact and lightweight, and with an older, bigger car like mine, you have to make…modifications…to get it to move fast. Other than that, I fix other people's cars here and there."

He makes his money from racing?

"You make your money from racing?" I blurted my thought out.

He chuckled, "Some of it. I also work at my dad's shop."

There went that heart pang again. He must've been close to his dad. "Is that where you learned about cars? From working in your dad's shop?"

33

"Towards the end, yeah. But most of my free time as a kid was spend in our family garage, watching him rebuild old cars, and learning how to do it in the process."

How ironic that our pasts had some similarities. I didn't want to pry into his history, or make him feel uncomfortable so I didn't push the topic. Instead, I looked around trying to come up with a change of subject.

"What's the blue button for?" I asked, glancing at the steering wheel.

He looked at me with a grin, then back at the road. "That's for the nitrous."

I remembered seeing nitrous in the *Fast and the Furious* movies. "Isn't that dangerous? We're not going to blow up, are we?" I said, suddenly concerned.

"Don't worry. I spend a lot of time researching safety and proper installation. You're right, it is dangerous, if not taken care of properly."

"Oh, great. I'm riding in the death mobile."

He watched me as I shifted in my seat, and he chuckled. "It's just for speed, Liv. It's not going to kill us."

I anxiously bit my fingernails the rest of the way home, and I breathed a sigh of relief when we pulled into my driveway safe, sound, and in one piece.

"Looks empty. Is anyone home?" Logan asked as he looked at the dark house.

"No, they're at the pub," I answered.

"Which room is yours?"

I leaned over him and pointed. "The one with the balcony there. I think my mother took pity on me the last time we moved, and I got the best room out of it." I turned my head to look at him and realized just how close I had leaned into him. When I saw his eyes on me and not my balcony, I froze.

The appropriate reaction would have been for me to pull away, but nope, I was stuck there, staring back and getting all hot and sweaty again. The thing was, nobody had ever looked at me quite the way he was looking at me right now. Yeah, the lust was there. That part I had seen a number of times before in guys. Physically, his lips wanted to close the gap between us just as much as mine did, but I got the definitive feeling that there was more to it. Like he had a genuine interest in me...as a person, too. Like he was searching for answers.

It freaked me out just as much as it intrigued me. Especially considering, I wanted to know more about him, too. What was he like as a kid? What kind of food did he like to eat? What was he more passionate about in life than anything else?

Why was I so damn interested in him?

I wanted to lean back into my seat, I wanted to run, but I still couldn't move. His pupils darkened and my heart began to pound hard in my ears. Keeping his eyes on mine, he slowly began leaning toward me. My skin burned as he began to close the gap between us and, oh hell on a stick, this beautiful man was going to kiss me.

I closed my eyes and took a deep breath, trying desperately to keep control. "Thanks for the ride," I whispered huskily, thankful that my voice worked.

I opened my eyes to see a small grin form on his face and amusement occupy his expression. He opened his mouth to say something, but stopped himself. A second later, with a wide grin, he simply said, "Anytime."

My body came to and I leaned back into my seat, taking a moment to gather my wits. I've never felt anything like that with the boys I've kissed before...and that wasn't even a kiss. It was an almost kiss. Thoroughly confused by my reaction to him, I opened the door and turned to face him. "Bye."

I stepped out of the car, giving him a quick smile before closing the car door, and I began walking toward the house.

"Hey, what are you doing tomorrow?" he asked through his open window.

Knowing that he wanted to see me again ignited a surge of excitement in me. My eyes lit up and a smile immediately took over my face in response. Fortunately, I was able to get it under control, to a cool-moderate level, before turning around to answer him. "Cleaning the pub, working at Frank's, then getting ready for school on Monday. It's going to be a busy day," I shrugged.

I felt disappointed, yet relieved at the same time, that I wasn't going to be able to see him. I was concerned by the fact that I could feel myself letting my guard down around him. The feeling he gave me every time he looked at me, the way my body temperature rose at the slightest touch, and the fluttering in my stomach every time he said my name, were all valid reasons to keep my distance.

I couldn't let myself fall for this guy. I wouldn't. This unwanted attraction that I felt toward him needed to get under control.

With what I perceived to be a look of discouragement in his eyes, he nodded and smiled. "Have a good night, Liv."

Chapter Five

The first day of school came and went. Most kids bustled with energy upon their return, but not me. To me, school was nothing more than an item on the checklist of things to do. Switching schools during third quarter last spring, after Mom married Jeff, and moving to an incredibly affluent town had been a challenge.

Maybe it was just me, but kids seemed more "cliquey" here. They weren't mean…They just didn't meander far from their herds, and the only person who made an effort to talk to me when I came here was Melody, another transfer student. We hit it off right away. The last day of the school year had been a relief, and the summer was a blast–but now that summer was over, I felt nothing but apprehension.

My routine, which consisted of school, work, homework, and sleep, was established within the first few days of school. It had already gotten mundane by Thursday, which is why I was elated when Melody suggested we have some girl-time that night after work. Her relationship with Nate had become more serious over the summer and most of her free time was now spent with him. I didn't mind. Mel had a heart of gold, Nate treated her well, and she deserved to be happy.

Mel's car pulled into the parking lot just as I walked out of Frank's. I quickly jumped into the passenger seat, and Mel took off onto the strip the moment my door closed, leaving my car behind in the lot as usual.

We didn't have any specific plans on where to go or what to do, so we drove up and down the strip a few times with our windows down and music up while we decided. We were on our third lap when Mel's attention diverted to Milo's, a popular burger and ice cream place.

"Is that Logan's car?" Mel shouted over the music.

My attention immediately turned to the parking lot of Milo's, where a yellow classic car rested under a dim orange light. There were several tables outside, in front of the strip, occupied by a considerable number of people of all ages...but I didn't see Logan. Mel didn't wait for me to respond before making a U-turn and pulling into the parking lot.

"I feel like having some ice cream, don't you?" Mel questioned rhetorically after she had already parked and turned off the car.

I rolled my eyes and laughed. "Do I have a choice?"

We entered Milo's and after quickly scanning the inside of the restaurant, it was clear that Logan wasn't within these walls. A combination of relief and disappointment came over me. It had been less than a week since our almost kiss and my reaction to him still shook me up enough to want to keep my distance, while at the same time...I wanted to see him again. We ordered our ice cream and headed outside. All the tables were occupied, and several people were sitting on the brick ledge that surrounded the seating area. Others were standing. Then, a familiar blond-haired, blue-eyed, friendly face caught my eye.

"There's Isaac," I nudged Melody.

As we walked towards his table, I noticed he was with the same girl that he had met at River Fest. Chloe was sitting next to her...and that's when I realized that the man who was sitting

38

with his back facing us was actually Logan. Isaac looked up as we approached and gave us a warm smile.

"Come on over. We'll make some room for you," Isaac said. His companion smiled brightly and began to scoot over to make some space. Chloe, however, looked as if we had just killed her cat. Out of the corner of my eye, I saw Logan turn his head to look at us, but I made a point not to look in his direction. Still baffled by the effect he had on me, I was apprehensive of what his eyes might do to me.

Isaac introduced me to Jess, his new "interest." I had seen her at River Fest from a distance and at Gavin's party but had not yet officially met her. I could tell by her demeanor that she was the type of person who could get along with anyone, just like Isaac. With her hair pulled back into a high ponytail with short bangs and an eyebrow ring, she had a punk style that matched Isaac's, even though her black hair strictly contrasted with his light blond hair. She extended her hand to me and said "hello" with a genuinely friendly smile.

Chloe, gave us a not-so-genuine smile and clung to Logan's bicep when we were formally introduced to her. I finally glanced at Logan, who appeared to be completely comfortable with her on his arm. I wondered if they were a thing. When I sat down across from him, he looked at me and nodded with a smile as if to say hello. I don't know why, but it irked me that he didn't say hello…verbally.

The people at the table next to us began to stand up from their seats.

"Chloe, c'mon, we're out," called one of the girls from the table.

"I'm gonna catch a ride with Logan," Chloe replied, turning around to face the group.

"Sorry, Chlo, can't tonight," Logan said, as he casually pulled his arm away from her to take a drink from his soda.

She pouted at him for a moment, then shot daggers at me. "Fine. Have fun," she said as her gaze bore a hole in my face. Then she got up and left with her group, shooting me one last evil glare as she walked to the parking lot.

"She's not with you?" I thought out loud before I could stop myself. "…You guys…She's not with you guys?" I tried to recover, but it didn't sound right.

"She wishes she were with Logan!" Isaac teased.

I looked at Logan, thinking he would be embarrassed by Isaac's remark, but instead, he chuckled and nodded in agreement.

"You guys suck. That poor girl probably really likes you! You shouldn't lead her on like that," I scolded toward Logan. Why was I defending her? And why was I imposing some sort of moral lecture on them? Why did words just come out of me like that?

"Lead her on?" Logan repeated as if he had to in order to make sure he heard me right. "All I'm doing is sitting here!" he said, pretending to be shocked.

I rolled my eyes. "Uh-huh."

He grinned, "Chloe's just a friend, and she knows it."

That sparked my interest, and I wondered if he had a conversation with her about it. If he did, it obviously didn't stop her from trying to get more out of him than friendship. Or, maybe that was the type of "friendship" they had.

I reminded myself that this was none of my business, and dipping my spoon into my caramel sundae, I let it go.

Isaac, Jess, and Logan were done eating, and they began to get up to leave.

"Hey, we're going back to Gavin's. You guys want to join us?" Isaac asked.

Melody and I looked at each other, and I gave her a quick shrug and head-shake, indicating that I did not really want to. She seemed to agree. We both had school in the morning, and it was tough to get through the day on little sleep.

"No, we've got school tomorrow, but let's catch up this weekend!" Melody replied.

*

My parents were already asleep when I got home. They must've had the night off from the pub. I slipped into some comfortable shorts and a tank top and crawled into bed. After plugging my iPod into the speaker on my bedside table, I curled up under my comforter and dozed off to my favorite rock ballads.

Shortly into my dream state, I began to hear what sounded like thunder. It was constant, never silencing, and it kept getting louder. Stirring awake, my eyes opened, and I realized there was a tapping noise coming from my balcony door. Someone was knocking on its window. My body sprung up to a sitting position.

Mace.

Pulling open the drawer on my bedside table, I grasped the bottle of pepper spray that I had purchased a week after my parents opened the pub. Even though we lived in a safe neighborhood, I learned that when you're alone in the house late at night and you've fallen asleep after watching a scary movie, the pitter-patter of animals scurrying across the roof can sound more like axe murderers and rapists trying to scratch their way in. The pepper spray made me feel more in control. Besides, you can never be too safe, and bad things happen everywhere. Even in safe neighborhoods.

I looked at the balcony window and saw a man's silhouette in the moonlight through the sheer curtain. I watched a hand rise up and tap at the window again, and I gripped the mace tightly.

"Who's there?" I called.

"It's Logan."

I released the air that I had been holding in my lungs, and after a moment of regaining my composure, I put the mace back in the drawer.

The thunder noise must've been his car. I hoped it didn't wake my parents. They wouldn't be too happy about a boy on my balcony. I got out of bed and opened the door to see him leaning, with his hand against the door jamb. Our eyes met immediately. His glowed in the luminescence, and his features were shadowed in all the right places. I may have even gasped at the sight of him and before I knew it I was holding my breath again.

"Hey," he said simply.

Hey? He came here to say hey?

"What are you doing here? I thought you were an ax murderer." I scolded in a half-shout, half-whisper as I held the door open. "I'm sleeping. My parents are home. I'm sleeping."

He smiled and poked his head in the door, looking around. "So, this is your room, huh?"

"Hey, get out!" I nudged him. Keeping my eyes on him, I scanned my brain to make sure there was nothing embarrassing in my room that would be in his view, like underwear or my childhood Scooby slippers. I didn't think there was. "What do you want?"

42

"I feel like racing tonight. You wanna come?" Then he looked down at what I was wearing, and I immediately crossed my arms, realizing that I wasn't wearing a bra.

"You woke me up for *that*?" The last race was exhilarating, and I wanted to go with him, but I had school in the morning. Looking over at the green glow from the alarm clock by my bed, I found out just how late it was. "You're going to a race at midnight on a Thursday? You just say you want to race and you find people who will race you? Just like that?"

He shrugged. "Pretty much. I get a lot of offers, so it's not hard to find a race when I want one."

"Yeah, well, some of us have responsibilities," I teased. "I have school in the morning. I can't. Why don't you go ask Chloe? I'm sure she'd be happy to be your escort." It came out more bitter than I intended, but it didn't seem to faze him.

"Chloe's cool, but...you make an awesome flag girl..." He raised one brow. "C'mon, it'll be fun." Then he gave me a flirtatious smile which melted my irritation.

I sighed. "I really can't, Logan. Maybe next time." I began to close the door on him.

He looked up at the sky for a moment, then back at me. "Hey, will you come out here for a minute?"

I looked into his glowing eyes. Why did he have to be so irresistible? I supposed it wouldn't hurt to spend a few minutes outside with him. I went to my closet to grab a sweater while he waited at the door. Once we were on the balcony, we leaned on the rail overlooking the neighborhood.

He didn't say anything, and I wondered what his true intention for coming to my house was. He couldn't possibly have a thing for me. I was much too ordinary for someone like him. Not to mention, he didn't seem like the type to have to chase after girls. He seemed like the type to have girls knocking on *his* door at late hours of the night, not vice versa.

At least, those were the things I was telling myself since the "almost-kiss-night." Truth is, I was scared that he *did* want me. Because I kinda wanted him, too. And *that*—us wanting each other—could lead to something else. Something that was not in the cards me, *ever*.

"Logan, there's something you should know." I dreaded what I was going to say next. Shit, I *liked* him, and the thought of alienating him so soon was…strangely disturbing. Hopefully, he would accept what I had to offer. Maybe, if we just hung out as friends with no extra added pressure to try to turn it into more than that, this unusual pull I had toward him would eventually fade. Maybe it's even what he wanted, too.

"Oh, really now. And what would that be?" His interest had clearly been sparked.

I took a deep breath. "I don't do the boyfriend/girlfriend thing." Before I could say anything else, a stifled laugh escaped him, and he turned himself to face me, seeming genuinely interested in what I would say next as he leaned his side against the balcony rail. He appeared to force himself to stop the laughter, but he couldn't get rid of that grin and look of wonder in his eyes. He didn't say anything, so I continued. "I like you, and I had fun with you last weekend, but I'm just not looking for more than friendship…What's so funny?!" By now, several laughs had escaped him.

"Nothing, I'm sorry," he replied as he shook his head and let out a few more chuckles. "It's just…do you know how many times I've given the 'I don't want a relationship' speech? This is the first time I've been on the receiving end of one. It's kind of ironic. Trust me, I'm totally fine with being friends." He rubbed his chin, giving me a thoughtful look. "Since we're being so open, maybe we should define our friendship."

He said 'our' friendship. He's okay with this!

My elation from the fact that he wasn't resentful or running away from what I said overshadowed his words. "What do you mean *define*?"

"Well, you don't do relationships, right?" He cocked an eyebrow. "What is it that you do?"

I knew then from his tone exactly what he meant, and I proceeded to smack him in the arm. "What the hell? I'm not some whore, Logan!"

Rubbing his arm in mock pain, he continued to chuckle. "Well, that's why we're talking about it, right? We don't want any misunderstandings."

"I'm not talking about friends with benefits. I'm talking about straight up friends." Cringing at my Paula Abdul reference, I sighed and rolled my eyes. This type of embarrassment was new to me. Something about this boy brought out things in me that I had never experienced before.

He gave me a reassuring look. "Well, friends it is then, Olivia Evans." And he reached out to shake my hand.

It surprised me that he knew my full name. I placed my hand in his, trying to ignore that thing that happens to me when I touch him. "Friends it is, Logan Tanner."

He turned to climb down from the balcony, but before he did, he looked at me one last time. "You know, the race tonight was just an excuse. I was planning on coming here to sweep you off your feet and find a way to kiss you passionately in the moonlight." He pointed up, directing my attention to the brilliant full moon that I hadn't noticed until now because I had been solely focused on him. My attraction to him seemed to have intensified in the single moment it took me to look back at him. "But I think this will be much more interesting." He smiled just before he turned away from me.

My legs became cement blocks as I watched him climb down from the balcony. The guy had guts, that's for sure. My elbows leaned on the rail and my hand found its place on my chin, which was a good thing because my jaw needed to be lifted from the floor.

Just before getting into his car, he turned around and looked in my direction with disappointment behind his eyes at first, but then when he noticed me watching him, it melted into warmth.

I stood on the balcony for several minutes after watching his car drive away. Finally, I slipped back into my room, and with the mental image of Logan's intention still fresh in my mind, I drifted to sleep.

Chapter Six

I was glad to have a day off from Frank's on Friday. Mel and I stood at our lockers at the end of the school day, stuffing our backpacks.

"Do you work tonight?" Mel asked.

"No, why?" I replied.

"Let's grill out at your house."

"What? Mel, I don't know…"

With my mom and Jeff being gone in the evenings, my house was the perfect place for a gathering, but I had made an agreement with them that I wouldn't have more than a few people over at a time when they weren't there.

"C'mon, Liv. It'll just be a few people, no big deal," she said, as if she read my mind. "Don't worry, I'll help you clean up."

It did sound like fun. "Fine, but it can't be a big party, and we have to stay outside. I don't want the house trashed."

Mel grinned from ear to ear, unable to control her excitement. I grabbed my phone out of my pocket and started texting invites when Logan popped into my mind. I wanted him to come, but I hadn't gotten his number.

Mel noticed my hesitation. "What's wrong?"

"Nothing." I didn't want her to think I had a thing for Logan, so I stayed silent about it.

*

Nate was the first to arrive at my house, and then came Isaac with Jess and her friend Hailey, who immediately took a liking to Nate. Melody and I were in the kitchen, preparing the sides, while the boys grilled the burgers outside. Each time Hailey let out a giggle, Mel looked up with a murderous face.

"Mel…" I said. "Nate loves you. You love Nate. He doesn't care about anyone else."

"I know," she huffed. "I'm being stupid. It's just…Those bitches didn't even offer to help us. They're just sitting out there, flirting with my man."

"Hey, if you want me to kick them out, I will. It is my house you know," I said, raising my eyebrows.

She laughed, putting her hands up in the air with the knife she had been using still in one of them. "Whoa, no need to go to extremes. Jess seems cool, actually, and I'm not going to cause drama for Isaac." She pointed the knife at me. "Would it be fair to just kick Hailey out?"

"Just say the word, sister." I pointed to what she was holding and smiled. "Maybe you should let me slice the tomatoes now."

My attention digressed to the sound of a low rumble in the distance. The second I heard it, I knew what it was. The corners of my mouth curled up as I bowed my head down so that Mel wouldn't see my delight. The rumble came closer until I could hear it in my driveway, and then it stopped.

How did he know?

I looked up at Mel. A huge grin spread across her face. She heard the rumble too.

"Did you tell Logan about this?" I asked.

"I may have mentioned to Nate that he could tell Logan about our little get-together tonight," she shrugged.

"Seriously, Mel, you've got to stop trying to set me up with people. It's not going to happen."

"Well, who am I gonna double date with? I need you to get a man so we can all hang out together!"

I disregarded the comment and headed to the door, catching Logan's eyes through the screen as we both approached it at the same time. Gavin was with him.

"Hey, come on in!" I opened the door. "Nate and Isaac have the grill started out back, help yourself to drinks in the coolers. Grab a chair, grab a drink, and make yourself at home. Bathroom is over there. Mel and I will be right out with the food. It's burgers. You guys like burgers, right? We've got lettuce, cheese, tomatoes, sautéed mushrooms, the works..." The information spewed out of me at the speed of light. I needed to talk and point to things to keep from making a fool of myself by staring at his heart-stopping hazel eyes and perfect face. I really needed to get a grip and stop thinking about the mental image that Logan left with me last night.

"Burgers are the shit," Gavin declared.

Logan looked around, then grinned. "You've got a nice place here, Liv...When do I get a private tour?"

"A *private* tour, huh? Well, I guess I'm not sure." I beamed back at him. "When are you going to stop using cheesy lines?"

"Oh! Burn!" Gavin laughed as he headed out the back door to join the others.

Logan looked towards the kitchen to make sure Melody wasn't listening, then playfully leaned toward me. "Liv, I wasn't trying to get you into a room. We're just *friends*, remember?"

"Friends don't use lines on friends."

He laughed, "Ok! I get it. No more pick-up lines, I promise."

"Thank you."

"Hey Liv?"

"Yeah?"

"You're really fucking cute when you're nervous."

"I'm not nervous," I lied as I handed him the ketchup and mustard to take outside.

Melody and I followed him out with the rest of the burger fixings. The moment we stepped foot onto the patio, one single sarcastic laugh escaped Melody when she saw Hailey sitting on the patio bench next to Nate so close that their arms touched, gazing at him with a flirtatious smile. In true Mel fashion, she placed her items on the table, then casually walked over to Nate and found her own seat on his knee.

"Hey, baby," she whispered to him just before she wrapped her arms around his neck and placed her lips on his in a passionate kiss.

Hailey looked down in defeat, then get up and take a seat next to Gavin, transferring her full attention to him. It didn't take long for the two of them to get comfortable with each other, and the next time I looked over, Hailey was sitting on Gavin's knee.

After we ate, the summer air began to cool, and shade enveloped the yard as the sun set. The boys had started a bonfire in the fire pit, and by the time they had it going, it was dark. We all took a seat around it with Logan taking the seat next to me.

Gavin shooed Hailey off his knee to grab his buzzing phone out of his back pocket. After answering it, he looked to Logan. "You in tonight, man?"

"Hell no, man," Logan replied.

"Nah, not tonight," he said into the phone.

*

The night ended early. Our chill night clashed terribly with Hailey's full-on party mode. I never want to judge someone on the first impression, but the girl had been guzzling wine coolers like they were going out of style and had spent most of the night between belting out off-key renditions of the music we listened to, and plunging her tongue down Gavin's throat. Not that Gavin minded.

Melody, however, held her grudge from earlier and in addition to shooting Hailey the evil-eye all night, she had been making smart-ass remarks, like "nice job Ariana Grande!" and "get a room, hooker!" The comments had been disguised as friendly jabs, but I was pretty sure everyone including Hailey knew she meant exactly what she had said.

The atmosphere was tense. Isaac, Jess and Hailey were the first to leave, and at Hailey's request, Gavin went with them.

Jess gave me a friendly hug before she left. "Thanks for having us, Liv. Sorry about Hailey. She's just had her heart broken and she's been on a bit of a bender ever since."

"Oh man, that sucks. Do you think she'll be okay?"

"Yeah, I mean, I'm trying to be supportive, but her roommate is giving her the worst advice *ever*. She told Hailey today that nothing soothes a broken heart like a good rebound and apparently Hailey thinks she found it in Gavin."

We both turned to where Gavin had her pressed against the brick wall of the house with his hand up her shirt and her hand in his pants.

51

"Gavin's a decent guy," I assured her. "Good with the ladies, obviously, but he'd never take advantage. Let him know what's going on. As much as it'll kill him at this point, to not…you know…close the deal? He'll do the right thing."

She eyed me curiously, "Did you and Gavin ever—"

"Nope." Flashbacks of another Melody-fix-up gone wrong filtered through my mind. "No sparks. We're friends."

She smiled, "Thank you Liv, for everything."

Melody helped me clean up, then I walked her and Nate out. Logan was still sitting by the fire, which had burned down to embers and a few small flames when I returned from the house. His features were stunning in the orange glow. He looked up and smiled, causing my heart to skip a beat as I walked past him to sit in the chair next to him.

"Are you sticking around?" I asked, somewhat surprised that he hadn't left with the others.

"I can leave if you want me to."

I shrugged. "Friends are always welcome here."

"Well, if we're going to be friends, I should probably stay and get to know you a little bit more."

I began playing with a loose string that was hanging from the arm of my canvas chair. There was something about him that made me want to share everything about myself. "There's not much to know."

"I doubt that. Tell me about your family…Any brothers or sisters?"

"Nope, it's just me."

"What do you want to do…after high school?"

"I have no clue. Just be happy, I hope."

He looked at the empty house, then back at me. "Who keeps you company?"

"Well, right now, you are."

He paused for a moment and squinted at me. "Most girls love to talk about themselves. I get the feeling you don't like to share."

I took a moment to digest that. He spoke the truth...I usually hated talking about myself. Especially when it came to my past. Mostly because I didn't like the way I felt when I remembered it. So why did I feel like everything about my past, present, and future, was on the tip of my tongue, ready to jump out?

"You're right," I replied. "I don't like talking about me very much. But, I'm a really good listener. Let's hear about you. Tell me about your family." Then I remembered about his father, and I immediately wished I had more of a filter.

Logan shifted in his seat and stared blankly into the fire. I sighed, inwardly scolding myself for making things awkward. I didn't want him to, but I was sure he would get up and leave now. I figured I would beat him to the punch. "My parents will be home soon..."

His gaze turned to me, his expression both serious and thoughtful at the same time, as if he were trying to decide whether or not he was going to say the next thing. "It's still early. Will you come with me? I want to show you something."

Yes.

"I don't know, Logan. I should probably call it a night," I said as I took a poking stick off the ground and began to push around the fire embers.

"What are you, *eighty*?" he laughed, lightening the mood. "C'mon, it's early. I promise I won't bore you."

Every part of my subconscious screamed that it was a bad idea to get close to this boy. Why did he have to be so endearing?

"Really, Logan? You want to *show* me something?" I grinned.

His jaw dropped as he feigned shock. "Nothing inappropriate, *friend*," he teased. "You're not gonna make me beg, are you? Cuz I don't beg."

I wasn't sure if he was trying to be funny, or suave, but the exaggerated puppy-dog look he gave me brought an unintentional laugh out of me. Actually, it was more of a snort, but the expression of victory in Logan's face after it came out of my mouth—and nose—made the embarrassing sound worth it. I was beginning to doubt he could ever bore me. My subconscious could shove it. Just for tonight. I had to have more of this boy. "Alright, Zoolander, take me away."

After putting the embers out with the garden hose, we climbed into his Mustang and drove off.

Chapter Seven

The colorful glow of the city lights reflected throughout the interior of the car as we drove. The night air was still warm enough to have the windows down, and the breeze felt refreshing on my skin. A blues song played on the car stereo while the waves of the wind pushed against my hand as I held it out the window

Logan's fingers tapped on the steering wheel to the beat of the music, then he looked at me and instantaneously busted out singing the words of the song. I laughed at the face he was making as he sang. He was so into it. The words were something about "riding with the king."

"Oh, now I know what you really think of yourself!" I joked.

"It's B.B. King, Liv! He's the king, not me!" he defended, pretending to be hurt.

I found it intriguing that someone my age would be listening to blues. Logan seemed so different from other people my age and, yet again, I found myself trying wrap my head around the idea that…for the first time ever, I was interested in finding out more about a boy. As the song ended, Logan turned the volume down.

"The phone call that Gavin took earlier…It was for a race, wasn't it?" I asked.

Logan looked at me and nodded.

"Why do they call Gavin? Why don't they call you?"

55

He shrugged. "Gavin is better with the negotiations. I'm better at the driving. It works well for both of us."

Negotiations. Gavin's expertise. I admit, experience would come in handy for when he dives fully into the real-estate biz.

"You didn't go tonight." It wasn't a question. More of an observation. Although, I did wonder why he passed up the chance.

He looked at me and smiled. "I guess I had better things to do."

"What about the police? Isn't street racing...?" I decided not to finish. We both knew it was not exactly legal.

He chuckled. "I've got nothing against cops. Police are good. We just don't want to see them during a race...or before or after a race, for that matter."

"Isn't it a little risky, though? You never know when they could show up."

"We take precautions. I don't race unless there are spotters around to let us know if police are getting close. We change the location as much as possible. There is always a risk, though." He paused. "The real risk is dealing with some of the idiots that want to race."

"What do you mean?"

He shifted in his seat, beginning to look uncomfortable. "You never know if the other guy is on something or if he even knows how to handle his car, among other things. The police are the least of my concerns." He looked at me. "I almost called off the race last week. The one that you came to."

"Why?"

He didn't answer right away. Instead, he started tapping the steering wheel again. "Derrick was more jittery than normal. I didn't have a good feeling about it."

"Why didn't you call it off?"

His expression became serious as his eyes fixated on the road. "I don't know."

He knew why. He just didn't want to tell me. "Why do you do it if it's so risky?"

He pondered the question for a moment as if he had never really contemplated that thought before. "It's easy. And fun. And a hell of a lot better than working nine to five, six days a week."

We pulled up to a two-story commercial building which had four overhead garage doors in the front and an entry door on the side. The sign above the overhead doors said "Tanner Automotive." We parked in the lot in front and walked towards the building.

"This is my shop."

"*Your* shop?" I found it hard to believe that a nineteen-year-old owned his own building.

"Yes, *my* shop. My dad left it to me and my uncle. My uncle runs the business. I help him out when he needs it, and I live in the apartment upstairs."

"Geez, must be nice," I teased.

"Actually, it is pretty nice," he grinned back at me. "Look, I may not work nine to five but that doesn't mean the shop's not important to me. It is. I train the mechanics. I'm here when we're short-staffed or overloaded with work and plenty of times when we're not, too. I've just been lucky enough that it's done so well and that Craig hasn't pushed me to be more involved."

"You don't want to be more involved?"

I watched as he unlocked the side door. "I'm cool with the way things are at this point. Maybe someday that will change, but for now it's all good."

We entered a hallway which had stairs to our left, and the garage was straight ahead. We walked into the garage, and Logan switched on the florescent lights, revealing a sizable object underneath a grey canvas cover in the very first car bay. The remaining three car bays were empty, making the room appear enormous. Against the walls were shelves and peg boards stocked with tools and auto supplies. Each bay had its own tool station which included several different tool chests.

We moved to the back of the garage, and Logan tossed his keys on a metal desk. I took a seat in the swivel chair in front of the desk and stared curiously at an old-time movie poster that hung on the wall.

"It's John Wayne," Logan explained, noticing my interest in the poster. "My dad was a huge John Wayne fan. He always had those movies on when I was growing up. We even had a room in our house specifically designated for all the John Wayne memorabilia that he collected."

He leaned back against a tall Craftsman tool chest directing his attention to the grey canvas cover in front of us, silently staring at it for a moment.

"Why did you bring me here?" I asked softly.

He turned his face to me, meeting my eyes. Slowly he shook his head as if he wasn't sure he knew the answer. My heart skipped a beat. What was it about looking into his eyes that made me feel so…at peace…and thrilled at the same time?

He stepped toward the canvas cover then slowly removed the cloth, rolling it up along the way to reveal an old white muscle car with black racing strips which traveled from the front bumper to the back bumper. The condition of this car wasn't nearly as pristine as the Mustang. The dull finish had several nicks and scratches, and a few small spots of rust lined the bottom.

"It's a '72 Nova," he disclosed as he walked around the car, taking in the sight of it as if it were for the first time.

"Your current project?"

"Not really," he shrugged. "This one's been on hold for a while. I've barely looked at it since…" He didn't finish. Just got lost in thought. After a moment, he cocked his head to the side. "Hey, do you wanna go upstairs and get a drink?"

I frowned at him suspiciously. "Is that why you brought me here? You know you're not going to get lucky with me, right?"

He let out a laugh then bowed his head down as he shook it, trying to hold back any more laughter. He couldn't hold back the gigantic smile on his face, though. "Don't worry. I'm not going to try anything with you. I think you're cool, Liv. You're someone I could hang out with, that's all, nothing more. Friends have drinks together, *right*?"

I nodded, feeling embarrassed that I jumped to conclusions. I stood up from the chair. "Alright then, let's go."

"Usually it's the guy's mind that goes there," he teased as we walked up the stairs to his apartment. "I like the way your mind works."

"Oh, please! You have to admit, it sounded a bit forward," I counter attacked.

The apartment was only half the size of the garage downstairs. The décor consisted of a few posters on the wall, a couch with a coffee table in front of it, an oversized round wicker chair in the corner, and a giant TV. A breakfast bar separated the kitchen from the living room. I took my shoes off, sat down on the couch, and brought my knees up, resting them on the cushion.

59

Logan handed me a beer, sat down next to me, and raised a brow. "Now it's my turn to ask the questions."

He didn't ask anything too deep or too personal, and I was grateful for that. We spent the next few hours laughing and talking about everything from our favorite foods and music, to embarrassing moments, places we've been and want to go, and a rather extended round of "would you rather." I found out that he would rather get a cardboard cut between the toes than get poked in the eye. And I informed him that I would rather drink pickle juice than sour milk.

There were no awkward silences or lulls in the conversations. I showed him that I could walk across a room with a full bottle of beer on my head without spilling it, and he showed me that he could spin a pen around his fingers so fast that it looked like moving helicopter propellers. Towards the end of it all, as we started to get tired, I asked him about the blues music that he was playing in the car earlier.

"There's such a raw emotion behind the really good blues music. The guitar speaks to you in a way that doesn't happen with any other genre," he explained.

"So, let's hear it. Play me your favorite blues song," I challenged.

He turned it on, then looked at me with a small smile. He stepped over to the couch and sat down beside me, as the track started. It was a mellow song with no vocals. I didn't expect it to have such an effect on me, but he was right. The guitar's voice had a way of grasping my emotions, squeezing them tight, then pulling them out of me. I was hooked no more than thirty seconds into it.

I faced him, somewhat shocked that this beautiful music moved me in such an intense, hypnotic way. He stared straight ahead, looking at nothing in particular absorbed in the melody.

Slowly, he turned his face to me, and our eyes locked. We stared at each other for several moments, taking each other in. The friendly smile I attempted quickly faded as the intensity in his eyes increased and the atmosphere became much more than friendly. His brows furrowed as his gaze moved slowly from my eyes, to my hair, to my lips, and back.

I'm not sure if I leaned into him, or if he leaned into me, but we slowly inched closer until I could feel his minty breath on my face, his nose on my nose, and my heart pounding rapidly in my ears. I longed so badly for him to kiss me, yet hated my lack of control. Was it the music that was causing me to lose myself in him or just...him?

Heat emanated from his lips as they gently touched mine, hesitating in place for several moments, and igniting a surge of fire through my blood. The longer the kiss lingered, the more my skin began to burn, and when my lips parted and his tongue slowly discovered mine, I felt the rush of the touch throughout my body.

My hands slowly moved to his face, then the back of his neck, and I pulled him toward me. His fingers weaved up the hair at the base of my skull as he drew me closer. My body and mind were completely enraptured in the moment, my self-control rapidly fading away to nothing with each passing moment. Logan Tanner was kissing me in a way I had never been kissed before. It was happening, and although it was going against my plans, it was so fucking right.

He began to lay me down onto the couch and then stopped, abruptly pulling away, forcing himself back up to a sitting position. Following his lead, I sat back up, too. His eyes focused on me for a moment, the confusion in his them matching that which was in my heart, the look on his face mirroring my thoughts…*Holy shit, that was intense.*

He took me behind the neck and drew me closer to him, his lips no more than an inch from mine. Then, just at the moment I thought he would continue our kiss, he closed his eyes and placed his forehead on mine, taking a deep breath in.

My heartbeat was almost deafening as it pounded throughout my body, my chest moving up and down as I tried to catch my breath and regain composure. Pulling away, he opened his eyes and looked at me with intensity, passion, and…confusion.

"This isn't why I brought you here, Liv," he whispered. "I didn't mean for that to happen."

Then he kissed me softly on the forehead and slowly leaned back into the couch cushion. Maybe it was the music, maybe it was the drinks, but a mixture of emotions flooded my senses. I was both grateful and disappointed that he stopped and baffled at why I couldn't. I was mad at myself for being so irresponsible, but at the same time, I couldn't deny the feeling of both peace and excitement that he gave me.

My head found a place to rest in the nook between his chest and his shoulder, as my arms held him. Closing my eyes, I became lost in the music.

Chapter Eight

The car screamed of familiarity. The soft, cushioned fabric of the passenger seat which I occupied was more comfortable than that of today's cars, and I wondered why car companies decided to make newer cars with such firm seats. That was a bad choice.

With the engine off, and with only myself in the car, it was quiet. Dead quiet. So quiet it was almost eerie. Taking in my surroundings, I realized this was a car I knew well but hadn't been in for at least eight years. The multi-CD holder in the driver's side sun visor still rested in its place. The miniature dream catcher still hung from the rear-view mirror. The coffee stain still marked the driver's seat from when Kevin had to slam on the brakes because his laughter from my joke had distracted him.

Looking out the window, a thick fog surrounded the car, making any visibility nonexistent. It was morning but still dark out, and an orange glow from the streetlight above laced the fog. The door clicked open, letting in the brisk, misty air. The car bounced slightly as Kevin sat down in the driver's seat, and he closed the door once he was in.

Even though I just saw him last night, my eyes filled with happy tears as I beamed with elation from the very fact that he sat here next to me.

I've missed him so much.

A thin layer of stubble covered his cheeks, and his tangled shoulder-length hair had been pulled back into a low ponytail with the shorter parts tucked behind his ears. He wore the same flannel shirt he had on last night. It had become routine for him to drive me to school on the mornings after he spent the night at our house…which had become more frequent lately. I couldn't wait for him to move in with Mom and me. I cherished the close-knit family feeling I got when the three of us were together.

After starting the car, he turned to me with a kind smile which quickly disappeared when he noticed my tears. "What's wrong, hon?"

My brows pulled together in apprehension as the words he spoke registered in my mind. Everything about them was wrong. Not because of the words themselves, but because it's wasn't Kevin's voice that came out of his mouth. It was Logan's.

I shook my head. "Nothing. I just had a bad dream last night, and I can't stop thinking about it."

"You wanna tell me about it?"

No way. Telling him that he died in my dream—that he was gone and buried in the ground—might make it real. "No. It's okay. I'll get over it." I didn't like that his voice sounded wrong. It made me nervous. Suspicious. But his face exuded warmth, and seeing him made me feel an enormous sense of relief.

He nodded as if he understood, then directed his gaze to the dream catcher. Removing it from the rearview mirror, he handed it to me. "Do you know how these things work?"

I shook my head, becoming distracted by the little circle of white light coming from beyond the driver's side window.

"It's a dream catcher," Logan's voice said through Kevin's mouth. "If you hang it above your bed, it'll filter out the bad dreams and only let the good dreams enter your mind."

The light was getting bigger...brighter. It mesmerized me, and I couldn't take my eyes off it. My eyes squinted, trying to get a better look through the fog. Logan's voice continued to speak, but I couldn't make out any words. Only muffled echoes. Then the light parted, becoming two bright circles, and as they got bigger, they began to move sporadically from side to side. That's when I realized what was happening, and I had to stop it. I took hold of Kevin's arm, but it wasn't his arm anymore; it was Logan's. "Get out of the car!" I begged, "You have to get out!"

It was Logan's hazel eyes that stared back at me, but he continued to speak calmly as if he didn't hear me. "Your mom means the world to me, Livie, and so do you. I promise you can always count on me. For anything."

"Please get out! You have to hurry!" The light was too close. He'd have to get out on my side. I pushed my door open and tugged on his arm, causing him to look down at my hand. In the split second it took for us both to look back up at each other, a horn blared and headlights blinded me.

As glass shattered and metal screeched, everything became black, and in the darkness I screamed out to Kevin, "Liar! Dreamcatcher's are a myth!"

Nightmares are inevitable.

*

My phone buzzed in my back pocket, ripping me out of my dreams. I winced at the kink in my neck and as I tried to lift my head I became distinctly aware of my upright sitting position.

65

Forcing my tired eyes open, I focused on what was right in front of me. A huge ass TV.

Crap! I was still in Logan's apartment. Music still played, but it had changed from blues to some kind of old classic rock. My head slowly turned to the left to see Logan's chest rising and falling with each deep breath he took as he slept.

I lifted my head off his shoulder, pulling my phone out of my back pocket to look at the time. Darkness still blanketed the apartment, so it couldn't have been too late. The screen on my phone said 3:01AM. Two and a half hours after curfew, and I had one missed call from my mother. She and Jeff must've just gotten home from the pub and realized I wasn't there. Wanting to avoid an unpleasant conversation, I decided to text her, instead of calling.

Fell asleep @ a friends. Be home soon.

What friend?

No one u know.

Home. Now.

Coming.

Irritation swept over me as I thought about how incredibly stupid a curfew actually was for someone who would be eighteen in a few short months. Logan's sleepy eyes were already on me when I turned to wake him.

"Are you in trouble?" he mumbled.

"No, but I need to go home now."

66

"Alright."

We both stayed silent as we walked out the door. When we got in the car and began to drive, I replayed the evening in my mind, becoming even more irritated as I thought about how it ended. I couldn't believe I had fallen for Logan's charm. Or...his game? Had I just been played? I trusted him to keep his distance and he had just taken full advantage of my vulnerability. I let out one single chuckle and shook my head at the realization of how gullible I had been.

"You okay?" Logan asked.

"Oh yeah, I'm fine," I retorted.

He eyed me with hesitation. "Are you mad?"

"No. I'm not mad," I huffed. "It's just..." I tried to remain calm, but I was not the type of person to keep quiet when something was on my mind. "What the hell was that last night?"

"What was what?" he asked as if he were completely oblivious to the event I was referring to. He probably did this sort of thing with all girls, maybe even every night, and I was just one of many who fell for his stupid...bewitchery. And beautiful eyes. And heartwarming smile. And charismatic humor. And ripped body. And...*focus Olivia!*

"When we—you know—made out. What was *that?*"

As if I weren't already fuming enough, he grinned. "Are you mad that it started, or mad that it stopped?"

My jaw dropped. I was speechless.

"Hmm," his eyes twinkled. "You're mad that it stopped, aren't you?"

"No! I mean...yeah, kind of." *What? No!* "I mean, no, of course not! I'm glad it stopped. Really glad. *So* freaking glad. Ugh, what kind of question is that anyway? You said you were cool with being friends. You told me you weren't going to 'put the moves' on me! And then we—you know—"

"Made out?" he offered.

"Yes! I feel so stupid! I should've never—we should've never—I mean, is this what you do? Bring girls to your apartment and make them think you like them just to get them to—make out with you?"

His humored expression converted to one of frustration. "No, Liv, when girls come to my apartment, making out is just the beginning."

That shut me up.

He let out a deep sigh and ran his fingers through his hair, keeping his eyes on the road. "Shit, that came out wrong."

"Pull over."

"What?"

"You heard me, pull the car over. I'm walking home." What the hell was wrong with me? I didn't want to walk home. This man was making me crazy. Or maybe I was just tired and still a little buzzed.

"You're not walking home."

"I can't believe I fell for it, Logan. I have to admit, that last part, with the music, was pretty smooth. I bet that gets the girls to your bedroom every time."

"Liv…I had no intention of getting in your pants last night. I'm the one who stopped, remember?" He took a deep breath to calm himself. We stopped at a red light, and I placed my hand on the door handle, ready to bolt at any moment.

He continued, "What I meant to say was…I'm sorry. I *do* like you. You're right, I don't know what happened last night…when we—you know what? Making out doesn't even begin to cover what that was. It was fucking hot, Liv. Mind-

68

blowing, sexy as all hell, *blazing* hot. But as much as I want that to happen again, I'm letting it go because it honestly wasn't my intention. You're *nothing* like any other girls I've met. You're a million times more fun," he turned toward me with a damn sexy smirk, "even when we're not making out. And I'd rather stay friends with you than ruin it by complicating things," he sighed, focusing back on the road. "But clearly I've fucked that up."

As much as I wanted to stay mad, he said exactly what I needed to hear, in exactly the way I needed to hear it. He wanted to let it go, too. He liked me…as a friend, and wanted to keep it that way. We could work this out. Maybe even pretend it never happened. I let it all sink in as the light turned green and the car moved forward.

After a few minutes, he broke our silence, "I fucked it up, didn't I Liv?"

Nope. We had me to blame for that.

I shook my head, both of us staring at the road ahead, "No, Logan. You didn't."

It took the rest of the drive home, but I calmed down and felt normal again by the time we pulled into my driveway. I thought about our night together. I had fun with him too. In fact, I don't remember ever feeling such a connection with anyone else. Not even Melody.

"What *was* your intention, Logan?" I asked as his car idled in front of my house. "Why did you take me to your place last night?"

He brought his hand to his chin and brushed it back and forth as he contemplated what he would say. Then he looked me in the eye carefully. "Please don't take this the wrong way. You just seemed a little…closed off. I thought if you saw a little of my world, you would open up yours."

"Your apartment is your world?"

A chuckle escaped him as he shook his head. "I never planned on taking you up to my apartment. You asked me about my family last night, and the first thing that came to mind was the shop. My dad and I spent a lot of time there together."

He sighed, then his expression turned serious. His eyes were intense, with sadness behind them, when he looked at me. "I don't know why, but I wanted to show you the Nova. I haven't taken the cover off it since…The last time I saw it, my dad was standing next to me."

"Oh…" It must've been such a pivotal step in his healing process and he wanted me to be there for it? I wasn't sure how to respond to that. It should've been awkward for me, since I had only known him for a short time, but instead I felt oddly comfortable with it and thankful to be a part of it.

"Hey, are we good?" He asked.

I gave him a reassuring smile, "Yeah, we're good."

And it was the truth.

Chapter Nine

Logan and I really were good after that night. Great, actually. As the days passed, we began spending more and more time together. We saw each other every weekend, and if we didn't see each other during the week, we spoke on the phone or texted every day.

Some days he would pick me up after work and take me for ice cream at Milo's. Other days I would see him at Gavin's where he and Gavin would work on their cars while I did my homework on the couch in the garage. The more time we spent together, the easier it was to shake the attraction I had for him, but the electricity I felt when he touched me never fully went away.

I had mentioned to him one single time that I hated doing my homework in my quiet, empty house, and he made every attempt since then to make sure that didn't happen anymore, inviting himself over to my house to "study." His version of studying was working on cars or reading instruction manuals, while mine was actual school work.

Today, since I didn't have to work after school, I planned to go to his shop. I hadn't been there since the night I fell asleep on his shoulder, almost four weeks ago. As I pulled into the parking lot, I noticed that in contrast to the last time I was here, all four garage doors were open and several mechanics were busy at work on different cars. I parked my car in the lot and began walking towards the garage. I didn't see Logan at first, so I didn't know if I should enter through the side door or one of the front overhead doors. I decided on the latter.

Several of the grease-covered mechanics stopped what they were doing and turned their heads as I approached. One of them whistled.

"Shut-it Carter. Get back to work," Logan yelled as he appeared from behind the covered Nova and began walking toward me. "Dipshit."

"Show the lady some respect, man. Jesus–this is a business." another guy said. Carter laughed, and the men returned to what they were doing. It only took me a second to remember that Carter was the one with Logan on the night I met him. I glanced over and noticed that the other guy who came to my defense was the same one who was carding people in front of the beer tent that same night.

"Don't worry about Carter," Logan assured me as we met inside the garage. "He's harmless."

I shrugged. "No harm done." My gaze shifted from Carter to the other guy, who nodded to me with a friendly smile. "Isn't that the bouncer from River Fest?" I pointed.

The man came over, wiping his hands on a rag as he approached. He looked much less intimidating in his mechanic's clothes. "I'm Matt. I'd shake your hand, but you probably wouldn't like that too much." He held up his blackened, greasy hands. "I work security on the side."

"I'm Olivia. And thank you," I motioned to his oily hands.

Logan pointed individually to each of the men. "Carter's the ass-munch. That's Casey, James, Jimbo, and Steve." Each of them stopped what they were doing to give me a friendly wave as they were introduced. We walked to the back of the shop, and I dropped my backpack on the metal desk.

"You can do your homework here," he pointed to the desk. "My uncle couldn't be here today, and the shop is overloaded with work, so I'm helping out."

"Okay, let me know if I'm in the way. I can leave anytime," I said.

He looked at me with a reassuring smile. "You're never in the way, Liv. I like having you around."

I welcomed the clinking noises and zoot-zoot sounds of the power tools accompanied by the hard rock/heavy metal music that was playing in the background. Any background noise was better than quiet.

After finishing my homework an hour later, I walked around to watch the guys work on the cars. I quickly found out that Logan was the go-to person for questions. He went from car to car, motivating the mechanics and giving encouraging instructions, while helping hands-on when and where he needed to. He managed them well, and they clearly had respect for him, despite most of them being years older.

Carter began to struggle with the car he was working on. "Dammit!"

I stepped over to take a look. I had seen that model of car before. In fact, I had spent a considerable amount of time in my preadolescent years observing the reconstruction of one.

"Hey, Carter," I said.

He grunted in response, then appeared to feel bad about it. "Hey, Liv."

"Everything okay?"

"Fuck no. Shit. Sorry. I mean no, it's not okay. I'm stumped. I replaced the starter and the ignition switch and this bastard still won't start. All the wires to the starter look fine. The battery is fine. The radio, lights, everything works when you turn the ignition, just not the starter." He looked at me, remembering that I was a girl. "Sorry. Just rambling."

I grabbed the little flashlight that was sitting on Carter's Craftsman tool chest and looked under the hood, instantly remembering all those times helping Adam. The familiarity of the engine brought back memories of our talks.

Carter's face lit up as he watched me study the machinery under the hood. Clearly entertained, he chuckled. "You gonna save the day, princess?"

The power tool noises from the bay next to us stopped, and I noticed heads turn our way out of the corner of my eye.

I rolled my eyes at him and continued to examine the under-hood. As I tilted my head to get a better look at the back of the engine, I shined the light way in the back and noticed a white, rusty corroded wire attached to it. I remembered Adam talking about this same ground wire when he was replacing the engine on his car.

"You've got a corroded ground wire back there."

His amused expression quickly morphed into a *WTF* expression. "Huh?" He came up next to me and looked at the spot where my flashlight was shining. Reaching down to grab the wire, it broke into pieces from his touch.

"Well, fuck a duck. You've got to be shitting me." A dumbstruck Carter said, shaking his head as it dropped down. "I can't believe I didn't look back there."

"Looks like we've found your replacement Carter." teased James, as he walked toward us with a grin from ear to ear.

"Hell yeah," shouted Casey, "Knows cars and a hell of a lot easier on the eyes!"

74

Carter stood upright and pointed at Casey. "Fuck you, shithead!"

On the other side of the shop, Logan stopped wrenching under the hood of one of the cars and walked over to us. "What's going on?"

"Your girl knows cars, that's what's going on!" Jimbo laughed. "She just gave Carter a lesson!"

Logan studied me attentively as a smile crept onto his face. "Really?"

They were making this into something bigger than it actually was.

"No, not really," I shrugged. "It's no big deal."

"My ass it's no big deal!" Casey interrupted. "Carter was all 'oh what to do? What to do?' then Liv strolled over and dominated his ass *in zero point two seconds*! She's all 'it's the ground wire, dumbass!'" He used a feminine voice to portray Carter, and deep, manly voice for me.

The others all laughed hysterically at his remarks. Logan grinned and his eyes were slightly squinted as he watched me like he was processing information.

"It literally took her less than 30 seconds to figure that shit out, dude." Casey continued between laughs.

I shook my head. "As much as I love that interpretation, Casey, it was just a corroded wire, anyone could've missed it. It's no big deal!"

Casey's laughter filtered down to chuckles. "If you say so sweetheart."

After several more stabs at Carter, the commotion eventually died down, and the men went back to their work. Logan stayed by me. "Damn, a pool shark and you know cars? Any other surprises I should know about?"

"Nope, that's it," I replied. "And I don't know that much about cars!"

Defeated, Carter looked over at me, then Logan. "That was pretty fucking cool. For a girl." He patted Logan on the back. "She's a keeper." Then he excused himself to go have a cigarette out in the parking lot.

"We're just friends." Logan and I called after him in unison.

Carter turned around. "Sure thing, kids," he chuckled, then kept walking.

"Care to explain?" Logan asked.

I rolled my eyes. "There's nothing to explain!"

"It's not everyday someone like you"—he looked me up and down—"can school an experienced mechanic on auto repair techniques."

I sighed. "It was just a corroded wire," I said for the hundredth time. "Carter would've seen it eventually."

He remained silent, waiting for me to continue.

I looked down at the floor. "Someone my mom dated for a few years considered it a good bonding experience to have me watch him work on his car. It happens to be the same model as that one—" I pointed to the car Carter was working on. "—and he happened to have the same problem with it." Logan waited for me to continue. I shrugged, "Let's just say he ended up leaving us for a newer model."

His eyes narrowed. "What an ass."

"It is what it is. Nothing's forever."

Studying me, he leaned against the tool chest, crossing his arms and nodding slightly. "Yeah. I guess you're right. That's why it's important to live in the moment."

I smiled. "Life is for living, right? No regrets."

"No regrets," he repeated.

We were silent for the next moment. I looked over at the grey canvas-covered Nova. "Hey, Logan?"

"Yeah?"

"You know you have a pretty awesome car under there right?" I said, pointing to the canvas cover.

"Yeah, I guess it is." He looked at the covered car, then at me with a hint of anxiety behind those beautiful hazel eyes.

"What if today is the day you take the cover off and start fixing her up?"

He took his eyes off me to look at the Nova and stared at it intently for a moment. "I don't know, Liv."

"Come on," I said, taking his greasy hand, walking him over to the car. "A car like this is not meant to sit under a cover. Listen, she's calling to you! 'Logan, fix me. Drive me. Fix me, please!' How can you say no to that?"

He chuckled. "I can't tonight, I've got to help the guys…"

"We're good, man!" called James. "Just finishing up."

"Yeah, we've got it covered, Logan," Jimbo chimed in.

I sat down in the swivel chair and twirled myself around. When I stopped, I was facing the John Wayne movie poster. Logan sat beside me on top of the desk. He looked at the poster, then at the car. His eyes stayed glued on the covered car for several moments.

I leaned over and placed my hand on top of his. "There's no better time than now," I said, giving him an encouraging smile.

With apprehension mixed with warmth in his eyes, he looked at me. Forcing the corners of his mouth up, he shook his head and took a breath in. He slid off the desk and began removing the Nova's cover. After it was completely off, he placed it on the floor next to the desk, leaned against the desktop, and crossed his arms. And just stared at it.

With a peaceful grin, he eyed me with an expression that was as though an enormous weight had been lifted off his shoulders. "I'm going to have to start ordering parts." His smiled widened. "You know what that means, right?"

It meant he would need money for parts…which meant…"More racing?"

"More racing."

"Logan…" *Oh crap, what have I done?* "Are you sure that's a good idea? Isn't there a better way?"

"Other ways? Yes. A better way? Not really." He was amused now.

I hated the thought of him putting himself at risk. "Just be careful."

He grabbed the arm of the chair and swiveled me to face him. "I'm always careful, Liv." Then, with a gleam in his eye, he grabbed both arms of the chair, rolled me closer and quickly kissed my forehead. A chuckle escaped him as he let go of my chair, took a few steps to the Nova, and lifted the hood.

Chapter Ten

Women lusted after Logan wherever he went, and although he toned it down a bit when I was nearby, he was a natural-born flirt. I had accompanied him and Gavin to several more races and although Logan always insisted I be the flag girl, he had no problems mingling with his admirers before and after the races.

As he flirted with a group of three women, I stood near Gavin while he spoke with another man about the next race. Usually Logan raced at least three or four times in a night.

An attractive man with an athletic build, sky blue eyes framed by dark lashes, and medium-length caramel hair approached me.

"Are you having fun yet?" he asked.

I must've looked bored while I waited for Gavin to finish his negotiation. "I was having fun before…this is the boring part," I replied.

"I've seen you around a few times. Aren't you Logan's girl?"

Apparently, everyone knew who Logan was. An unsettling feeling overcame me at the thought of a rumor going around that Logan and I were involved in any way other than friendship. I looked over to Logan who had his arm around one girl as he flirted with the other two, wearing a charming grin.

He glanced up at me, then his gaze moved to the man who was with me, and his smile faded. I gave him a reassuring look to let him know I was fine, then I turned my back to the guy. "Now what would that say about me if I was?"

He laughed and held his hand out. "I'm Evan."

That sparked my interest. I took his hand. "Hi Evan. I'm Olivia Evans."

He smiled, not letting go of my hand. "Now if that's not fate, I don't know what is…"

"Are you racing today, Evan?" Tickled with the coincidence, I wanted to say his name again.

"Nah, I don't race, just here with friends. I ride that." He let go of my hand and pointed to a motorcycle that was parked at the curb across the street. "It doesn't really qualify in a car race."

There was a short pause. Then he continued, "You live around here?"

"Yeah. You?"

"I'm from here, but I've been living in Denver for the last two years. I came back to help with…with family stuff."

I felt an arm hook the back of my neck. "Hey, man." Logan extended his hand to Evan. The hand which was not attached to the arm on my neck. "Logan Tanner. You race?"

"Evan Phoenix. And no."

"Evan Phoenix? Dude, that's fucking awesome! It sounds like a porn name." Logan laughed. Whether intentional or not, his tone came across as derisive. And it kind of pissed me off.

"Well, I can assure you, I'm not a porn star." Trying to make friendly conversation, Evan continued, "I've seen you race a few times. You're good, man. What's your trick?"

"No tricks. When you've got it, you've just got it." He pulled me closer.

WTF?

Evan backed off after that. From the way Logan was holding onto me, he must've thought we were together.

"Alright," Evan said. "Well, it was nice meeting you, Olivia."

"You can call me, Liv," I interrupted.

"Ok, Liv," he said with a warm smile. Then he looked at Logan, his grin tapering off some. "Later." He turned around and walked towards his bike.

Once he was out of earshot, I grabbed Logan's hand and pulled his arm off of me and turned to face him. "What the hell was that, Logan?! He was nice!"

He looked confused. "I was just making sure you were okay. You don't know that guy, Liv. He could try shit with you. You should be careful."

"Are you serious?! We were just talking!" I was completely dumbfounded.

Gavin approached. "The next race is on, man. You ready?"

"Yeah, c'mon, Liv. Let's go," Logan replied, trying to take my hand.

I moved my hand out of his reach. "I don't think so."

His expression became angry. "What are you talking about? You need to start the race."

"I don't *need* to do anything, Logan. Ask one of your girls." I pointed to the three girls that were staring intently at our dispute. I was angry too. I didn't like being told what to do. I turned to see if Evan was still around. I spotted him on his bike, talking to another guy.

"Evan!" I called. Evan turned to look at me, and I began to step away from Logan, but my arm was yanked back. I looked down at my wrist to see Logan's hand grasping it.

He knew me well enough by now to know my intention. "Liv, don't go with him. You don't know that guy," he pleaded, still upset but with a morsel of fear behind his eyes.

"You don't know him either, Logan. He seems nice enough to me." I pulled my arm from his grasp. "And stop telling me what to do."

I ran across the street to Evan, who was straddling his bike, and he looked at me with an amused grin. "Hey," he said.

"Hey. Are you leaving?"

"Yeah." He nodded in Logan's direction. "I'm not really feeling this place anymore."

"Yeah. Me neither." I looked around nervously and realized that I wasn't normally this forward with people. "Any chance I might be able to catch a ride with you?"

His eyes lit up and a small grin crossed his face. "I think I can manage that."

"Good. But I've never been on one of these things before." I pointed to his bike. "Is there anything I need to know?"

He smiled as he reached down and pointed to some bicycle pedal looking things. "These are the foot pegs. Make sure you keep your feet on these. If you move them, you might get hurt."

He put his hand out to help me onto the bike. After crossing my modestly-sized purse in a diagonal with the strap on my right shoulder and the pouch by my left hip, I mounted the bike.

He continued. "When I turn right, look right. When I turn left, look left. If you do that, your body will naturally lean where it needs to." He turned to face me and placed his helmet on my head, adjusting it to fit. Taking my hands and placing them on his hips, he turned to face forward. "Stay close to me, and don't let go when we are moving. Try to be an extension of me when we ride."

"I can do that."

"Alright, I think that's it," he said. "Where to?"

My car was parked at Frank's, and I told him where it was. He started his bike, creating a loud, powerful roar that caused a great deal of heads to turn and glance in our direction. I didn't look back at Logan. Depending on what his expression would be, it would either cause me to feel guilty or hurt. Not only was the effect that Logan had on me becoming a problem, I didn't want to ruin the thrill I was feeling.

The thrill only increased as we sped off down the road, and when we reached the interstate, an exhilarating rush swept through me. I held on to Evan tightly, somewhat fearing for my life, while at the same time, with no barrier between myself and the elements, I felt truly free. And freedom was exactly what I needed.

We rolled into the parking lot of Frank's, and he pulled up next to the only car in the lot...mine. After he shut his engine off, I took the helmet off my head and handed it to him. "That was amazing. Thank you," I said.

"Anytime." He grinned as I dismounted his bike. "Maybe we can do it again sometime."

"Yeah, maybe we can." I smiled as I took my keys out of my purse and pushed the button on my car door remote, unlocking them. I opened my car door and paused, turning to face him. "Bye, Evan."

He continued to grin as he put his helmet on. "Later, Liv."

His bike growled as he started it back up. After giving me one last smile, he drove out of the lot and down the strip. My phone buzzed as I settled into the seat of my car. Three texts and one missed call. All from Logan. The last text read:

Plz just tell me if u r still alive.

A long sigh came out of me. There was no sense in making him worry about me all night, so I responded to him.

Evan's gone, I'm in my car, still alive. We need to talk.

A moment later, my phone buzzed again.

I know. Sorry for being an idiot.

*

The talk never came. It had been three days with no call or text from Logan. I didn't try to contact him either. We had been spending so much time together, and logically, I knew we both needed some space. The problem was that I missed him. It took all my strength not to pick up the phone and call him. He had become just as good of a friend to me as Melody had, and in the past several weeks since I met him, it had become a natural occurrence to speak with him at least once a day. And the more time that passed without a word from him, the more I thought about him.

"Hey, Liv," a guy's voice said from behind me.

I turned my attention away from the shampoo and conditioner bottles that I was stocking and directed it to the voice. I instantly lit up when I saw Evan standing before me. "Hey!"

"Everything okay? You look deep in thought," he inquired.

"Stocking the shelves is serious business, you know," I replied with an extra serious face.

He smiled. "Well, I would hate to keep you from such an important task. How would you feel about doing something a little less serious when you get off work tonight?"

"What do you have in mind?"

"I'm thinking…a Haunted House. If you think you can handle it."

I smiled. Melody and I talked about hitting up a number of haunted houses this year. "Do you mind if I bring friends?" I asked.

"Yeah, no problem. The more the merrier."

"Which Haunted House?"

He gave me the info. "I'll pick you up after work."

"See you then."

After he left, I took a quick break to text Mel. As expected, she was all for the plan, and she was going to tell Nate, Isaac, and Jess about it. They planned on meeting Evan and me there. My mind drifted to Logan. I wanted him to come, but things were so weird between us. If he came, it would be awkward, so I quickly brushed away the thought.

Evan was leaning against the side of a dark grey Nissan Altima, smoking a cigarette, as I walked out of Frank's after closing. A cold front had come through, and the autumn air had turned too brisk to be riding a motorcycle. A grey hood stuck out of the collar of his black leather jacket and a smile formed on his face as he watched me approach.

I gave him a hug. "Hey."

He took my hand and motioned for me to lean against the car beside him. "Hey. Before we go anywhere, I just need to touch base with you about something."

"Okay?" I said in more of a question than a statement.

"I need to let you know that I have a girlfriend back in Denver." He glanced at me to observe my reaction. I stayed neutral and quiet. He continued, "We decided to try an open relationship before I left, so she's cool with me dating...but...I made a commitment to her. I'm not going to get involved in any other serious relationships...emotionally."

I let out a giggle. Laughter was my inappropriate defense mechanism for uncomfortable situations—and this was awkward. "I'm totally fine with that, Evan. No worries." I continued to smile.

He looked so uncomfortable. It was kinda cute. "You seem cool, Liv. I just didn't want you to have any...expectations."

Oh, the irony. "You have no idea," I mumbled.

"What?"

"Nothing. It's fine, really." I brushed my hand on his arm. "I think it's cool that you're clearing the air right away. More guys should do that."

"You still want to hang out?"

"Yeah! Let's go get the crap scared out of us!"

During the car ride, I found out that before leaving school to help his family, he majored in bugs. *Bugs!* He had some big long scientific word for it, but the gist was that he studied bugs. Although it impressed me that he was incredibly attractive *and* extremely intelligent, I had an issue with the bug thing. It grossed me out. But he was cool and fun, so I would try my best to overlook it.

When we arrived, we immediately spotted the rest of our group by a concession stand. They didn't see us right away, so I snuck up behind Melody and poked her in the sides. "Boo!" I yelled.

"AAAHHH!!!" Her soda went flying and landed on the ground next to Isaac. We all erupted into laughter. Melody was not so amused. I instantly felt a little guilty, so I gave her a big bear hug.

"Aw, I'm sorry Mel!" I said as I squeezed her to me. "I didn't mean for you to drop your soda. I'll get you a new one I promise."

"Don't do that to me! I'm freaking out already!" she anxiously giggled. "Look," she said as she pointed to the haunted house exit. The people exiting had a look of terror on their faces. "Everyone who comes out of there looks like they just shit their pants. Nobody's laughing. I'm having some serious anxiety here!"

Nate came from behind her and wrapped his arms around the front of her. "Aww, baby, I'll be there to protect you."

Isaac chimed in. "This is supposed to be one of the scariest haunted houses in the state. I saw on the news that someone actually *did* piss their pants."

We all glared at him. His comment was not helping.

"What?! It's true!" Isaac defended.

Jess nervously chuckled then hooked her arm in Isaac's, and began patting his shoulder. "TMI, Isaac. T.M.I." she said, with an exaggerated tone.

In an effort to change the subject, I introduced Evan. "Guys, this is Evan. Evan, meet Mel, and this is Nate, Isaac, and Jess."

"Hey," Evan said, knuckle-knocking with the guys and giving a courteous handshake to the girls.

The haunted house had a number system, so we didn't have to wait in line. Nate and Mel were the first to arrive, so they had gotten tickets for all of us before we got there. We had a few minutes to spare before our number would be called, so we girls made a trip to the ladies room.

"Have you talked to Logan lately?" Mel asked as we touched up our makeup in front of the bathroom mirror.

"No, he hasn't called. Why?" I replied.

Jess joined in. "Isaac said he's had a huge stick up his ass for the last few days. He's not himself." Melody and I looked at her, shocked and delighted by her choice of words. She put her hands in the air with her cover-up still in one of them. "Isaac's terminology, not mine."

Melody and Jess giggled, but my heart sank at the thought of Logan having something going on that would put him in such a bad mood.

"Nate said he hasn't been himself since he lost that race," Melody divulged. "But I bet he misses you Liv."

"Wait, what? What race did he lose? And he's got fingers. That can push buttons on a phone. If he missed me, he would've called me, or at least texted me. He hasn't tried calling me once."

"He lost the race that you left him at," Mel continued. "It was against some rookie too, that just got his license the week before. It was supposed to be an easy win. Everyone's talking about it. They're saying you're his good luck charm and he can't win a race without you there to flag it."

"That's crazy," I said, rolling my eyes. "He's been undefeated for over a year. Long before I came around."

"True. But think about it. Since you met him, you've flagged *every* one of his races. The one race you're not there for…he loses. Sounds like he's getting attached." Mel nudged me with her elbow. Then, as if a light bulb went off in her head, she stared at me. "Speaking of attachments, you two are practically attached at the hip. Remind me…Why are you not *with* him?"

Jess stopped applying mascara and looked directly at me. "That's a good point. You both seem so happy around each other. You'd be good together."

I shrugged. "We just don't feel that way about each other."

"Oh, *please*! I've seen the way he looks at you," Mel refuted. "That boy is into you. And I've kept my mouth shut long enough, but you look at him the same way. He's gorgeous! Why resist it?!"

I sighed. "Jess, help me out here."

"Sorry, hon," Jess said. "She's right."

"One-thirty-nine," we heard over the loudspeaker.

"Oh shit! We're next! Shit!" Mel frantically cried.

Jess and I guided Melody out of the bathroom with our arms hooked to hers at the elbows. We rejoined the boys in front of the entryway to the haunted house. The attendant took our tickets and motioned for us to enter.

"Good luck. See you soon," the attendant said. Then he lowered his voice dramatically. "If you make it out alive." We all chuckled. Except for Mel.

My hands firmly grasped Evan's arm as we felt our way through a pitch black hallway. Spooky music played, combined with the sounds of electrocutions and screams.

"Liv, I'm gonna kill you for making me do this!" Melody cried from a few feet ahead of me. She had wrapped her arms around Nate's middle and clasped her hands together on the other side of him before we entered. I assumed she was still clinging on to him for dear life. If she needed to blame me for her current state of horror, I was okay with that.

"I'm sorry Mel! I love you!" I assured her.

We entered a large room where a mechanical skull began to tell us the rules between electrocutions. No running or pushing. No flashlights or lighters. Don't touch the monsters, and they won't touch you. Each rule was given in a very horrific, dramatic, yet comical fashion.

After all information was given, we entered a hallway lit up by strobe lights. A zombie jumped out at me from nowhere.

"Aaarrrgggh," it snarled. I screamed bloody murder and jumped into Evan's arms while he laughed. Jess and Isaac were getting a kick out of this too. They seemed to be much more entertained than scared.

"They better not fucking do that to me, Liv!" Melody was near hysterics. "They better not do it. I'm not kidding! They need to stay away, Liv!"

"They're not gonna do it, babe," I heard Nate try to comfort her. "I won't let them do it."

We entered a room where there was an exorcism going on. An actor in a priest outfit held out a cross in front of a woman's face. She laid in a bed screaming as if she were in excruciating pain. Wanting to get through the house as quickly as possible, Mel immediately began moving along to the next hallway. She had no interest in witnessing an exorcism.

The rest of us followed her and Nate into another pitch black hallway. A monster jumped out and screeched at Jess and Isaac, but it only caused them to laugh hysterically.

"Fuck! I'm next, baby! They're coming for me!" Melody cried to Nate.

"Geez, Mel, language!" I teased.

"I'm too freaking scared to have a brain-to-mouth filter right now!" she replied.

Evan pulled me close to him. Still pitch black, I felt his nose by my ear. "Your friend is pretty freaked out," he whispered. "Is she gonna be okay?"

"She's tougher than she's letting on," I quietly responded. "She'll make it."

We made it through the cemetery, the butcher shop, and the electroshock therapy room. Jess and I got spooked by monsters and zombies a few times, but Melody had managed to escape them, which only intensified her anxious anticipation. The boys and Jess weren't nearly as freaked out as I was, yet I was nowhere near as terrified as Melody.

It seemed like we had been in there forever, and I was ready for it to be done. We entered another hallway that was lit up by black lights.

"Roooaaarrrrggg!" A monster jumped out, right in front of Mel.

"AAAAHHH!!!" Mel jumped frantically in the air, then slapped the monster directly on the face.

"Ow!" the monster shouted.

Still horrified, Mel repeatedly punched the monster in the shoulder. We all began to roar in laughter.

"Ahh! Hey, that hurts! No touching!" the poor actor cried. "Hey, Joe! We've got a hitter here!!!"

Two more actors dressed in monster and zombie attire came out from the shadows. There was nothing spooky or scary about the way they approached. Annoyed, they kindly asked Mel to follow them, to exit the haunted house early. She and Nate followed them through a door in the hallway.

Knowing Mel would be safe with Nate, Jess, Isaac, Evan, and I decided to finish. The last scene was a scientific lab where an actor dressed as Dr. Jekyll and Mr. Hyde was performing mad experiments. Jess and Isaac chuckled briefly and kept walking. Evan and I stayed and watched the actor drink his potion and turn into crazy Mr. Hyde.

Once we lost interest, we headed through the door to the final hallway, which was illuminated by a string of pink neon lights on the ceiling.

"I have to admit, that was pretty awesome," I confessed. Just before I was about to push the handle of the exit door, my hand was pulled back.

"Liv, wait," Evan whispered as he pulled me into the corner, not easily visible to the passersby. The force of his tug caused my body to press against his. Confused, I looked up at him. His expression was a mixture of playfulness and desire.

"Hey," he breathed.

Holy crap, he looks good in this light.

"Hey," I softly replied, as my arms found their way around his middle.

With a slight grin, his fingers took my chin, and his lips lowered onto mine. His hand moved behind my neck to pull me closer. He was a good kisser, and I enjoyed the moment fully until my mind brought me back to the kiss between Logan and me. It was the only time I had ever felt such electricity, and I became upset at the thought that I wasn't feeling the same kind of intensity with Evan. Yet, at the same time, I was glad because it meant that Evan was safe. Our involvement with each other would remain on the surface, nothing more, and I already knew there was no way we'd get emotionally invested in each other. Which was exactly what I needed.

I smiled as he pulled back. Even without the intensity, the kiss was good. Maybe even great. "Is that allowed?" I asked, remembering his confession from earlier.

92

He smiled. "Yeah, that's allowed. Listen, I know it might sound weird, but my girlfriend and I are really open with each other. We don't keep any secrets. I'll probably even tell her about you."

My eyes squinted at the thought. "Yeah, that's pretty weird. She'll be okay with this?"

"She sees other people, too. It's okay. I promise."

"I'm not going to pretend to understand it, Evan. But I do like you. I think you're fun. And I don't know why…but I believe you."

He gave me one last soft peck on the lips before taking my hand and leading me out the door where the others were waiting for us. Isaac had his phone to his ear.

"Did you see what those jerks did to me?" Melody asked when she saw me. "I should get a refund!"

I couldn't help but laugh.

"You guys want to go to Gavin's?" Isaac asked, his phone still on his ear. We all looked at each other, shrugging and nodding. He turned away, talking into the phone. "Yeah, we're in, man. We'll be there in a bit."

I turned to Evan. "Do you want to go?"

"Sure, why not?" he replied.

Chapter Eleven

Logan's car was the first thing I noticed when we pulled into Gavin's driveway. Part of me was apprehensive to see him again since the last time we were together, we argued over the very person who happened to be sitting in the car next to me. But mostly, I was excited to see him. I hated that we hadn't talked in so long and made a mental note to end our stupid standoff tonight.

I could hear the music pounding before we entered the house. Gavin, Hailey, Logan, and Chloe were at the bar doing shots as we came down the stairs. Matt sat on one of the couches, looking at his phone. I chuckled at the sour face Chloe made after she took her shot. It must've been something strong. Logan smiled as he watched her, and my heart dropped.

Then, he turned to me. I swore I saw relief in his eyes, but it quickly turned to frustration when he stared past me, seeing who I was with, his smile quickly fading. Chloe noticed his expression change, then glared at me.

"Hey, stranger," I said, ignoring Chloe, as I approached him.

"Hey," he replied coldly. My heart sank at his standoffish tone.

"I'll take one of those," I tried again. "What is it?"

"Whiskey," he replied. "You sure?"

"It's So-Co, Liv, your favorite," Gavin divulged, remembering my drink of choice.

"Well, then yeah, I'm in. How could I say no to that?" I said with a smile.

"SHOTS!!!" Gavin called out to everyone.

I passed out the shots to everyone as Gavin poured them, giving Matt a quick hug during the process. He became less intimidating every time I saw him. Considering I had been spending time at Logan's shop, it had become almost non-existent.

Once everyone had their shot, Gavin toasted, "To friends!"

"To friends!" everyone else repeated, and then we all downed our shots. The liquor burned slightly going down, but it was a sweet burn that I hadn't tasted in a while. It felt good.

"Holy shit, that stuff is disgusting!" Melody choked. Nate laughed until Melody glared at him. Then he abruptly stopped.

"Yeah…Nasty whiskey," he agreed.

Mel rolled her eyes then glanced at the pool table. "Let's play doubles. Evan, Liv, you want to play?"

"I'm game," Evan said.

"I'm in," I said.

"One more round first?" Gavin asked, already pouring more shots. Logan, Chloe, Gavin and I were the only ones who did the next round. Hailey took a seat on the couch and started flirting with Matt.

"I've never seen a girl take a whiskey shot like that without flinching. I think you might be the coolest chick I know." Logan looked at me, a little out of focus. How many shots did they have before we got there?

Chloe let out one single sarcastic laugh.

"Are you equating my coolness with my alcohol preferences?" I asked.

"Not at all," he replied. "I'm equating your coolness to your lack of wincing while shooting your preferred alcohol."

"Oh, okay. To cool chicks!" I toasted. I clinked Chloe's shot glass with a smile, trying to be nice, then we slugged our second shots. "Hey, wait, I'm not a chick."

"Are you sure about that?" he laughed.

"Yes. I'm just a girl. Just a girl in the world." I smiled at my Gwen Stefani quote.

He nodded in Evan's direction. "I see you're with the porn star."

"Not a porn star!" Evan called out, as he chalked his cue, completely unfazed by the remark. "Liv, you want to break, or should I?"

I wanted a minute to talk to Logan and clear the air, but Chloe stayed tightly glued to his side. It looked like I would have to wait for a different moment.

"I'll break," I said to Evan, leaving Logan and Chloe at the bar.

As the pool game progressed, so did the closeness between Logan and Chloe. I saw them take at least two more shots together.

"Nice one, Liv!" Evan said as I sunk my second stripe. Evan was good at pool too, and we had a strong lead.

"This is so unfair!" Melody said. "Next game we're playing boys against girls!"

I missed my next pool shot but not on purpose.

"Good try, babe," Evan said as I sluggishly walked over to him, acting much more disappointed than I really was. Out of the corner of my eye, I saw Logan turn his head towards us. Why did I have to be so overly aware of every move he made?

Evan finished the game on our next turn, sinking the final two stripes and the eight ball. I went to give him a congratulatory hug, and when I put my arms around his neck, he took me by the waist with one hand, by the neck with the other, and dipped me down, planting an unexpected kiss on my lips. I smiled as he lifted me back up to a standing position, holding on to him for balance. Those whiskey shots had clearly kicked in.

"Ok, Liv. Let's kick some boy ass," Mel said.

I leaned back against the wall, waiting for the next pool game to start and looked over at the bar. Logan's eyes were on me with an expression I couldn't quite figure out. It wasn't a happy one. His intense stare made my heart flutter. For a few seconds, the world seemed to go away, and it was just the two of us, staring.

What the hell is going through his mind?

A moment later, he looked down at the floor, breaking the stare. His shoulders lifted up from a small chuckle as he shook his head, snapping himself out of it…Whatever *it* was. Turning to Chloe, he brought his face close to her ear and whispered something. Her eyes widened, and she nodded with a smile. The corner of Logan's mouth turned up as he looked at her and raised one eyebrow.

Oh no.

He took her by the hand and led her to the back room. A knot tightened in my throat. What typically happened in the back room was no secret.

"Logan," Matt called from the couch area, where Hailey, Jess, Isaac, and Gavin were also sitting. Their heads all turned toward Logan. Logan turned to look at him.

"Just think, man. Think about it."

Giving Matt an expression that said *"whatever,"* Logan lifted his middle finger at him and turned back around, stumbling into the back room with his arm around Chloe's neck, closing the door with a bang. Matt looked down and shook his head.

Mel and I looked at each other simultaneously.

"We should go," Mel said. "Let's go. We could go get something to eat."

We stopped for food on the way here. I knew she wasn't hungry. "Mel, don't worry, it's fine. Do you wanna break or should I?"

"Are you sure?"

"Yes!" I replied. "Of course. There's no reason for us to leave."

Mel nodded. "Okay. I can break. Lord knows I need the practice."

That's when I noticed the stares. It seemed like everyone in the room had their heads turned in my direction, all trying to gauge my reaction. *What is everyone's problem?*

Logan was allowed to have fun, and they all knew I was not his girlfriend. I was here with another guy for God's sake. My mind told me that Logan was doing what needed to be done—to confirm our friendship. What I didn't understand was why my heart was suddenly in my stomach and why tears begged to escape my eyes.

As Mel took her shot, giggling noises came out of the back room. Gavin went to the stereo and turned the music up, looking in my direction just before returning to the couch. I got the feeling he felt the need to protect me. As Gavin sat down, Matt stood up from the couch and walked toward me.

"Liv, I'm going outside for a smoke. Do you want to come with me?" Matt asked.

"I don't smoke. It's nasty," I replied.

"Okay, then will you just come out for a minute? To talk?"

Not that I needed permission, but I turned to Melody who was staring intently at me, as was everyone else.

I sighed. "Fine. Hey, Jess, would you want to step in for me?"

"You got it, hon." Jess replied.

I turned to Evan. "I'll be right back."

"Yeah. No problem," he shrugged.

Once we were outside, Matt lit up his cigarette. I waited patiently as he seemed to be finding the right words. After a few moments, he finally spoke.

"Don't take this the wrong way, but you know Logan is doing what he's doing to prove a point, right?"

All the muscles in my body tensed. "Sex to prove a point, huh? That's always a good idea." I thought for a moment. I didn't want to ask why, but I had to know. "Exactly what is he trying to prove?"

After a long pause, he turned to face me. "That he's not into you."

I felt as though the wind had been knocked out of me. My mind imagined all the things Logan and Chloe might be doing in the back room. I wanted to stop thinking in graphic detail about the acts that were taking place back there. It was making my stomach turn. Why was my mind so focused on it? I hated that I had become so affected by another person. I *hated* it so much that I wasn't ready to admit it.

"Well then, that's where you're wrong," I replied, trying to keep my cool. "Because he's not 'into me' in that way. So there's nothing to prove."

Matt took a drag from his cigarette. "I've known Logan for over ten years. He's like family to me. Trust me. He's into you. And it's tearing him up because..." He shook his head and dropped his smoke to the ground, stepping on it to put it out. "Has Logan ever talked to you about what happened after his dad died?"

"No, we've never gotten too in-depth about our pasts." Logan and I had an unspoken understanding that talking about our "sad stories" was out of the bounds of our comfort zones.

He sighed. "There are some things that you need to hear from him...it's not my business to say anything. But you need to know that he's been hurt, Liv. By his own family none the less."

I continued to stay quiet. This conversation seemed to be difficult for him, and I wanted to make sure he had the opportunity to say what he needed to say.

"Since he met you, I've seen changes in him that I never thought would happen. With the exception of the last few days, that is. Since you came around, he's been...happy. I just think...I can tell that you're a strong person, Liv. I just hope you can be strong for him, okay?"

Matt was obviously a good friend to Logan, and it made me feel good to know that he had Logan's back. It was sweet. It suddenly hit me that no matter what, Logan had become a part of my life, as well. He was—first and foremost—my friend...and losing him scared the hell out of me. "Logan is my friend, Matt. I'm not going to abandon him if that's what you're worried about. I don't know why everyone is acting so weird tonight. Logan is allowed to have fun. I'm not his girlfriend. He's not my boyfriend. We're *friends*. Nothing's going to change that."

I hooked my elbow in his. I needed this subject to change. "And, by the way, you are officially not creepy anymore."

"When was I ever creepy?"

"Are you kidding? I was scared shitless when I first saw you at River Fest. You had veins bulging out of your neck!" I giggled. "But you're not so bad. I guess."

He looked at me with a friendly smile. "You're good for him, Liv. I hope you stick around."

I laughed. "Why wouldn't I?"

As we headed back down to the basement, I heard a door slam. Chloe came storming out of the back room, her face flushed and eyes wet. When she saw me, a look of fury flooded her face, and she stomped over to me and slapped me hard.

"Ow! W-w-what in the ever-loving hell?" I screamed. As if this night wasn't weird enough already.

"You need to wake the fuck up and realize what you've got, you stupid bitch!" she angrily shouted as Matt quickly came between us. Then, her fury melted into sadness as she began to cry uncontrollably. She grabbed her cell phone and keys off the bar and barreled past me, up the stairs.

I looked at Matt. "She's not driving, is she?"

"I'm on it," Matt said and quickly chased after her.

Confused beyond belief, I went over and sat down on the couch next to Gavin. Mel came and sat down next to me. "Holy shit, Liv, are you okay?"

"Yeah. Just...Ugh! What the hell?" I replied.

As I rubbed my aching cheek, Gavin reached for his phone, which was lighting up on the coffee table, and answered, "Yeah, what's up? Nah...tonight's not a good night."

"Who is that?" Logan asked from behind us. I hadn't heard him come out of the back room, and his voice startled me.

101

Gavin, Melody, and I turned around to see Logan looking completely disheveled with messed up hair and bloodshot eyes. "If it's a race, I'm going."

Gavin nodded and began his negotiation.

"Are you kidding me?" I asked in disbelief. He had been drinking all night. Logan glared at me but didn't say a word. He didn't need to. I could tell that he blamed me for whatever happened in that room with Chloe. Instead, he turned and took his keys off the bar just before bolting up the stairs. Terror set in my blood at the thought of him driving in his condition.

Without thinking, I stood up. "So help me God, Logan, if you take another step I'm going to sic Matt on you!!!" I shouted in a panic-stricken voice. "Don't you *dare* drive tonight!" Tears stung my eyes, and my entire body began to tremble as every single conflicting emotion from the last few days came raging to the surface.

I didn't know what I would do if something happened to him.

He stopped in the middle of the stairs. Facing away, with his hand on the railing, his head dropped, then his shoulders lifted up and down slightly. Was he laughing? He *was* laughing! He seemed to take a deep breath to calm himself down. When he turned around, his intense gaze met mine immediately. Even bewildered and drunk out of his mind, he was flawless.

"You're going to *sic* Matt on me?" Then he said it again as if he needed to make sure he heard me clearly. "You're going to *sic* Matt on me." He shook his head and let out a single laugh as he started to walk toward me, keeping his eyes on me. He stopped a foot in front of me, causing my head to tilt up slightly in order to meet his eyes. "Who says that, Liv? Who…in the hell…says things like that?"

Embarrassed, I searched for anything else to focus on, but I didn't want to look at anyone else either, so I just looked down at the floor, doing my best to fight the tears that were creeping up. My restraint held up for the most part, except for the trembling, but then I thought about how important he had actually become to me. If he drove drunk tonight, the chance of losing him was huge. And the thought of him being buried in the ground, like Kevin, was too much to bear.

With all my strength, I nervously looked up and met his confused glazed-over eyes. My eyes burned, and I could no longer hold back the single tear that escaped down my cheek.

"Just don't drive tonight, okay?" I whispered, just loud enough for him to hear. "Please."

Our eyes locked for a moment, mine pleading with his. His expression softened as he brought his hand to my cheek and wiped away my tear with his thumb. My eyes instinctively closed from the incredible feeling of his touch. Finally, he took a deep breath. "Fine," he said, defeated. My eyes opened as he removed his hand from my face and pointed at Gavin. "I'm crashing in your room."

"No way, the guestroom is under construction. Where am I gonna sleep?" Gavin retorted. Isaac threw a couch pillow at him while the others shouted words of protest at him. Apparently, they had all been watching our transaction. "Fine, asshole, sleep in my bed! Don't enjoy it too much, you pansy."

Logan ran his fingers through his hair in exasperation, then turned around and walked up the stairs. I watched as he turned into the kitchen when he reached the top, instead of going outside. Relief washed over me, knowing that he was safe.

103

It took everything in me not to chase after him. I wanted nothing more than to lay beside him and fall asleep next to him, wrapped up in his warm embrace. I stood staring at the stairs, the realization that he meant so much more to me that I had previously allowed myself to believe hitting me at full force. But I had seen this story play out more than once. I watched it happen several times, with each ending being just as devastating as the last, if not more. There was no way in hell I would let it take place again. I knew in my heart that getting too close would be the first step towards the demise of us. If I wanted to keep him, I had to let him go.

My attention turned to Evan. Despite the situation, he appeared incredibly calm. He leaned his pool cue against the wall and walked over to me, placing his hand on the small of my back. "You wanna get outta here, babe?"

"Yeah," I nodded. "Would you mind taking me home?"

"No problem."

We said our goodbyes and climbed into Evan's car. He kept the mood light, and kept the conversation going strong. After a few minutes of talking with him my spirits lifted a little bit. I liked Evan. I wasn't sure I had ever met someone so laid back. His attitude throughout the evening had been remarkable, and I felt I owed it to him to address the awkward ending to our night.

"I'm sorry things got weird before." I said as we stopped in front of a red light.

"No worries. I had fun," he replied.

"Really? Even that last part?"

He laughed, "Yeah, I guess that last part was interesting. But I'm cool with it." He looked at me. "Are you okay?"

"Yeah, why wouldn't I be?"

He shrugged. "I don't know. Just checking."

"Well, I had fun too. Up until that last part." I smiled at him.

His eyes beamed as he glanced at me. "Fun is good."

"I like fun."

His smile widened as the light turned green. His eyes returned to the road as he drove ahead. "Since we both had fun, and it's good to have fun, maybe we could have fun again sometime."

I laughed. "Sounds like fun."

Chapter Twelve

The music was on full blast at the pub the next morning, just the way I liked it. My mind wouldn't stop thinking about the things that took place last night. I didn't like what was happening with Logan and me. We definitely weren't the same, but I didn't know how to fix it.

I made sure to pick more upbeat songs on the juke box, in an effort to keep my mood light, so when my favorite Katy Perry song came on, I took a break from my pub cleaning duties to jump on top of the bar and pretend I was her. My body moved to the music as I clenched my invisible microphone and belted out the lyrics at the top of my lungs. Then I heard a knock at the door.

It wasn't unusual for pub patrons to try to come in, thinking the pub opened earlier. I jumped down from the bar and looked over to tell whoever it was that we were closed, but then I saw Logan through the glass doors with an amused grin on his face.

He clearly saw me dancing. I glanced down at what I was wearing…an old t-shirt, yoga pants, and sneakers. Lovely. I looked back up at him and shrugged.

As I walked toward the door, I a pang of apprehension flowed through me. Things had been going downhill with us lately, and I was nervous about what was going to happen. Way more nervous than I should've been.

I opened the door. "What are you doing here?"

"I was thinking about you cleaning bar bathrooms, and I came to help," he replied, still grinning slightly. "Someone like you shouldn't have to do a job like that."

"Someone like me?" I asked, becoming defensive. "What's that supposed to mean? I'm a big girl, Logan. I can handle it."

"I know. No, that's not what I meant," he sighed. "Just let me help you. Please."

The bathrooms were the worst part of the job, and I hated cleaning them.

"And what, exactly, do you get out of helping me?" I asked.

"Can't a guy do a good deed? I don't expect anything in return, Liv. I promise."

I supposed it wouldn't hurt. "Well, if you insist."

I showed him where the supplies were and what to do. I turned around to start my work when he took my arm, forcing me to face him. "Hey, Liv?"

"Yeah?"

"I'm sorry about last night." His hopeful eyes awaited my response as he held my hand. I couldn't seem to look away from them. But if I looked at them another moment, I would surely break. So I forced myself to look down at the floor.

"There's nothing to be sorry about, Logan. We're good." Taking a deep breath for strength, I looked back up at him with the most reassuring smile I could conjure up, hoping it was believable. He didn't seem too sure of my comment, so I continued, "Let's just never do that again, okay?"

"Do what?" he awaited my response, but I didn't say anything. I wasn't sure what to say. All I knew was I wanted things to be back to normal. "Liv, tell me what you don't want us to do."

"Not speak to each other for so long. I missed you. It sucked." I pulled him by the hand and wrapped my arms around his middle, resting my cheek on his chest. If only I could hold on to this feeling of being in his arms.

He sighed and tightened his hold on me. "Yeah, it sucked pretty damn bad. I promise. It won't happen again."

Relief washed over me. "Good. Now, I've got work to do," I said, pulling away. "Some of us have jobs, you know."

He grinned. "Yeah. Suckers."

I turned around to get started at the bar area.

"Nothing happened," he said. I turned back to face him, not sure what he was talking about. He continued, "With Chloe. We just kissed."

"None of my business, Logan," I said, as I walked away from him with my hands in the air.

"And there was some touching."

I faced him again to see him grinning like an idiot. "Logan! Stop!"

"What? I didn't bang her, okay?"

"Oh. My. God." I turned around with my fingers in my ears and went behind the bar to turn the music up. I cranked it high. When I looked back at Logan from across the pub, he still had a grin on his face. Whenever he tried to say something, I cupped my hand behind my ear and mouthed, *"I can't hear you,"* then shrugged. His head tilted back as he laughed, and then he entered the men's bathroom and went to work.

We spent at least an hour working separately. When he finished, he came out with a disgusted look on his face.

"That's it, we're hiring people to do this," he said. There was something in his voice and in his demeanor that made me feel like we really were good. We really were back to normal.

"Yeah, *I'm* the hired help, remember? I'm not doing this for my health. *I* get paid to do it."

"Well then, I'm going to do it for you. You are not doing that job anymore."

My eyes rolled as I handed him a glass of water, and he sat down on a bar stool. He watched me as I finished the dishes on the other side of the bar. I felt water dripping on me from somewhere, and I looked up to see a mischievous grin on his face. Then I watched him put his fingers in his water and flick it in my face.

"Hey!" I shouted. Then he did it again, so I took the water gun from under the bar and pointed it at him. "Stop it if you know what's good for you."

He eyed the water gun, then me. "You wouldn't."

"Try me," I challenged.

He studied me for a moment, as if he were trying to decide whether or not I was bluffing. Then he slowly put his fingers in his water glass and deliberately flicked the liquid in my face again. I pushed the button for only a split second, but that was all I needed to drench his t-shirt with water. His eyes widened and his jaw dropped as he looked down at his soaked shirt, then looked up at me as he shook his head.

"Oh, that's it. You're gonna get it," he warned with a playful smile, and he jumped over the bar to my side.

"Stay back! I'm still armed!" I laughed.

"So am I," he responded as he took his glass of water and dumped it over my head.

"Hey!" I pushed the button on the water dispenser, this time holding it down for good, making sure he was as drenched as I was. He came after me, causing me to squeal and step back quickly. Suddenly, I lost my footing and stumbled in an effort to stop myself from falling. Logan grabbed me just before I lost it and pulled me toward him with so much force that it caused both of us to fall to the floor.

After the initial shock wore off and I realized I was ok and nothing was broken, I busted into laughter, which in turn caused him to start chuckling. Once we settled down, I became aware of how we landed. We were close. Extremely close. And soaked. I had fallen on top of him with his arms around me. His eyes locked with mine, and the laughter ceased. His touch gave me a feeling of comfort. It felt good, and I realized I didn't want him to let go.

The feel of his heartbeat on my chest caused my own heart to start pounding hard. Slowly, I lifted my head, trying to somehow pull myself off of him and saw his eyes darken. His breath tickled my face, and the longer we stared at each other, the weaker I felt, even though all my senses became heightened.

"Are you okay?" I whispered.

He gave me a slight nod, keeping his eyes on mine, as I was pushed upward with each breath he took. We were frozen, immersed in each other's eyes. His hand slowly inched its way from my lower back, and up to the back of my neck, causing my body to pulse. Then he closed his eyes and dropped his head back to the floor. He took a deep breath in and stayed that way for a moment. When he opened his eyes, they seemed to have a glimmer, and a mischievous grin crossed his face. He had regained control.

"We better get you up so you can clean up this mess you made," he teased. Then he gently pushed me off him and stood up, pulling me with him to a standing position as if I was light as a feather.

I breathed deeply. "I was just defending myself." My voice had come out more breathy than I anticipated. It must have caught his attention because it caused him to turn his head to look at me with a thoughtful expression, just before it quickly turned into a slight smile.

"Don't worry, Liv," he said, as he pulled me into a hug. "I'm not going to let you do it on your own." Then he kissed my forehead and released me.

Chapter Thirteen

My head pounded as I rose from my bed. After six consecutive sneezes and a number of nose blows, I realized I would be out of commission today. There was no way in hell I was going to sit through school feeling like this. Too lazy to move, I reached for my phone and texted my mom to call the school. I knew she was downstairs getting ready to go to her day job, but I couldn't bring myself to get out of bed.

Knowing how rare it was for me to miss school or work, she texted me back.

No prob. Feel better.

After calling Frank's to let them know I wouldn't be at work tonight, I plopped back on my bed and drifted off to sleep.

A familiar tune woke me a few hours later. It was the B.B. King song that Logan sang in his car two months earlier. He had programmed the song and his picture into my phone the night I fell asleep in his apartment. Into his phone, the same night, I had programmed a picture of myself with my fingers in a peace symbol in front of my face with Katy Perry's song "Last Friday Night." I smiled as I took my phone and looked at the overly sexy face he made for my phone picture.

"Hey." I answered.

"Hey…who is this?" he replied, confused.

"It's me. How do you not know who you're calling?" I attempted to laugh, but it came out as a cough.

"Holy shit, it doesn't sound like you. Are you okay?"

"I'm sick. I'm home, wallowing in my own misery at the moment." My voice sounded like a man's. No wonder he didn't recognize me.

He paused for a moment, and I wondered if he was really concerned about me. If he was, he made sure not to let on.

"Playing hooky, and you didn't tell me?" he teased.

"Yeah, it's a big party over here. You're really missing out." I took my glass of water from the mounding pile of tissues and cough drop wrappers on my nightstand and tried to take a drink. While holding the phone on my face with my shoulder, my other hand messed with my iPod, attempting to turn on some music.

"I'm just teasing, Liv. I was going to ask you something, but I'll wait until you're feeling better."

The glass slipped, water pouring everywhere. "Shit! Logan, I have to go. I just spilled water all over myself."

With my phone still on my ear, I leapt out of bed, and headed towards the bathroom to get a towel. My hand held on to the door frame as a massive head rush ensued, and I reminded myself never to do that again. *Never spill water on yourself. Never get up that fast when you are sick.*

"Another water incident?" he quipped. "Hmm, I'd love to come over to help you clean up but I'm *pretty* busy here watching an *American Muscle* marathon." When I didn't respond, he continued, "Uh, Liv? You okay?"

"Yeah, sorry, just a head-rush. What the heck is *American Muscle?*"

"It's a car show. Are you sure you're okay?"

113

"I'm fine, I really have to go, though. I'll talk to you later okay?"

"Yeah. Okay."

I figured since I was already soaked, I may as well take a shower. And holy hell, it felt good. I let the hot water massage me and the steam clear my sinuses until the hot water ran out. As I stepped out of the shower, I heard the doorbell. Still relaxed and not wanting to rush, I ignored it. Then there was a knock. Annoyed, since I was in no mood to be in a hurry and the only people who would knock on the door in the middle of a weekday were sales or delivery people, I quickly wrapped a towel around my wet hair and a bathrobe around my body, stepping out of my self-made sauna into the frigid air of the hallway.

Goosebumps prickled my body, and a shiver ran through me as I peeked through a closed window blind to see who was at the door. Logan stood in the icy rain, waiting, holding a white paper bag in one hand and a white plastic bag in the other. A smile formed on my face as my annoyance instantly turned to contentment.

When I opened the door, he looked down at what I was wearing, then up at my head, and I remembered I had a towel on my head. I quickly took it off, instantly realizing how horrible I must look with my tangled wet hair now stuck to my face. Not to mention my sick, puffy, makeup-free eyes.

Logan just stared at me, making me feel even more self-conscious.

He pointed at me up and down. "You shouldn't answer the door like that. I could've been anyone. There's a lot of douchebags out there, you know."

"What do you mean? I'm completely covered!"

114

He sighed and shook his head. "I know, never mind." His expression changed to compassion, and he walked through the door, passing me, and headed toward the kitchen. After he laid the bags on the table, he began to empty the plastic one. An assortment of boxes and bottles were lined up on the table, all different kinds of cold, cough, and flu medicines. The final thing he pulled out of the bag was a box of Puffs tissues.

"If you're not into drugs, there's a bunch of herbal crap here too," he informed me as he pointed to the non-pharmaceutical vitamins and remedies. "The lady at the vitamin store was incredibly helpful."

I'm sure she was. Logan never had any problems getting women to "help him" with things. I glanced down to see Echinacea, Elderberry, and Thyme supplements next to a box of "Breathe Easy" tea. I silently stared at the assortment, shocked, and not sure if I should laugh or cry. It may have been the nicest thing anyone had ever done for me.

"What's that?" I whispered, pointing to the white paper bag.

He opened the bag and pulled out a Styrofoam container with a plastic lid on it. "This..." He lifted it up and proudly pointed to it. "This is the best chicken noodle soup in the city." Then he began to tell me about a restaurant that his family used to go to before his dad died and how his mom would get take-out chicken noodle soup from there every time he was sick. It was the first time he talked about his mother.

Maybe it was my feeling like crap that made me so emotional, but tears began to creep up behind my eyes as I thought about how incredibly considerate it was for him to do all of this for me. I had become accustomed to taking care of myself. It had been a long time since anyone took care of *me*.

115

I quickly pushed the tears back and walked a few steps over to Logan, placing my arms around him, inside his unzipped leather jacket. With my head on his chest, I squeezed him tightly.

"Thank you," I croaked, my voice still manly.

He didn't hug me back at first. His hand was still holding the Styrofoam container in the air, but I didn't let go. He was so warm. I wished I could smell his intoxicating scent, but my nose was too plugged up.

Maybe it was the combination of my headache, congestion, and muscle pain that had invited this moment of emotional weakness. Whatever it was, I just needed to be close to him. He slowly placed the chicken soup back on the table and wrapped his arms around me. He rested his cheek on my head and breathed out, letting his body relax. "You're welcome, Liv."

A moment later, he released me. "Now that you have everything you need, I expect a full recovery within twenty-four hours," he instructed, as he let go of me and began walking towards the door.

"You're leaving?" I asked.

"Yeah, I was going to…"

"Stay," I cut him off. "I mean, you can stay if you want to. I was going to watch a chick-flick, but we could watch something else. Or do something else." He cocked an eyebrow and smirked. I knew what that look meant. "Jesus, Logan! Not that! You're such a damn flirt. Never mind, go if you must."

He laughed. "Hey, you said it, not me."

"I meant play cards or something, you dope. As if you'd even consider doing anything with someone who looks like this." I pointed to my makeup-free face. "All puffy eyed and sickly."

His eyes widened, as his smile faded, his intense gaze locking with mine. "Are you kidding?" He paused and began looking around the room as if he were struggling to decide if he wanted to say what he was thinking.

Then, he stepped towards me and placed his fingers under my chin, forcing me to look up into his contemplative eyes. "Trust me, Liv. I've considered plenty when it comes to you. I consider you every damn day, actually. And you look fucking hot as hell right now which baffles the shit out of me considering you *are* sick. In fact, you in that bathrobe, with your wet hair is making me consider taking you right fucking here."

He took me behind the neck and pulled me closer with one hand, as he used the other to grab my bathrobe tie. His face was only inches from mine. His voice deepened. "But I'm not going to do that because I know it's not what you want." He hesitated and took a deep breath. "That's not what you want...is it?"

Holy crap.

My cheeks burned as I watched his eyes darken. My skin flamed, and the tears I had pushed back began to creep up again. Thoughts were not forming in my mind, let alone words. All I could do was feel, and I'd never felt so wanted. My body wanted his. He wasn't letting go, and I didn't want him to, but was I ready for this? Did I even know what I wanted?

I knew I cared about him too much to hurt him—or be hurt by him—but the way he was looking at me washed away any bit of sense I had. I breathed in and bit my lip as I did what felt natural. I placed my hands on his abdomen, then slid them around his sides, under his leather jacket and up his back. He slowly began to pull at my bathrobe tie as I brought my lips closer to his.

Then, I sneezed. Three times.

A look of remorse overcame him as he let go of me. He quickly grabbed the box of tissues on the table, opened them, and handed one to me. I sneezed into the tissue two more times. Then, just when I thought it was over, I sneezed again.

When the sneezing fit was finally over, I looked up at Logan's distressed face. We both knew the moment was gone and there was no going back to it now. Not knowing what to say or do, I felt a smile form on my face, and then a small laugh came out of me. It was my typical inappropriate subconscious escape method for uncomfortable situations.

He grinned. "Oh…I'm sorry…is this funny to you?"

"Come on, you have to admit, it's a little funny." I held up my thumb and pointer finger in reference to the 'little' as I continued to laugh. "I must've looked like a fool with all that sneezing."

He took my hand and pulled me into a hug. "I don't think you could ever look like a fool, Liv. Adorable, yes. Fool, no."

"So, do you want to stay or not?"

He paused. "It's been a while since I've seen a chick flick. If you still want me to stay, I'd be happy to watch one with you."

I looked up at him with a smile and nodded, then we went to the couch. He took his jacket off and sat down while I sifted through DVDs. "You say 'fuck' a lot," I informed him, not really sure why I felt the need to blurt that out in that particular moment.

He let out a single laugh. "Well, you sound like a frog," he retorted.

After inserting *Dirty Dancing* into the DVD player, I went to my room to get dressed, deciding on an oversized sweatshirt and sweatpants. I slicked my damp hair back into a bun. When I came back, I stopped and inwardly chuckled. Logan's expression as he watched the beginning credits of the movie was one of annoyance mixed with boredom. He clearly was not the chick-flick type, and it warmed my heart to know that he would watch one with me.

I sat down on the couch next to a TV tray that had been set up with the box of tissues, the chicken soup, no longer in the Styrofoam bowl but a regular one, and a glass of white soda. Logan must've set it up while I changed into my clothes.

He was taking care of me.

"Hey, Logan?"

He turned to look at me. Afraid to say the next thing, I hesitated.

"You…you mean a lot to me. You know that, right?" I asked.

His piercing eyes looked into my soul in that moment. He could look at me in a way nobody else ever could. Words were irrelevant. It didn't matter what I said, he knew what I needed, what *we* needed. And we needed to keep our friendship intact at all costs. It was too important to screw up. Simply nodding, he said nothing.

"Thank you for this." I motioned to the soup and the TV.

"Of course, Liv."

Five minutes into the movie, I took the remote and changed it from the DVD setting to the TV setting.

"What are you doing?" he asked.

"Look, Logan, I know Dirty Dancing is a classic and it'll physically pain you to *not* be able to watch it, but the sick girl gets to choose the programming, and I'd much rather watch *American Muscle*. What channel is it on again?"

His big, genuine smile warmed my heart. "Forty two."

Chapter Fourteen

The freezing winter wind burned my ears as I walked to my car. Relieved that school was over for the day, I collapsed into the driver's seat of my car and threw my backpack on the passenger seat, quickly closing the door. I turned the ignition, but the only thing I heard was a click. I tried again, and nothing.

What the hell?

I pondered what could possibly be wrong for a few minutes, but nothing came to me. Logan would know what to do. I texted him.

Car won't start. What do I do?

After a moment, the B.B. King song played on my phone with Logan's picture lit up on it.

"I'm stranded!" I answered.

"I thought you were a car expert."

"I knew one thing about one car! That's it! Help me!"

What happens when you turn the key?"

"Nothing. It clicked once, then after that, nothing…" Then, as I looked at the little knob attached to the left side of the steering wheel, I realized what the problem was. "Oh, shit!"

"What?"

My cheeks began to burn in embarrassment as I realized the problem. I turned the knob to the off position and let out an enormous sigh. "I left my lights on all day."

"You've got to be kidding me." He paused, then asked, "Is there anyone there that can give you a jump?"

I looked around. There were a few kids quickly walking to their cars. I stepped out of my car, and my hair immediately whipped up as the icy blast of air stung my face. I approached one person after the other while Logan was still on the phone, but nobody had any jumper cables. Logan seemed to be getting impatient.

"Liv, just wait there. I'll be there in a few minutes," he huffed.

"You don't have to…." He hung up before I could finish.

My teeth chattered as I sat in my car where I could be protected from the wind and waited for Logan to get here. Finally, his car pulled up next to mine. I stepped out to greet him and watched as he immediately opened the hood of his car then went to his trunk to get the jumper cables. Without a single word to me.

When he finally looked at me, his brows crinkled together, and he looked at me as though I had done something to upset him. "Liv, get in my car. You're freezing."

"No, I'm fine. I'll help." I began to walk towards him.

"Your lips are fucking blue." He pointed to his car, demanding, "Get in my car."

Taken aback by his tone, I squinted at him, confused. "No, I'll help."

"For the love of Christ, you're going to get hypothermia!" he snapped. "I can handle a jump start. Get in the fucking car and warm up."

Wondering where in the world that outburst came from, I decided to let it go, and I got in the car. It only took a few minutes for Logan to get my car started. He closed the hood of my car, then his, and came into the car, sitting in the driver's seat next to me.

"Stay here for a few minutes until your car warms up," he ordered, staring straight ahead.

Why was he so mad at me? "Logan, I'm sorry, I didn't mean for this to happen. I know it was stupid."

He looked at me with guilt. "Shit, I'm sorry. I'm not mad at you. You can call me anytime you need help. With anything."

I sighed. "Does that mean we're good?"

"Yeah. Of course. We're always good."

"Then what the heck is up with you?"

He leaned back and rested his head on the seat. "Nothing's up."

I stared at him, waiting for a real answer. Still, he remained silent. "Hey, Logan?"

"Yeah."

"I'm here for you, too, you know." I reached for his hand which rested on his thigh and held it tightly. "What's wrong?"

"Your hands are freezing, Liv. Why didn't you wait inside the school for me?" He took hold of both of my icicle hands and covered them with his nice, warm, toasty ones, and began to rub them together.

"Stop changing the subject."

One corner of his mouth turned up, and his demeanor visibly relaxed. "I don't know...My mom is having this birthday dinner for me tonight, and I don't really want to go."

"It's your birthday?!"

"Not 'til next week, but yeah."

"What day?"

"December 15th, why?"

122

"Shut up."

He let out a laugh. "Okay, this I've got to hear."

"Mine's the 13th."

"Get the fuck out, are you serious?"

I nodded. "This means you are almost exactly 2 years older than me. You old man, you."

"At least I'm not a *dirty* old man." Then he looked up at the roof of the car as if he were contemplating the validity of that statement.

An idea came to me, and I took my hands out of his and grabbed his arms in excitement. "Let's have a party! For both of us!"

"A birthday party?" he asked as if the idea were ridiculous. "I'm not into that, Liv. I haven't had a birthday party since I was a kid."

"What's tonight then? Sounds like a family birthday party to me."

"More like my own personal hell."

Confused, I gave him a questioning look. "Why don't you want to go to your mom's tonight?"

"Because her husband is going to be there. I hate that prick."

"Her husband? I thought your dad…Wait, when did they…Huh?"

"Yeah, exactly. It doesn't quite add up, does it? Turns out she was with him when my dad was…dying."

"Oh my God, Logan. I'm so sorry."

"My dad had a rare form of cancer. He passed away three months after we found out he had it." Pain mixed with anger was in his eyes as his gaze met mine. "My mom has been with this douchebag for a long time. I'd cut them out of my life completely if it weren't for my sister."

"Your sister?! Logan, why didn't you ever tell me you had a sister?"

"You never asked."

He was right. I was a horrible friend to not know these things. "Well, tell me about her!"

"She's eleven. As much as I hate the guy, Robert is actually good to her. I'd kick his ass if he weren't."

"Are you close…with your sister?"

He nodded silently. I took a moment to let the new unexpected information, and the fact that he was just now sharing it with me, sink in.

"You want to meet her?" he asked.

"Yes! I would love to."

He hesitated. "Come with me tonight."

To meet his family? I had to work tonight. Looking into his afflicted eyes, I realized that he needed support. And I wanted nothing more than to make sure he got it.

"Okay," I agreed, smiling. "I got your back."

He chuckled at my remark. "I know you do. Dinner's at six. I'll pick you up at five. Sound good?"

"Sounds good. See you then." I pulled on the door handle and stepped into the icy wind. Before closing the door, I dipped my head back down so I could see him. "Thanks for rescuing me, by the way."

"It was no problem, Liv. Really, I want you to call me if anything like this ever happens again, okay?"

"Okay." I grinned. "Later."

I closed the door and immediately jumped into my car, grateful that it had a chance to warm up. I took a deep breath and dialed the number to Frank's, hoping that my manager wouldn't be too upset with me for missing work tonight.

*

The doorbell rang as I put the finishing touches on my makeup. I had decided on dark blue jeans and a fuzzy black sweater. Having no idea what Logan's family was like, I figured a casual chic style would be appropriate. The top portion of my hair was up in a clip with a few chunky wisps hanging down from my hairline.

I grabbed my coat on the way to the door, wrapping myself in it just before turning the knob. Logan held the storm door open as I locked up. We climbed into his Mustang, and I grinned at the low rumble it made as it started up.

"Are you ready for this?" Logan asked as if we were going into battle.

"It's your family, Logan. They can't be that bad," I reassured him.

"Just wait. You'll see."

The drive was longer than I had anticipated. After jumping onto the interstate, the number of city lights gradually lessened until there were none at all. Finally, we exited onto a country road. Gravel crackled under the tires as we rolled up the long driveway to Logan's childhood home a few moments later.

After exiting the car, I gazed up at the sky, astonished at the multitude of stars that could be seen. The wind had died down and just a small breeze remained.

"You don't get out of the city much, do you?" Logan asked. From his tone, I could tell he was on edge.

"It's beautiful!" I answered, still looking up. "I've never seen so many!"

I hooked my arm in his, giving it a supportive squeeze before he ushered me into the house. The home had been recently renovated. The smell of new carpeting and wood work mixed with home cooking filled the air. To my right was a large living room, and to my left, a staircase. We advanced straight ahead, down the hall to the kitchen.

"Logan's here!" a young voice shouted. An adolescent girl, whom I assumed to be Logan's sister, hopped off her chair and rushed towards us, meeting us in the hallway. Her straight shoulder-length hair was the same dark chocolate color as Logan's, but her eyes were pure emerald. The resemblance between the two was unmistakable. She would be a heartbreaker in a few years, if not already.

"Hey, squirt!" He lifted her into a huge bear hug. Her feet dangled back and forth as he playfully swayed with her. Setting her down, he placed his hand on top of her head and messed up her hair.

"Logan! Stop it!" she giggled, giving him a nudge.

He directed his attention towards me. "Lanie, this is my friend, Liv."

She smiled and gave me a big squeeze. "Hi, Liv."

"It's a pleasure to meet you, Lanie," I laughed. This girl was irresistible.

"We're in the kitchen. Mom's making your favorite," Lanie said.

As we followed Lanie towards the kitchen, I noticed several pictures on the walls, and I stopped to stare at one that caught my eye. It was of Logan and a man in front of the Mustang. They looked happy.

"It's the only picture in the house of my father," Logan said from behind me. "My mom took the rest of them down when Robert moved in. It was taken the day we finished restoring the Mustang."

"You look exactly like your dad," I said.

"Yeah, we got that a lot."

"There he is! Happy birthday!" shouted a man walking into the kitchen from the back patio door. He carried a platter with something huge on it, wrapped in tin-foil. The aroma of a charcoal grill followed him in. I smiled at the thought of grilling in the winter. It was something Adam used to do.

Logan's mother was at the stove, stirring some sliced red potatoes in a skillet. "Hi, sweetheart."

"Hi," he coldly replied, staying by my side. Tension filled the air from his lack of affection. After what he told me, it didn't surprise me that he didn't show her the same warmth that he did with his sister. She continued to smile, but Logan's indifference elicited disappointment in her eyes.

Her gaze turned to me, and her expression lightened. "You brought company!"

"Liv, meet my mother," Logan said.

"You can call me Jen." She smiled, and I politely shook her hand. "And that's Robert." She pointed to the man who had placed the platter on the counter, and I waved to him.

"Can we help with anything?" I asked.

"You two just relax. We'll take care of everything," Jen replied.

A phone started ringing to the tune of a Justin Bieber song that I frequently heard playing on the radio. Lanie jumped up. "That's Cody!" She rushed to where the phone was sitting on the kitchen table and answered it. "Hey, Cody," she said in a flirty voice.

Jen and Robert shared a knowing smile and shook their heads as Lanie walked out of the room, twirling her hair with her finger. I turned to Logan, seeing anger build behind the calm façade he was trying to maintain.

"Please tell me an eleven-year-old does not have her own cell phone," Logan said in an overly calm voice. Jen looked at him with an uncertain expression. "And please tell me that was not her boyfriend on it."

After a silent, awkward moment, Jen spoke. "She's growing up, Logan. Robert and I discussed it with Lanie, and we all agreed that as long as she kept up on her schoolwork and housework, she could have the privilege of a phone." Jen took a deep breath. "And yes, Cody is her boyfriend. But you know how kids are at that age. So-called 'boyfriends' change weekly, and they barely even talk to each other. It's nothing serious."

"Clearly, they're talking to each other now," Logan replied. "I hope you've at least met the kid."

Oh, this is not good.

"You have a beautiful home, Jen," I said, trying to change the subject.

Logan answered sarcastically, "Yeah, beautiful. It's been completely remodeled. I barely recognize it."

An ear-piercing clanking noise, coming from where Robert was standing, caught our attention. Robert's palms were on the counter. His head dropped down as he took a calming breath. He turned to face Logan.

"Your mother and your sister have been looking forward to this night for weeks. Regardless of how you feel about us," he said, motioning to himself and Jen. "I think you can agree that it

128

would be in Lanie's best interest for us all to have a nice time this evening."

Oh dear.

Logan's face turned a shade of red as his fury began to build.

"Uh—Logan, do you want to give me a tour?" I asked.

Through clenched teeth he replied, "Sure, Liv, I'd love to."

"We'll be right back," I said to Jen and Robert.

I took the hand that he extended to me and he led me back through the hall and up the staircase. We entered a room with dark blue walls, a bed with a grey comforter, and mission-style dressers.

He began to pace as I closed the door. If this evening had been planned for weeks, it meant Logan had weeks to let this apprehension build up. Now that he was here, his emotions had come to a boiling point. Jen and Robert hadn't said or done anything too horrible, but given Logan's history with them, any little thing seemed to set him off.

He grabbed his hair. He sat down on the bed, then instantly got up and started pacing again. "What the fuck was that?" He half-shouted, half-whispered. He turned to me. "Who does that asshole think he is? Did you hear him, Liv?" He pointed to the door. "Did you hear that shit?"

"I know…" I started.

"We're here two minutes. *Two* minutes!"

"Logan…"

"I mean, why does he think I'm here? It's sure as hell not for him! And it's not for my cheating mother. I can't believe that asshole is living in my father's house, I mean…"

"Logan!"

"…Of course I'm here for Lanie! Do you know how much I want to put my fist through his smug face right now?" His anger intensified.

I tried again. "It was uncalled for, I…"

"She's the *only* reason I'm here. I would NEVER do anything to upset her!"

"Logan, I know…"

"What the hell do they think they're going to accomplish with this stupid dinner anyway? Do they think they're going to make us a family? My dad would never allow his eleven-year-old daughter to have a boyfriend. What the hell are they thinking, Liv?"

"It sounds like…"

"Since when is it okay, for an eleven-year-old girl to have a boyfriend? Boys are douchebags, even eleven year olds."

He continued his rant with anguish in his beautiful eyes. I couldn't bear the thought of him struggling this way, but I couldn't get a word in to even attempt to help him. Without thinking, I grabbed him behind the neck and pulled him down to me so that his lips firmly pressed on mine. At first, he didn't move. It took him a moment to realize what was happening. Then, as our lips parted, his hands took my waist, pulling my stomach into his, intensifying our embrace.

I instantly regretted my thoughtless action, but I needed to get him to calm down. As his hand drifted to the back of my neck, his anger melted away. A low moan rumbled deep in his throat, which made my own heart begin to pound hard, and I was immediately reminded of what his touch does to me.

Before I lost all my senses, I pushed him away and instinctively brought my fingers to my lips from the tingling.

"I'm sorry. I didn't know what else to do," I breathed, trying hard to pretend I wasn't fazed by what just happened. "You weren't listening to me."

He stared at me with intensity for several seconds. "That's an interesting way to get my attention."

I hesitantly replied, "It was either that or slap you. And I'm not a violent person."

One corner of his mouth turned up, but his eyes weren't behind the smile. His eyes matched how I was feeling. Shocked. Confused. "Well, you've got my full attention now."

As he stared at me, waiting for me to speak, my mind drew a blank. Shit, I didn't know what to say. All I knew was that he was buried under a mountain of hurt as he still mourned his father's death. As irrational and impossible as it was, the only thing I wanted to do was make his pain go away.

I took his hands. "You're here for Lanie, right?"

He nodded, his eyes remaining deeply focused on me.

"Then nothing else matters. Put all your energy tonight into her. Into making this a great night for *her*. Nothing that Robert or your mother says matters. Only Lanie matters. It's a shitty situation, Logan, plain and simple, but Lanie is stuck dead in the middle of it, and she needs you." He remained silent, so I continued, "Reacting to Robert isn't worth it."

He took a deep breath, staring at nothing in particular.

I gave him a comforting smile. "And just so you know, when I need to keep my cool, I Taser people in my mind. Robert got a good zap downstairs."

Laughter came out of his throat, and I giggled at his reaction to my comment. Pulling my hands, he drew me close and planted a small kiss on the top of my head. "I'm so glad you're here, Liv."

"I wouldn't miss it," I replied, resting my cheek on his chest.

"Alright," he said after several moments. "We should get back. For Lanie."

I pulled away from him, "Yeah. Okay."

I tried to walk away but he tugged on the hand he still held, forcing me to meet his playful stare, "I don't know, I'm still kinda pissed off though. Maybe we should make out one more time. You know, to *distract* me."

I laughed, "Nice try. That was an accident. A one-time deal."

"One time, huh? Only, it's happened *twice*. And, damn girl, it gets better every time."

"Logan!" I couldn't help the stupid smile that formed on my face. "Stop making this awkward, I'm immune to your charm remember? That only works on your groupies…not your *friends*."

"Trust me, if Matt kissed me like that, I'd be charming the shit out of him. Wait, do you kiss Mel like that? 'Cause if you do, you should really film it next time. Or better yet, invite me—"

"Okay," I said, walking out of the room. "I see my job here is done."

"Wait," his hand on my shoulder stopped me in the hall. "Thank you, Liv."

I nodded in response and we heading back downstairs. Jen's nervous expression as we entered the kitchen receded once she saw that Logan had calmed down. Logan and I joined Lanie in setting the table while Robert and Jen quietly finished with the food. After the food was on the table, we all took a seat.

132

Jen and Robert had made quite an effort with the dinner. Grilled steak tenderloin and potatoes were accompanied by a tossed salad, dinner rolls, and steamed asparagus, all accented by fancy dinnerware and fabric napkins. The aroma made my mouth water. The atmosphere started out slightly uncomfortable but became much more breathable as the dinner progressed.

Mostly, we listened to Lanie talk about school and her boyfriend. She was the common ground. The one thing everyone had a vested interest in. If Logan had any sort of issue with Lanie's boyfriend, he kept it to himself, listening intently with a delighted smile as she talked about him.

After dinner, Logan and Lanie began a game of *Guitar Hero.* Robert went to his office, and I began to wash dishes as Jen cleared the table.

"You and Logan seem happy together," Jen said.

"Oh, it's not like that," I replied. "We're just friends." If I had a nickel for every time I said that...

"Oh...really?" she hesitated. "You two just seem so...close."

"I suppose we are close. He's my best friend," I said without thinking. It was the first time I said it out loud. It was true. Logan was my best friend.

Jen gave me a curious look, then smiled. "Well, you seem like a very nice girl, Liv. I'm glad he has you."

I peered out to the living room and watched Logan with his sister, and a warmth came over me at the sight of his undeniable devotion to her. It occurred to me that I really did care very deeply for him.

"It didn't happen how Logan thinks it did," Jen said.

"Huh?" I asked, having no idea what she was talking about.

"My relationship with Robert."

133

"Oh." I tensed. This conversation was taking a very sharp turn. Why was she telling me this? It was in none of my business in any sort of way.

"Robert has always been a good friend to us. To Logan's dad too. He was around the kids as they grew up. He was devastated with Andrew's passing, just like we were," she sighed. "Logan misunderstood something he saw, and he's hated Robert ever since. And me. I just wish..." She didn't finish. As I set a plate in the drying rack, I gave her a reassuring smile. She collected herself, then let out a nervous laugh. "...I'm sorry Liv, I'm sure this is the last thing you want to hear."

"It's okay. Really," I said. Jen seemed nice. She and Robert seemed to truly love each other and Lanie. They had made such an incredible effort with this dinner for Logan that it was clear they cared about him too. "Sometimes things just take time."

Logan entered the kitchen with a murderous expression. "When were you going to tell me?" he fumed at his mother.

Jen let out a sigh. She knew exactly what he was talking about. "I was going to wait until after your birthday. Logan, I'm sorry."

"Bullshit. Your apologies mean nothing to me, Mom." He faced me. "Let's go."

I dried my hands on a towel, gave Jen an apologetic look, and followed Logan to the living room.

He lifted Lanie off the floor in an embrace. "See ya, squirt."

"Lanie, you rock," I said as I squeezed her. "We have *got* to hang out sometime."

Her eyes got wide as I let go of her, and she nodded her head vigorously. "That would be so awesome!"

After slipping on our coats, we exited the house into the brisk winter air. As we sat down and closed the doors to the Mustang, Logan let out a sigh. "Thank fuck that's over." He started the engine and waited a moment for the car to warm up.

"Everything okay?" I asked.

"It is now." He ducked his head and looked out the window, taking a look at the house. "They're selling the house. They didn't even have the balls to tell me themselves. They had an eleven-year-old do their dirty work," he laughed sarcastically. "Can you believe that shit?"

I took his hand. "No, I can't."

"It's my home. I grew up there. It's gonna be gone."

"It's just a house, Logan. It's just a bunch of drywall and two-by-fours. A home is so much more than just a building. It's where you're...most comfortable...most at peace...free to be yourself. A home is where you belong." I looked upward, trying to think of more things that made a home just that. "And that house seems to stress you out." I brought my thumb and pointer finger together. "Just a little." When I looked back at him, his gaze was fixed on me.

"Liv, thank you for coming tonight. I don't know what would've happened if you weren't here. You're an angel." He squinted his eyes at me like he had just figured something out.

"Trust me, I'm no angel."

He shook off whatever thought he had, put the car in reverse, and backed out of the driveway. As we sped onto the interstate, I fidgeted with the stereo, trying to find a good song.

"You kissed me," he blurted out.

I froze. Why was he so fixated on that? Maybe for the same reason I couldn't stop thinking about it...because his kiss was better than any other kisses...ever. Still, I was hoping it would be forgotten because I didn't want things between us to change. I liked our relationship the way it was.

"Yeah," I replied. "I guess I did."

"All joking aside, you're a damn good kisser, Liv. We should really do it again sometime."

"Oh no. No way. Uh-uh. I told you, it was a distraction method only."

I thought he would chuckle at my remark or tease me about using my 'method' on him anytime, but instead he frowned and became distant. After a while, as we neared my house, he began tapping on his steering wheel. Then he turned to me with a flirtatious smile.

"So, about that birthday party…," he said.

"What birthday party?"

"Ours. It's still early. Matt is working at Rain tonight…Let's go celebrate. It would just be us, you and me, but…"

"Yes! Let's go!"

He made a U-turn and headed for downtown.

Chapter Fifteen

The pounding bass could be heard a block away. The sound increased the closer we got, sending a feeling of excitement through my body. A line formed in front of the entrance door, but Logan led me to the front of the line where Matt was carding people under a heat lamp. Not having to wait in line was a definite perk since we had left our coats in the car. I would've froze.

Logan and Matt exchanged a manly handshake/fist bump. Knowing Matt needed to keep up his distant, bad-ass image, I refrained from giving him a hug. Instead I simply smiled, which softened his eyes for only a split second. He gave me a friendly wink as we walked past him and into the club.

I followed Logan down the short dim hallway and into the club. People bounced in unison on the dark dance floor straight ahead. Laser and strobe lights flickered to the thump of the bass. Only a few laughs and shouts from the club-goers could be heard over the music. Each beat pounded hard in my heart, which only increased my exhilaration.

Not wanting to lose Logan in the crowd, I took his hand. He ushered me to the bar through the clusters of people. On our way, several female heads turned, appraising the man I was with. I wondered if Logan took notice of their lustful glances.

He leaned on the bar and faced me with a huge grin. "What'll it be, birthday girl? Let me guess...So-Co."

I nodded and dug into my pocket. Logan brought his lips to my ear. "This one's on me."

"Fine, I'll get the next one," I shouted over the music. He shook his head in a non-verbal *"whatever."*

We lifted our shots in front of us in a silent toast, then downed them, placing the shot glasses hard on the bar when we were finished. Logan took my hand in an attempt to lead me elsewhere.

"Wait! It's your turn," I yelled. "Name your poison."

Logan placed his finger on his chin pretending he had to think about it. "Patrón," he said with one brow up.

"Hmm, tequila? Sounds like you're on a mission."

"If you mean a mission to let loose and have some fun, then hell yeah, I'm on a mission," he smiled. "It *is* our birthday party, right?"

The bartender poured the shots, but when I tried to give him my money, he shook his head and pointed to Logan. Logan leaned into me. "I've got an ongoing tab here."

"What? That's not fair! I wanted to pay!"

He shrugged, unconcerned, "Consider it a birthday gift. Eighteen is a pretty big birthday, you know."

"I suppose so. I'll finally be legal." I thought for a moment. "I can get my own apartment!"

He appeared to be in thought before grinning widely. "You could buy tobacco."

I scrunched my face up as my palm playfully hit his arm. "Ew, gross. Hmm, what else does one do when they're eighteen? I know. I could die for my country."

He looked at me like I was being ridiculous, "Hell no, I cannot picture you as a military chick."

"Why not? Military chicks are the shit. I could totally do it if I wanted to."

"No argument there. Trust me, I know how bad-ass you are," he teased. "But wouldn't you rather commemorate the occasion by doing something a little less...life-altering? Like...buy some lottery tickets?"

"That would be life-altering, but in a completely different way."

"Only if you win."

"Exactly. Oooh," I took his arm. "We could live in a mansion on a private, tropical beach. That'd be nice."

"We?"

"Uh, yeah," I said, momentarily faltering. Was I really picturing myself *living* with him? Yep, I was and I could totally see it. It looked damn good. Man, that kiss from earlier did a number on me. "I'd split my winnings with *all* my friends. We could *all* live in *neighboring* mansions. Separately. In our *own* mansions. On the beach."

He laughed, "If you say so."

I barely heard him before grabbing his arm again as the best idea *ever* struck me. "I could get a tattoo! Let's do that!"

He eyed me suspiciously as if he didn't think I would ever do something so audacious.

"You don't think I'd do it, do you...?" I challenged.

"*Maybe* I could see you getting a tiny little heart on your hip or some other discreet place that no one would ever see. But it's highly unlikely."

I huffed out an exaggerated sigh, "Oh, you know nothing about me. This girl?" I pointed my thumb at my chest, "Is bold. So bold that I'm not even opposed to a full sleeve. Just wait, you'll see."

Chuckling, he continued. "Geez, you're all about the long-lasting transformations, huh? Well, how about this...you could get *married*."

"Pfff." Still smiling, I gave him a *'whatever'* glance. "And divorced."

"Right? The way I see it, marriage is for suckers. I mean, *you* know it and *I* know it, how come the rest of the world is oblivious it?" Just as I was about to concur, he changed the subject, "Hey, you could go to the porn shop!"

"*Yipee!*" As he laughed, I rolled my eyes and glanced at the bartender, busy at work, a new idea popping into my mind. "I could bartend."

"Yeah," he thought for a moment just before his eyes lit up. "Or...you could go to a strip club!"

"Really Logan? First you want me in a porn shop, then a strip club?" I grinned. "You're such a guy."

"Exactly, which means I can't be held responsible for the things that go through my mind."

"True. But you can control what you say. It's called a filter."

"Eh, filters are overrated."

"Besides," I persisted. "I thought you had to be twenty-one to get into a strip club."

"Oh," he raised his brows. "So you *are* interested."

"No! Of course not!" I looked away, taking a sip of my drink.

"Yes you are! I see those wheels turning in that mind of yours. You're curious, aren't you?"

"Nope." I forced myself to look as disinterested as possible. "I could not care less."

"Well," he pondered a thought. "We could go to one that doesn't serve alcohol."

"Is there such a thing?" I asked.

"Oh yeah," his face was all teeth, his grin was so big. "You wanna?"

"No."

"You sure? I promise you'll have fun."

"No!"

Staring at nothing in particular, his grin widened as if that was even possible.

"What?" I asked.

"Nothing. I'm just planning what we'll do on your birthday. It's going to be a day you'll never forget."

"I'm not going to a strip club, Logan!"

After the shots, he ordered us some drinks. While we were on our second drink, our attention became diverted to a cackling sound. Seriously, it sounded like a distressed chicken. The second we heard it, we looked at each other, clearly thinking the same thing. *WTF was that?* We both turned to face the noise, but all we saw was an attractive young brunette with her group of girlfriends.

Suddenly, the cackling noise came out of her. It was her version of a laugh. Our first reaction was shock that such a noise could be coming out of a person. Once the surprise wore off, we looked at each other with the same confused expression, then immediately busted into laughter. Then, she did it again, which intensified our amusement. The next time she did it, I grabbed onto Logan's arm to steady myself as I giggled uncontrollably, and the time after that, I almost fell to the floor.

Logan fared no better. He was laughing just as hard as me. Between chuckles, he leaned into me. "You're terrible. Laughing at that poor girl."

He was right, but I couldn't help it. It was funny, and the drinks had kicked in. Still laughing, he took my hand and led me through the crowd to the dance floor.

"I love this song!" I proclaimed as we began to dance. Logan's body flexed and moved to the beat perfectly. His movement was slight, not overdoing it. It was sexy. Looking around, I noticed that I wasn't the only girl watching him.

A few moments later, the music took me over. Nothing could be heard over the rhythm. I closed my eyes as I moved to the beat, the bass pounding throughout my body. When I opened them a few moments later, the first thing I saw was Logan's bemused eyes burning into me. In the last few minutes, the mood between us had done a complete one-eighty. Humor no longer coated the air, and instead was replaced with a potent fervency that had me craving things. Things like Logan's lips. His taste. His touch.

I smiled, trying to diffuse the intensity, but it didn't work. The way he looked at me as he moved so flawlessly made my heart skip, and my smile quickly faded as our gaze deepened.

He took my hand and slowly drew me closer to him as our movement slowed, no longer following the beat of the music. With our eyes locked, taking each other in, he placed my hand on his lower back, and put his on mine, pulling me so close that our legs intertwined and our bodies pressed firmly against each other, his thigh grinding between my legs, and mine between his, as we continued to dance.

He brought his other hand to my face, delicately moving my damp hair behind my ear with his fingers. My eyes closed shut from his intoxicating touch as my cheek instinctively buried itself into his hand. I needed to stop this, but I couldn't. I wanted it to happen so badly.

His hand moved from my cheek to my chin, pulling it up so that I would look at him. Our bodies stilled, even though the music continued. His gaze moved to my mouth, as he slowly brought his face closer and pressed his warm, wet lips lightly on mine. Even though it was only a slight touch, it sent a shiver down my spine and a quiver through my stomach. A moment later, our lips parted and began moving in harmony. What was it about his touch that gave me such a euphoric feeling?

I wanted to keep kissing him so badly that a wave of pain washed through my chest at the thought of having to stop. But he had already become too important to me to lose. My eyes squeezed shut, and a whimper escaped my throat as I shoved him off me. My body shook while my chest rose up and down from each heavy, fast breath. It took everything I had to push him away.

Seeing the pain in his eyes after I abruptly shoved him brought tears to mine. I shook my head to tell him no, and his pain was replaced by anger. He took my elbow, pulling me off the dance floor and to a corner of the club where it was somewhat quieter, although the music still pounded in my ears. With a mixture of impatience and confusion, he stared at me for a moment.

"I'm going to say something. And it's the only time I'll say it because I don't ever want things to be weird between us." He looked me in the eye. "I like you, Liv. A lot. And I know we've got something here."

"Logan, please, don't."

"Just hear me out. There's something here. Between us. Why are you so dead set on staying friends?"

I swallowed, trying to get the lump out of my throat. Staying friends meant having a future with him. If we crossed the fine line between friendship and…more than friendship, the chance of us having any sort of future together would be practically non-existent. I hated what I would say next, but it had to be done if I wanted to keep him.

"Because that's all I feel, Logan."

The devastation in his eyes killed me. I knew he cared about me, but I didn't know how much until this very moment. It was a horrible feeling to know that I was the one making him feel this way.

I could tell he wanted to say something, but he simply exhaled and shook his head. "Okay. You can't get any clearer than that."

"I'm sorry, I..."

"No…You know what? It's *not* okay. I *know* you feel it, too, Liv. What are you so afraid of?"

"What do you mean? I'm not afraid of anything. I told you, I don't do relationships."

"Bullshit! That's an excuse. You kiss other people, why can't you kiss me?"

"What the hell, that's a rude thing to say!"

He ran his fingers through his hair in exasperation. "Tell me. Help me to make sense of it because I don't fucking get it! You say you want to be friends, but the way you look at me when I touch you is not just friendly, Liv. Do you know how hard it is for me to control myself around you? You're beautiful, smart, you've got spunk. And Goddammit, you're *fun*. I've never met anyone like you before." He took my hand. "We could be good together. Don't you think it's worth a try?"

He was right. We would be good together. We'd be phenomenal. The thought occurred to me to do what every part of my body and soul wanted to do…give in. Be his and have him be mine. But I knew if I did, it would be only a temporary euphoria. History has shown that, for me, having a mutual love for another person means having to say goodbye. It was like some sort of cruel genetic defect. Being more than friends would never last, and once we crossed the line, there would be no way of going back. We'd be done. And the thought of losing him terrified me.

"And then what?" I pulled my hand out of his and took a step back. "What happens when we become more than friends? Do you think we'll just stay idling in happy-relationship-land forever? No! One thing will lead to another and no matter which road we take, it'll always end up the same…it ends with us *apart*. You *know* it won't work if we cross this line. You know as well as I do that if we take this step, there's no going back and I *care* about you. You're too important to lose! And I don't care about Evan or any other boys the way I care about you, that's why it's okay for me to kiss them!"

He was silent for several moments as he stared at me. "Do you know how back-asswards that is?"

"I'm sorry. Being in a relationship is just not in the cards for me—for us—okay?"

He studied me for a moment, defeat slowly devouring his expression. "Fine. I get it. I understand. As fucked up as it is, you're absolutely right. I promise, I won't mention it again."

145

He turned away from me and started towards the bar, but I grabbed his wrist. "Logan, stop!" He turned to me with hope in his eyes. "Are we good?"

He looked down at the floor. "Yeah, we're good."

It was the first time he lied those words to me.

*

It didn't take long for me to find out just how *not* good we were. I stepped out of the ladies room and spotted Logan at the bar doing shots with two beautiful blonds standing on each side of him. His eye caught mine as I approached, and he smiled at me as if he were having the greatest time of his life.

"Liv, this is Kelsey and Candace," Logan politely introduced us.

"Is this your girlfriend?" a confused Candace asked.

"No, baby," he looked at me with a smile. "She's just a friend."

He called her baby.

I politely shook their perfectly manicured hands, then stood off to the side, not really sure what to do with myself now that Logan was otherwise occupied. Several minutes passed as the girls giggled and cooed, staying attentive to Logan's every word. The music was too loud, and I wasn't close enough to them to be part of the conversation.

"We're gonna go dance," Logan informed me as the girls pulled him away. "You wanna join us?"

My heart sank at the indifference in his voice. Unable to speak, I shook my head. For a moment, I thought I saw a pang of compassion in his eyes, but he quickly brushed it off as he was tugged to the dance floor.

I tried not to watch, but I couldn't seem to stop. While Candace took her place behind him and Kelsey in front, they swayed in unison with him, their hands exploring every part of him. By the amused, lustful expression on his face, I could tell he was enjoying every moment of it.

As Candace brought her hands to Logan's stomach, under his shirt, he took Kelsey by the small of her back, bringing her close so that their legs bumped against each other's. With his other hand, he swept her hair behind her ear, then delicately pulled her chin up and brought his face to hers.

That's when I looked away.

I flagged the bartender and ordered my favorite shot. I reached into my pocket to pay for it, but again, he didn't take my money.

"It's on him," the bartender said as he pointed to a gorgeous man, who looked to be in his early twenties, on the other side of the bar. His light brown hair was tucked behind his ears. I smiled and raised my shot glass to say thank you, then swallowed it down.

My buzz increased, as well as my boredom. This was supposed to be our birthday celebration. Why was Logan the only one allowed to have fun? I made a conscious decision to stop wallowing and began to subtly move to the music as I stood by the bar, searching for something to entertain me. I took one last look at the dance floor and met Logan's eyes. He turned away the very moment it happened.

"Is that your boyfriend?" a voice from behind me said into my ear. I spun around to see the man who had bought the shot for me.

"No, apparently, I'm more like his wing woman," I replied.

He laughed. "Well, then who's *your* wing woman?"

147

"Again…me." I smiled.

"You're obviously someone who doesn't need any help."

I looked at him, confused.

"You're strikingly beautiful," he clarified as he smiled, showing a dimple in his left cheek and perfect white teeth.

Normally that sort of line would turn me off. But this man had an enticing confidence, and I was bored. I extended my hand. "I'm Liv."

He placed his hand in mine with just the right amount of firmness. "Tyler."

We stood in place, neither one of us letting go.

"So, Liv, tell me what you love to do?"

"Well, that's a pretty broad question, don't you think?" I replied, finally releasing his hand.

"I don't think so. It would be broad if I asked you what you *like* to do. I asked you what you *love* to do. That cuts the options down drastically."

As I thought about his question, the only thing that came to mind was Logan. I loved spending time with him. I loved the way he laughed at my stupid humor. I loved the way he looked at me and how I felt around him. I looked down at the floor as I thought about the irrefutable fact that things might not be the same with us anymore.

Tyler's comforting hand touched my shoulder. "Hey, it's just a question. How about I tell you what I love instead."

I smiled. "Okay."

"I love quiet places."

"Huh?" Confused, I glanced around at our noisy surroundings.

"There's a coffee shop next door. You want to go?"

"Oh! I don't know, I came with…"

"Just one coffee. I'll have you back in a half hour. I promise. Your friend seems occupied anyway."

I looked back at the dance floor where Logan's angry eyes were on me, or maybe Tyler, while Candace and Kelsey's hands were on him.

"Sure, why not?" I said, shrugging.

Tyler offered his arm, and I latched my hand around it. The thought crossed my mind to tell Logan I was leaving but that would surely cause a scene that I did not want to deal with. I would just tell Matt instead.

As we approached the exit hallway, I was yanked backwards by a tug on my sweater.

"Hey!" I shouted.

"What are you doing?" Logan's expression exuded fury. And fear.

"Logan, this is my favorite sweater!"

"Is there a problem here?" Tyler said in an authoritative voice.

"Yeah, there is. She's with me," Logan challenged, bringing his face close to Tyler's.

"It didn't look like it," Tyler responded condescendingly, then he turned to me. "Liv, it's up to you. But I'll tell you this. Whoever you are 'with' should treat you like their first choice. Not their last." He faced Logan. "Any idiot can see that."

Logan's fists clenched tightly on each side of him. His eyes narrowed just before he lunged at Tyler, fisting his shirt and pounding him in the jaw with his other fist. Tyler stepped back, confused, and lost balance for a moment, then immediately reciprocated with a blow to Logan's face.

"STOP IT!!!" I screamed, trying to get between them. An elbow bashed into my mouth, thrusting me back a few steps. My fingers examined my lips which were wet to the touch, and when I drew them away from my face, they were bright red. I cringed at the rusty taste in my mouth. The fighting continued in front of me. Logan and Tyler kept at it, delivering blow after blow until they were both on the ground.

"Break it up! Break it up!" A familiar voice approached. Relief washed over me when I saw Matt. He took hold of Logan, pulling him up off the floor, while another bouncer gripped Tyler. It took a moment for them both to calm down.

"Real fucking mature, asshole!" Tyler shouted. "You really think that shit is going to impress her?" He forcefully pulled himself off the bouncer and reached into his pocket, pulling out a little white card. He turned to me and handed me the card. "Liv, you deserve better. Call me if you ever want to hang out." Then he turned and left.

"Yeah, keep walking, asshole!" Logan shouted.

Tyler kept walking but lifted his middle finger in the air in response to Logan's comment.

"Ah shit, Liv," Matt said as he let go of Logan. He took some cocktail napkins from the bar and placed them on my bloody lip.

"I'm fine, it's nothing," I lied. My face was throbbing.

While Matt dabbed my lip, my gaze found Logan's. Completely still, with utter shock mixed with regret in his eyes, he watched me. A drop of blood trickled down the side of his face from the cut on his left eyebrow. Even battered and bruised, he was immaculate. I took another cocktail napkin and walked to Logan, stopping inches in front of him.

The pain in his eyes as he gazed down at me brought tears to my eyes. I took the napkin and dabbed the corner of his eyebrow as his eyes searched mine.

150

"*Fuck*, look at what I've done." He brought his hand to my face and brushed the corner of my mouth with his thumb. "I'm *so* sorry."

My hand fell to my side, and I let the napkin slip out of my fingers. Without a thought, my hands found a place on his sides which only caused more anguish in his perfect face.

"It was an accident," I said.

I cautiously moved my hands to his back and placed my cheek on his chest. His breaths, heavy and deep, moved me as my body pressed against his. My eyes closed as I breathed his intoxicating scent, a mixture of deodorant, sweat and blood. After a moment, he carefully took hold of me and brought his lips to my ear.

"I'm sorry, Liv...He's right, I'm an idiot." He pulled his face away so that he could look at me. "You are my first choice. You're my only choice."

His eyes pleaded for forgiveness. And yeah, the fight was totally uncalled for, but I knew in my heart that he did nothing else wrong. He didn't owe me any explanations for hanging out with those other girls tonight. I didn't belong to him, and he didn't belong to me. He was free to do whatever he wanted with whomever he wanted.

"Let's just go, okay?" I urged.

He nodded, then took my hand and began to walk me toward the door.

Matt stood in front of us. "Oh no, neither one of you are driving. I'll call you a cab."

Chapter Sixteen

I waited next to Matt under the heat lamp as Logan retrieved our coats from his car. I was thankful to have a sweater and jeans on. Some of the girls in line were wearing nothing but mini dresses. They must've been freezing.

The cab pulled up to the curb just as Logan returned. I gave Matt a hug and a quick peck on the cheek before remembering that he was supposed to be a tough guy tonight. "Thank you, Matt. For everything."

He smiled without any hint that my thoughtless affection had bothered him. "Anytime, hon. Take care of that lip."

Logan held the cab door open for me as he nodded a goodbye to Matt. I scooted in and moved to the other side while Logan entered behind me.

"Where to?" the cabbie asked.

Logan gave him my address, and the cab started down the road. With no radio on and none of us talking, the only sound was the heater vents and the tires on the road.

I turned to face Logan. His gaze was overly focused on the nothing that was straight ahead, with his elbow on the window ledge, his temple resting on his knuckle. The city lights lit up his face as they moved, his scowl apparent in their glow. He knew I was watching him, but he wouldn't meet my stare.

"Logan?" I whispered.

"Yeah," he said, still looking ahead of him.

I hesitated. I wanted to ask him if we were good—really, truly, honest to God, good—but I already knew what the answer would be. He took a chance tonight. He put himself out there without getting the result he had hoped for, and part of me knew that after tonight, we would never be good again. At least not in the way we were. Tonight was a turning point.

For the first time, I questioned my resolve. But I couldn't tell him what I was thinking without giving him mixed signals. He deserved better than that.

I sighed. "Never mind."

I looked straight ahead as tears began to well in my eyes and a huge rock formed in my throat. We had to be okay. There was no other option. All my attempts to keep him couldn't have been done in vain. This situation needed to be rectified, but how?

A friendly gesture?

I placed my hand, palm down, next to my thigh and took a deep, hopeful, breath. Slowly, I extended my hand to the center of the seat, between the two of us, hoping, praying that he would meet me halfway.

Logan remained motionless.

The minutes passed. My intention for him to take my hand was obvious and he had never had a problem holding my hand before. *Shit.* I glanced at him in an attempt to get some sort of reaction, but all I noticed was his eyebrows pulling closer together, his chest lifting up and down with heavy breaths, and his jaw clenching tightly. I knew he felt my eyes on him. And I knew he saw my hand between us, waiting for him to take it. Still, he stared straight ahead.

Each moment that my reconciliation gesture continued to go unanswered, my hope slowly dissipated. What we had was gone. It would never be the same.

My head bowed down as my hand found its way back to my thigh. As I attempted to gather my senses, an involuntary sniffle came from my nose. Out of the corner of my eye, I saw Logan turn his head towards me. I turned to look out the window to hide my glossy eyes from him.

It was late and the roads were free of other cars. Empty. I knew emptiness like an old hollow friend that I had pushed away years ago. No matter how hard I tried, it always seemed to burrow its way back into my heart. Logan was making the choice to let me go.

Dammit!

An unexpected warmth encompassed my hand and squeezed tight. I looked down to see Logan's strong hand on mine. My gaze moved up his extended arm and to his defeated eyes. How was it, that one single look from him could make everything else in the world go away? The corners of his mouth turned up slightly in an attempt at a compassionate smile.

"C'mere," he said as he pulled on my hand.

A sob of relief escaped me, pushing a tear out, as I unbuckled my seat belt and nuzzled into him. With my head on his chest, he swept my hair back with his fingers in a repetitive motion.

He let out a sigh. "You're making me crazy. I can't figure out how to get past the cluster-fuck in my mind when I'm around you." He seemed to be saying it to himself more than to me.

"I can't figure it out either," I whispered. "I'm sorry Logan."

"Don't be. Don't ever be sorry for the way you make me feel." He took a breath then rested his cheek on my head. "If friends is what you need, I promise I'll try. For you, I'll try."

He held me silently for the rest of the ride home. I began to think this might actually work out. We might actually be able to salvage our friendship.

As we turned onto my street, my phone buzzed. It was a text from Evan.

r u home?

I had no interest in responding. As I put my phone back in my pocket, we pulled into my driveway.

"Oh, you've got to be fucking kidding me," Logan grumbled.

I looked up to see a Nissan Altima in my driveway and Evan on my balcony.

Oh shit.

Evan and I had been spending time together every so often since we met. Although neither one of us had any sort of romantic interest in each other, and even though he had a girlfriend far away in Denver, our relationship was not exactly platonic.

My mind drifted to our last encounter about a week ago. He had come over to watch a movie, and although the movie played in its entirety, our time was spent doing something other than watching it.

"Mmm," Evan groaned as I straddled him on the couch and sucked on his earlobe. I was fully clothed, but his shirt was off, revealing his muscular arms and chest. My hands became magnets to his abdomen. As my lips moved to his jawline and

down his neck, my thumbs traced each valley of each muscle on his stomach, causing him to moan again. "How far are we going to go today, Liv?"

Not sure what he meant by that, I stopped and looked him in the eyes.

"I mean, I'll respect whatever you want to do," he breathed. "But if we can't take it any farther, we have to stop now. Because if we don't, I don't know if I'll be able to stop later."

"Oh," I said as I removed myself from his lap. "Okay."

I sat on the opposite end of the couch and tied my hair into a ponytail with the hair-tie from my wrist. I took the popcorn bowl off the end table and began to crunch on the contents while I stared at the TV. After he found his shirt and put it back on, I felt his eyes on me. When I looked at him, he was shaking his head at me with a smirk.

I rolled my eyes. "I'm not having sex with you. You have a girlfriend."

But that wasn't the only reason. The truth was that I wasn't going to give up my virginity to someone who didn't really care about me, or for someone who I had no interest in. Sure, Evan and I were friends, and he'd help me if I were ever in a bind, but he would never go out of his way for me. And the feeling was mutual. He was crazy hot, but I just couldn't see myself doing anything other than kissing with him.

"I told you, we have an open relationship." He explained for the thousandth time. "I've talked about it with her, and she's okay with it."

"Okay, for one thing, that's weird. And secondly, that doesn't change the fact that you do have a girlfriend. And thirdly, I'm not going to be someone's secret mistress." Without

156

a care, I stuffed another bunch of popcorn into my mouth and focused on the movie.

"But you're not a secret!"

I looked at him, grinning at how riled up he was getting. He let out a defeated chuckle and shook his head at me again. Then he put his coat on and came over to me, leaning his face into my neck. The wetness of his tongue behind my ear tickled, and I let out a giggle.

"Whoever lands you is going to be one lucky bastard."

I threw popcorn at him. "Hey! Be nice!"

He laughed as he walked toward the door. "See ya later, Liv."

Now Evan was here at my house, leaning on the railing of my balcony, waiting for me at the worst possible moment.

"Let me take a guess at what he's here for," Logan said sarcastically.

"Logan, I had no idea he would be here. I'm sorry."

"You know what?" he said as he all but shoved me off of him. "Go. Enjoy yourself. I guess as your *friend*, I'll have to get used to this at some point."

"I don't want to."

"You don't want to what? Go and have some fun? Well, you can't stay here in this cab all night."

If I left this cab and went to Evan, it would put a barrier between Logan and me that could never be broken. I couldn't let that happen. "Come with me."

His confused face glared at me. "I'm not sure what you want here, but I'm not into dudes. Two girls is fine, but…"

"No! Oh my God. I'm not going to have any 'fun' with anybody." I used my fingers as quotations. "I'm going to tell Evan to leave. Logan, come with me. Stay with me tonight. I

157

don't feel good leaving things like this between us, maybe if we just talk it out."

"I really don't think there's anything more to say." He stayed silent for a moment. "Besides, I don't think your parents will enjoy finding me in your room in the middle of the night."

"Fine, then we won't talk about it, we'll just…I don't know, hang out…or talk about something else. And they won't know. I'll lock my door. You need someone to take you to get your car in the morning anyway."

The cab driver grew impatient. "Let's go! Clock is ticking!"

"Give us a minute!" Logan and I responded together.

Logan glanced out the window at Evan, then back at me. "Liv, I want to. Trust me, it's all I want to do right now. I just don't think it's a good idea."

My heart stopped. *Why?* Maybe this was his way of keeping his distance. Of not getting too close. Of not confusing things more than they already are. Then I realized he was right. He was doing what was right for our friendship.

"Okay," I whispered. "I understand."

His jaw clenched. The conflict in his eyes was obvious. He looked out at Evan again and shook his head slightly.

I reached over and embraced him. "Bye, Logan."

He didn't say anything when I let go of him, but his afflicted eyes stayed focused on me. I looked down to break the stare and stepped out of the cab, into the cold, closing the door gently behind me.

Evan had already climbed down from the balcony and stood waiting for me by the front door. I heard the cab drive away as I approached him.

"Evan, what are you doing here?" I asked.

He looked at me apprehensively. "I see my timing sucks right now. Sorry." He squinted at me. "What happened to your face?"

I stepped past him and began to unlock the door. "Nothing, I'm fine. My parents will be home soon, so you can't stay."

"I know. Can I come in for a minute? Just one minute. There's something I want to tell you."

The anxiety in his voice caught me off guard. He was normally so calm. "Yeah. Sure. Come on in."

After taking my coat off and downing two Tylenols with a full glass of water, I took a seat on the couch next to him. It was then that I saw the dark circles under his eyes.

"Are you okay, Evan?" I asked.

He turned to face me. "My grandmother passed away today."

"Oh my God, I'm so sorry." I immediately reached out and pulled him into a tight hug. The tension he was holding relaxed almost instantly.

"It's okay. It's for the best," he said as he released me. "She's been suffering for a long time. She's in a better place now." Seeing the quizzical look in my face, he continued, "She's the reason I'm here Liv. When I told you I was here helping my family, I meant her. She's been on hospice for months. My mom couldn't do it on her own, so I came back to help. Now that she's gone…"

"You're leaving," I finished.

He looked at me and nodded. "I just wanted to say goodbye. Cassie's—my girlfriend's—flight arrives tomorrow morning. She'll be here until the funeral, then we're going back to Denver together. This was the only chance I had to say goodbye to you." His expression turned nervous again. "I know

159

it's shitty timing. Did I fuck things up for you? I saw Logan out in the cab."

I shifted in my seat. I wasn't sure this was something I wanted to discuss with Evan. "I don't know. Some crazy stuff happened tonight with us. He told me things."

He gave me a knowing look. "He loves you, you know. I can tell by the way he looks at you. And not that I'm complaining because I've enjoyed every moment that I've spent with you, but I've always wondered why you weren't with him."

His statement surprised me. "He's my friend. I'm not going to ruin that." This conversation was getting way too personal. He nodded, appearing to want to say something else, but decided against it. I stood up from the couch and smiled. "I'm gonna miss you, Evan. Take care, okay?"

He stood and took me by the waist, embracing me tightly. "Take care, Liv."

Chapter Seventeen

With my eyes wide open, I stared intently at my alarm clock. An hour had passed since I came to bed, and I had grown frustrated that I couldn't fall asleep. All I could think about were the events of this night and the things that Logan said to me. I heard the front door open downstairs. Mom and Jeff were home from the pub. After some clinking of dishes for their after-work snack and the sounds of the bathroom medicine cabinet opening and closing, all was silent again. Still, my eyes stayed open.

Another hour passed. I pictured Logan at his apartment. Was he able to fall asleep easily after everything that happened tonight? The look of pain in his face when I left the cab to go to Evan caused a lump in my throat that wouldn't go away. I wondered what he thought happened between Evan and me tonight.

After another half hour and not an ounce of sleepiness in my system, I sat up in my bed. I needed to do something to stop this gut-wrenching, gnawing sensation in my stomach. So I put my shoes and coat on, grabbed my keys, and walked out of my house.

*

I hesitated before ringing the doorbell of Logan's apartment. What if he wasn't alone? What if he needed something, or someone, to take away whatever it was he was feeling? Or—what if he didn't want to see me? He did tell me he didn't want to stay with me tonight…what if my showing up on his doorstep only makes things worse? I braced myself for the ten thousand reasons I shouldn't be here and pushed the button anyway. Why? Because I needed him right now and I was pretty damn sure he needed me, too.

A few moments later, the lock unlatched, and the door opened. Logan stood with his hand on the door, and his tired, annoyed look melted when he saw me.

"Hey," he breathed with relief.

He was shirtless, wearing only sweatpants that hung just low enough to see the V of his lower abdomen. I wanted to run my fingers through his perfectly messed-up hair. The way he squinted at me from the light in the hallway was irresistible.

"Are you okay?" he asked.

I nodded. "I couldn't sleep."

He continued to stare into my eyes, the way he does, keeping his distance with his hand holding the door. I hadn't planned what I would say and now I wish I had because I was drawing a complete blank.

"Me neither." He mumbled as if he were saying it to himself. He looked down at what I was wearing and the corners of his mouth turned up slightly. I hadn't thought about changing into clothes before I left my house. I was still in my pajamas. "Spur of the moment decision, huh?"

I shrugged.

He opened the door a little farther and motioned for me to come in. He followed me up the stairs and into his apartment. The stove light from the kitchen and the streetlights coming through the window in the living room were the only things illuminating the space. I took my coat off and placed it on the

162

arm of the couch as he closed the door, then he walked toward me, stopping a foot in front of me. We stared at each other for a moment.

"Nothing happened with Evan tonight," I blurted out.

His eyebrows pulled together. "Okay."

"I don't know why I'm here," I confessed. "I guess I just felt like I needed to be here right now."

He took a breath. "Okay."

It took all my strength to muster up the courage to say the next thing. "I don't want to lose you. If things change. If we change…" Tears welled in my eyes at the thought of that very thing occurring. "It just can't happen, Logan."

Being this close to him, and seeing the way he was looking at me, I could no longer control the fear inside of me, and I began to tremble. I had been able to hold myself together rather well until now. Something about being near him caused my strength to crumble. My head dropped as tears trickled out of my eyes.

What the hell was happening to me? I did not see this emotional outburst coming *at all* and to be honest, I felt like a complete idiot for breaking down in front of him like this.

He pulled me into his arms and held me while I let out everything I had been holding in. After a few moments, he released me and cupped my cheeks with both hands, wiping my tears with his thumbs, and bringing my gaze back to his.

"Don't cry," he whispered. "It kills me to see you cry." He leaned down and kissed my forehead, lingering there for a moment. Then, he gently kissed my eyelids, one after the other. My tears ceased, and my breathing became shallow. His touch felt amazing.

"I'm sorry, I don't know what's wrong with me. I haven't cried in years. I feel like such a baby."

"Stop apologizing. I'm glad you're here." He pulled away. "You're fucking exhausted. *I'm* fucking exhausted. I really think we should just get some sleep. Don't you?"

Just being near him had calmed my anxiety. Sleep sounded like heaven right about now. "Hell yeah."

He took my hand and led me to his bedroom. Music played through the speaker on his bedside table. He sat me down on the bed, then lifted my foot, removed my shoe, and repeated the process with the other foot.

"This song is beautiful," I said.

He hesitated. "It makes me think of you." I couldn't hold back the grin that formed on my face from his words. When he saw my expression, he relaxed. "Damn, Liv, I'd do anything for that smile." He pulled down the bedding. "Lay down. Get some rest." He rose up and began walking towards the door, turning to face me just before he exited the room. "I'll see you in the morning."

"Where are you gonna sleep?" I asked, confused.

"The couch. It's fine. I don't mind."

I knew how selfish I was for what I would say next but I wanted him to stay by me so badly that I didn't stop the words from falling out of my mouth. "Please stay here."

"I shouldn't. Friends don't sleep in the same bed together." He sighed and bowed his head, shaking it slightly. "But I can't seem to say no to you." He looked back into my eyes. "I don't want to say no."

"So say yes," I pleaded.

As I stared into his brooding eyes and waited for his answer, the song repeated from the beginning and the lyrics shouted an unspoken question. It asked about the future. It asked about belonging. It spoke of everything in the world going away, and finding solace in the person you love.

"For the record," I blurted, "sometimes girlfriends sleep in the same bed together. Mel and I do it all the time when we sleep over at each other's' houses."

He laughed. Loudly. "Do you have any idea of what kind of visual you just put in my mind?"

"What? OMG, you perve, I meant the kind of sleep you do when you close your eyes and drift away to dreamland. Not sleep *together*, as in get-it-on. We stay on opposite sides of the bed, no touching involved!"

He walked back to the bed and slowly pulled the covers up, sliding under them, next to me. "I like my version better."

"I bet you do." I nuzzled my head in the soft spot between his chest and shoulder and placed my arm around his middle, sticking my cold hand between his warm body and the mattress.

His heart pounded hard in my ear as his arms folded over me. Being this close to him…touching him exhilarated me, while at the same time, I became immersed in a feeling of tranquility. His warmth comforted me and within minutes, I drifted to sleep.

*

"Liv, wake up," Logan whispered softly. A hum came out of my throat as I shifted off his shoulder and turned away from him, burrowing my face in the cool pillow beside us. The soft fabric smelled like him and I took one more deep, heavenly breath in. How long had I been asleep? Based on my current comatose state, not long.

His hand casually brushed up and down my arm. "You've got to see this."

Intrigued, my eyes cracked open, just enough to see the blurry orange and purple hues reflect on the bare walls of Logan's bedroom. His fingers brushed my hair off my face and behind my ear.

"Open your eyes, baby. It's beautiful."

He called me baby.

I turned to face him as I opened my eyes, confused and unexpectedly delighted by his term of endearment. When my eyes finally focused and saw his beautiful face lit up by the colors of the sunrise, my bewilderment grew incredibly. His eyes glowed as he studied me. I had never seen him look this peaceful and content. He smiled at my expression then huffed out a single laugh.

"It slipped," he said as if he read my mind. "Get over it."

He moved off the bed and leisurely walked to the window, placing his wrist on the window frame above his head and his other hand on his hip, as he gazed out with a more contemplative expression. Then he turned to face me and the corners of his mouth turned up slightly. He extended his hand, motioning for me to join him.

I didn't need to see the sunrise. The beautiful man that stood before me, bare chested and painted in colors was enough. I couldn't take my eyes off him. His smile faded as he dropped his arm to his side, and he stared at me for a moment.

Slowly, the melancholy grew in his eyes. "I don't know what the hell to think when you look at me like that, Liv. Everything about that look says you want me. That you need me, like I need you. But something tells me you'd freak if I tried

166

anything with you right now. I've never been so fucking confused in my life."

Shit. I tried to snap myself out if it, but I still couldn't look away. I was being unfair to him. He deserved so much better than me, so much more. He deserved the world. He deserved something I couldn't give him. I sat up with my feet dropping down to the floor. He deserved an explanation.

I stood and walked towards him, resisting the urge to throw my arms around him and give in to the passion he ignited in me. Instead, my fingers found his, and we laced them together.

"There are no happy endings, Logan. Someone always gets hurt. It's inevitable." I fought the lump in my throat with an artificial smile. "The only way to prevent the hurt...is by not starting. It can't end if it doesn't start, right?"

His fingers grazed my cheek, "I get it. I really do. But don't you think it's too late for that? It already started, Liv. It started the day I laid eyes on you. How can you not see that?"

Tears welled in my eyes. When he saw my expression, he dropped his hand to his side and let out a breath through his nose. "I would love to get my hands on the asshole that hurt you."

I finally gazed out the window. I had never seen a sunrise like this one before. It was magical. The blue shade of the industrial buildings contrasted the orange sun peeking out above them. The orange was surrounded by a dark pink dome, with a deep purple sky above.

I gazed up at him. "This is perfect," I breathed. "Please tell me it won't end. Promise me." I knew I was forcing him to make a promise he couldn't keep. I didn't care. I wanted to hear it.

"What are you talking about? Promise you what won't end?"

"This…*us*…Just promise me it will stay like this."

I saw the resistance in his eyes. He took my face in his hands. "I promise I will do anything to make you happy, Liv."

"*This* makes me happy. The way we are right now."

The distress in his face intensified. After a moment, he pulled me to him, enveloping me in his arms. He kissed the top of my head. "Then yeah, I promise, it won't end."

I knew it was a lie. Everything ends in one way or another, but I didn't think he knew it yet. It didn't matter because right now, at this very moment, it was what I needed to hear, in exactly the way I needed to hear it.

Chapter Eighteen

The door chimed as I entered the coffee shop down the road from school. I hadn't gotten much sleep lately, and I needed the caffeine to get me going this morning. It had been a few days since the night I stayed with Logan, and although we still talked every day, I couldn't help but feel there was something missing. There was an obscure distance between us that we couldn't seem to shake.

In a zombie-like state, I wandered to the end of the line to wait for my turn. I vaguely noticed the man ahead of me move forward a step, and I instinctively followed. The door chimed again. Out of the corner of my eye, I noticed the man in front of me turn around to peer at the door. Then, I felt his eyes on me.

My gaze traveled from his dark tailored pants, up to his black wool button down coat. A white collar and tie stuck out the top. Then I noticed a familiar white dimpled smile and light brown hair tucked behind his ears.

"I see your lip is better," Tyler said smoothly.

I nodded, still in shock that he was here. I couldn't get over how his long-ish hair perfectly contrasted his business-like style. It should be completely out of place, but for him, it worked. "Yeah, it was no big deal, really."

After a momentary awkward silence, he continued playfully. "You never called."

"Oh, yeah, sorry, I lost your card." That was a reasonable excuse, wasn't it?

He glanced around at our surroundings. "Looks like we have a chance to get that coffee, if you're interested. Are you in a hurry to get to work?"

He had no idea how young I was. I thought for a moment. "You mean school. And no, I have a few minutes."

We ordered our coffees and then sat down at a table by the window.

He stared at me for a moment, leaning with his forearms on the table and both hands around his coffee cup. "I'm sorry I walked out on you at Rain that night. I had a bad feeling after leaving you with that...guy."

"Logan's a good friend. He'd never do anything to hurt me." I gave him a reassuring smile.

He nodded. He didn't seem to believe me, but he let it go. "So, what's your major?"

Oh crap. I looked around nervously, as I tried to decide how to tell him I wasn't majoring in anything. I leaned back in my seat and met his stare. "I go to high school, Tyler. Right up the street."

His eyes widened but only momentarily. He leaned back, crossed his arms, and let out a chuckle. "Are you shitting me?"

I shook my head. "I'm not joking. I'm missing first period at the moment."

He huffed out a laugh. "I'm going to assume that you weren't held back four or five times."

I shook my head again and grinned. "Nope. Sorry."

"Well, you're full of surprises, aren't you?" he asked, still shocked, but with a hint of amusement in his tone. He leaned towards me. "Exactly how old are you?"

"As of today, eighteen."

"Today's your birthday?"

170

"It is."

"And I didn't even buy your coffee. I feel like a jerk."

I smiled. "What about you? You look like you're living in the 'real world.' Are you some big company hot shot?"

"No, just an intern at a law firm. I'm sitting second chair in a trial today. Trying to look the part."

"Well, you look very handsome."

He smiled, then pulled his buzzing phone out of his pocket. His face dropped when he read the text. "Shit, I have to go." He looked back up at me and shook his head. "Eighteen, huh?"

I shrugged.

He placed his phone on the table and slowly slid it over to me. "Can I call you?"

I smiled. "That depends. You're not thirty are you? 'Cuz that would be weird."

He shook his head. "Twenty-two."

"That's not so bad, is it?" I took his phone and programmed my number into to it. Then, I called myself so that I could save his number and would know it was him if and when he called.

*

I arrived at school towards the end of first period. When I approached my locker I stopped in place. A ridiculous smile formed on my face when I saw the outside of it wrapped in wrapping paper, balloons, and streamers. I would have to thank Mel when I saw her.

When I opened the metal door, a white envelope with a purple bow on top caught my attention. I could tell when I picked it up that there was something inside of it, distorting it. I slipped my finger under the fold and ripped it open. Inside the envelope was a slip of paper and a pen. Taking the white pen in my hand, I examined it and laughed when I saw the Chippendale shirtless man on it. I clicked it, and his shorts came off, leaving him wearing only a G-string.

Instinctively, as if there would be anyone in the hallway in the middle of class, and as if they could see something so small, I looked around to make sure nobody could see what I was looking at. I took the slip of paper out of the envelope.

Since you won't play hooky today to go to the strip club (and other shenanigans), I figured it would all have to come to you.

Happy 18th

Logan

Oh great, what was he planning? The bell rang and kids started filtering into the halls. A moment later, I felt arms squeezing me from behind.

"Happy Birthday, Liv!" Melody chimed. "Where were you? Did you miss first period?"

I turned and smiled. "Did you do this?" I pointed to the locker decorations.

"Yes, you dork! I was waiting for you so I could see your face when you saw it, and you never came."

"I'm sorry, I ran into Tyler when I stopped for coffee this morning. We hung out for a few minutes. I just got here."

Her smile vanished. I had told Mel everything about the night I met Tyler. The same night Logan told me how he felt. The same night I fell asleep in Logan's arms. Mel rolled her eyes and started on her locker combo.

"What's wrong?" I asked, perplexed by her sudden detachment.

She turned to me, annoyed. "Are you crazy?"

"No! Are you?"

She huffed and shook her head. "I thought that you'd start opening your eyes now that Evan is out of the picture."

"Mel, I have no idea what you're talking about."

"How is it that you are not seeing what's right in front of you?" Her expression changed to pity, which put me on edge. "You're not fooling anybody, you know. I've seen the way you look at Logan and how he looks at you. What are you waiting for? Why are you messing around with these other guys? It's stupid."

"Judge much? Logan's not exactly Mr. Commitment either you know. He's never been in a serious relationship before. He goes through girls like…"

"Like you go through boys? See! You're perfect for each other."

I glared at her. She knew full well that I had my boundaries. "I think it's a little different with him."

"Oh please, he'd do anything for you and you know it. And he hasn't been with another girl for months."

"Not that we know of anyway."

She smiled at me. "You might change your mind by the end of the day."

"What do you mean?"

Her grin widened. "Nothing! Never mind. I've said too much already." She slammed her locker closed. "See ya later!"

Second period AP Psych and third period Spanish dragged on forever. Since the two classes were on the opposite sides of the building from my locker, I hadn't had a chance to stop there between periods.

I stood in anticipation of what I might find inside my locker as I turned the combination knob and opened the metal door. A women's camouflage military cap sat on top of my books. I took the note from the top of it and opened it.

Please tell me that you will never die for your country. I'd die if I lost you.

Logan

As I stared at his note, grinning like an idiot, reading it over and over again, Mel approached.

"Having second thoughts, are we?" she said.

I stuffed the note in my pocket, trying unsuccessfully to remove the enormous smile from my face. I laughed when I saw her entertained expression.

"You're behind this, aren't you?" I asked.

"No, he's behind it. I just happen to know your locker combo."

I sat through fourth period chemistry, my least favorite class, daydreaming about sunrises and flagging races and yellow Mustangs and almost-kisses in the moonlight, and the feel of his warm skin on mine, and for the first time in years, I entertained the possibility—just the possibility—of changing my mind. I saw a glimmer of hope. A potentially attainable light at the end of the dark, phlegmatic, tunnel.

His words from the club repeated in my head. *"We could be good together. Don't you think it's worth a try?"* An irresistible urge to do just that overcame me. For him, maybe I could try.

I watched Mel close my locker door as I approached it after fourth period. She turned to me with a smile. "Good timing. That was close."

"You should've just left it open for me!" I teased.

After my nervous hands fidgeted with my combo for several moments, I finally opened my locker. A small red box with a white bow immediately caught my attention. I pulled off the top box cover and crinkled my face when I saw what it was. "Ew!" Mel's phone clicked as it snapped my picture. I looked at her quizzically. "What was that for?"

"*Someone* wanted to see your reaction to this one." She peered at the contents. "What is it?" Her face crunched up when she saw it. "Are you serious?" She looked around nervously. "Don't let anyone see that."

A Skoal chewing tobacco container rested inside the box with a white note sitting on top of it.

"What is he thinking?" I asked, disgusted. Then I remembered one of his suggestions for an eighteen-year-old's rite-of-passage and smiled. *Chewing* tobacco never crossed my mind. I took the note and opened it.

I wish I could be there to see your face. Hopefully Mel is on top of that. Don't worry. Open it. It's not what you think.

I twisted the lid off the Skoal container. It was empty except for another white note, and…something else. A picture of something. Wings and a halo. Was it a sticker? Laughter escaped my throat when I picked it up and realized it was a temporary tattoo. I placed it back in the box and read the note.

An angel for the angel.

Logan

P.S. I am SO there when you want to do this for real.

After sixth period, in my locker waited a Powerball ticket and two scratch-offs with a note that said:

Don't forget about me when you win it big. God knows I'll never forget you.

At the end of the day, Mel watched closely as I opened my locker for the last time. By her enormous grin, I knew it would be something good. The hallways bustled with kids packing their backpacks to leave for the day.

My favorite coconut caramel chocolate bar rested on top of my books with a bow on it and a single red rose placed next to it. My smile immediately faded. And there it was. Fear. A red rose had meaning. A meaning which I immediately realized I wasn't ready for. I took the note and opened it.

I know this has nothing to do with you turning 18.

I also know how much you love this chocolate

bar—you can't get enough of it. And I'm happy

when you're happy. Come over. I'll wait for you.

Logan

Come over? My heart began to race. Why did he want me to come over? What did he expect to happen if I came over? *Crap!*

"I thought you'd like that for sure!" Mel said, surprised at my reaction. "You look like you're going to be sick."

"I do like it. I'm just a little overwhelmed, I guess." I handed her the note. "It's just so much. And he wants me to come over."

She read it and looked at me, still confused. "What's the big deal, you go over there all the time."

"I know, but...He's never done anything like this for me before." I held up the chocolate bar and rose. "It's like he's making a declaration or something. What if...What if..." I sighed. "I feel like if I go over there...I just don't want to. I don't want anything to change."

Mel rolled her eyes. "You can't live your life based on 'what-ifs,' Liv. And change is inevitable. It's the one thing you can always count on. Stop worrying about what might or might not happen and follow your heart. How can you expect to ever be happy if you don't?"

We closed our lockers and began walking down the hall. "Besides, don't you think everything has already changed?"

"No," I lied.

Mel huffed. "Ugh! You are impossible!"

Chapter Nineteen

I stared blankly at the steering wheel, contemplating my next move, as my car idled in my driveway. Do I get out and walk into my house? Or go to Logan's? I had been so deep in thought during my drive home that I barely recalled how I got here or how much time had passed since school let out.

I glanced at the digital clock on my dash to see that it was already 5:18PM. Logan knew I had the night off work, since I had told him I requested off for my birthday. I hated the fact that he was waiting for me. I took my phone out of my jacket pocket and began a text to him.

Thank you

My finger hit the send button. Then my palm smacked my forehead. *Shit! After everything he did for me today, that's all I could say?* With my phone still in hand, I crossed my arms on the steering wheel and rested my head on them, as I inwardly scolded myself. My hand buzzed, indicating an incoming text.

Welcome

That's it? I supposed I shouldn't have expected much more after the brief, heartless text I sent to him, but for some reason, his response infuriated me. Then I realized my fury had nothing at all to do with his text and everything to do with this awkwardness between us. Or was it the corner I felt I had just been backed into that was causing my blood to boil?

Was this how it was going to be between us from now on?

All I wanted was my friend.

The thought occurred to me to give in, but if I did, it knew would be the beginning of the end. And I couldn't bear the thought of losing him. Suddenly furious and determined, I put my car in reverse, backed out of the driveway, and headed to Logan's.

My phone buzzed on my way to his place and without looking to see who it was, I answered. "Hello?"

"How was your birthday-day? Did you get everything you wanted?"

"Tyler?" I looked at my phone and saw that it was him. "Um…Yeah…It was good. How was court?"

"Long. I'm still at the office and probably will be for a while, but I've got the night off tomorrow. I'm planning on seeing a band with some friends. You should come."

"Oh. Yeah. Okay. Where is it?"

"Eagle's Club. You'll like them…at least I think you will. It's a local band. Do you like rock?"

"I do."

"Then you'll have a good time. They start at eight. Do you want me to pick you up?"

"How about I meet you there? I can call you when I get there."

"Sounds good. See you tomorrow."

"Okay. Bye."

I pulled into the lot of Tanner Automotive as I hung up the phone. The momentary distraction that Tyler provided caught me off-guard, but I hadn't lost my focus. I parked my car and stormed through the open overhead door of the shop.

The mechanics that I had grown so close to welcomed me with a friendly, masculine greeting. Half of them howled a low grumbling "Liiiivvvv!" while the others gave a single nod. I waved a hello and headed up to Logan's apartment and knocked on his door. A moment later, it opened.

"You came," Logan said.

His alluring hazel eyes immediately compelled my attention. The way they gazed into me with such intensity weakened every part of me, and I hesitated. Freshly showered, his messy, still damp hair glistened while the faint smell of shampoo mixed with aftershave—and seeing him—took my breath away. He caused my heart to speed up. The V-neck of his long-sleeved hooded grey t-shirt showed only a small portion of his collar bone and chest, but it was just enough to remind me of the warmth underneath it.

I took a deep breath, in an attempt to slow my heart, and I stormed past him into his apartment, forcing myself to stay focused on the reason I came.

"Stop making things weird between us!" I demanded.

"I don't want things to be weird either, but we can't keep…"

"I'm not your girlfriend, Logan."

He sighed, getting frustrated. "You don't think I know that, Liv?!"

"I told you what I have to offer. I thought you—of all people—would understand."

"Trust me, I do, but something changed…" He stared directly at me. "I changed the second I met you." He took a step toward me.

181

"No!" I didn't want to hear any more. "Why can't you just be my friend?"

His face reddened and twisted into anger as he stepped toward me.

"Because we're not friends." he yelled. "We were never friends, and we can never be just friends. What the hell is it going to take to make you understand that?"

"*Why?!*" I screamed, shocked. "You promised me we wouldn't change."

He growled and ran his fingers through his hair. Then, he took me by the shoulders and stared at me, furious, with his face inches from mine. "Isn't it fucking obvious? I *love* you, Liv! And I'm pretty damn sure you love me too."

My mouth dropped open as he let go of me and took a step back. He seemed to be surprised at his own confession. The deep aggression in his voice startled me but not as much as the meaning behind it. My cheeks burned as my anger quickly intensified, and before I knew what was happening, my hand struck his face with so much force that I had to immediately hold on to it with my other hand to ease the stinging sensation on my palm. His face turned to the side from the force of my hit, then it slowly returned to me, shocked.

He stood still and watched me silently as he calmed himself before he spoke. "I also promised it wouldn't end between us. We *have* to change. It won't work any other way. I don't care how much it pisses you off, Liv, it's time to stop pretending." He cautiously reached out to take my hand, but I pulled it away and took a step back.

Every possible emotion flowed through me, and they were all led by fury which was a thousand times easier than sadness or fear. "No. I'm not pretending. The only reason you want me is because I'm the only one you can't have. And you just ruined everything!"

I stormed past him towards the door. I yanked it open, then slammed it shut behind me and hurried down the stairs. My pace quickened when I heard his footsteps behind me. I bursted through the side exit door and sprinted to my car, relieved when I was able to get in and lock the door before Logan caught up.

"Liv, stop!" Logan's muffled voice shouted as he pounded on my window and pulled on the door handle, trying to get in. "Just wait!" I started the ignition and put my car in reverse, making sure not to look in his direction. "Goddammit!" he shouted with one last bang on the window.

My head turned so that I could see where I was backing up, and I saw Logan running to his car. *Oh shit, he's going to chase me!*

I pressed my foot on the gas, causing my tires to screech as I backed the rest of the way out of my parking spot. Then, I put my car in drive and sped out of the lot and onto the road. The faster my heart pounded, the more my foot pushed down on the gas pedal. Not having a plan for where to go, I weaved in and out of traffic, searching for an escape, while keeping my eye on my rear view mirror.

It didn't take long for Logan to catch up. Within minutes, he was directly behind me. Of course he was. Did I really think I could out-drive him? I pushed my sensibility aside and kept speeding forward until I saw a red light ahead of me. *Dammit! Now what?*

My car slowed down. I had no choice but to stop behind the car in front of me, which caused Logan to stop directly behind me. I peered in my rear view mirror and saw him step out of his Mustang and start jogging to my car. *Is he insane?* I clicked my

183

lock button to make sure all the doors were locked just before he arrived at my window. I wasn't about to give in now.

"Liv, *please* pull over somewhere so we can talk about this!" he shouted through the window.

Blinded by anger, I put my hands over my ears and stared straight ahead to block him out. The light turned green, and I heard him yell something just before he ran back to his car, but I couldn't make out what he said. A sign for the interstate caught my attention, and I decided that's where I needed to go. Traffic wouldn't be as much of a problem on the interstate.

I floored it when I arrived at the on-ramp to the freeway. It felt freeing to be away from the congestion of the city traffic. It was just after rush hour, so there were still plenty of cars, but it was easy to maneuver around them. Logan's driving mimicked mine, almost instantaneously, which kept his car glued to the back of mine.

I let out a sigh. This was ridiculous. There was no way I was going to get away from him this way. I didn't really want to anyway; I just needed time to think. As my adrenaline calmed down, my car slowed to just over the speed limit. There was no way he could stop me here on the interstate. Maybe if I just kept driving, he would get tired and turn around.

My gas gauge said the tank was half full. I had plenty of gas to drive for a while without stopping. I wondered how much Logan had.

The B.B. King song diverted my attention to my phone. I took it from my coat pocket and turned it off, then threw it on the passenger seat.

*

My eyelids felt like bricks. It took everything I had to keep them open. My lower back throbbed, and my right leg was starting to cramp. I had been driving for what seemed like an eternity.

What a way to spend my birthday.

I had no idea where I was but judging by the lack of cars and streetlights, it was the middle of nowhere. I glanced at my rearview mirror and saw two different sets of headlights, but I didn't know if either of them belonged to Logan's car. I had stopped keeping track of him when the need to focus on staying awake began to take all my energy.

When the urge to get out of my car to stretch became too much to bear, I exited at the nearest off ramp. Headlights followed me and when I came to a halt by the stop sign at the end of the ramp, I could clearly see that it was Logan behind me. I took a deep breath and braced myself. Pulling into the nearest gas station, I parked by one of the pumps and turned my car off. Logan did the same.

I shuffled through my purse for several moments trying to find my debit card, but it was nowhere to be found. I checked my wallet to find only two dollars in cash.

Please tell me I have money for gas!

I peeked up to see the gas pump next to me, with its hose attached to Logan's car, and him leaning against the yellow metal. His arms were crossed in front of him as he stared at me dead-on. His expression was difficult to read. Mostly, he looked exhausted.

I continued to look through my purse without any luck. Finally, I tipped it over, letting all of its contents fall onto the passenger seat. After sifting through everything and not finding what I was looking for, I remembered that I had left my debit card in my other coat pocket. The coat which currently hung in my bedroom closet.

My heart sank to my stomach. I was on "E." I needed gas to get home. I looked up at Logan, who was in the process of removing the nozzle from his car and returning it to the pump. After grabbing the two dollars from my wallet, I stepped outside and pumped two dollars' worth of gas into my car.

"That's not going to get you very far," Logan announced.

"Thank you, Captain Obvious," I rebutted as I walked to the convenience store to pay, trying desperately to come up with a way home that did not involve Logan's help. On my way back to my car, out of the corner of my eye, I saw Logan still leaning against his car, watching me.

"Stop following me," I said as I opened my door.

"Someone's gonna need to rescue you when you run out of gas."

"I don't need to be rescued. I don't need anything." I sat in my seat, closed the door, and turned the ignition on. I didn't want to, but I couldn't stop myself from glancing back at Logan. With his head down, he pinched the bridge of his nose as he shook his head. Then, he looked at me, annoyed, which would've fueled my own irritation if I weren't so damn tired.

The feeling of being trapped and vulnerable provoked my frustration. "Dammit!" I said to myself as I clasped the steering wheel so tight that my knuckles were white. "Ugh!" I turned the car off and stepped out, slamming the door behind me. I stomped over to where Logan stood.

"Why are you following me anyway?" I yelled.

He narrowed his eyes. "I've been trying to figure that out for hours. Apparently, I've turned into a psycho stalker."

"Well, apparently I've turned into an abusive slapper. And don't say that means we're meant for each other."

"You are the most stubborn person I've ever met, you know that?"

"Ditto."

He peered down, staring blankly at nothing, as if he were trying to figure out what to say. Just as I was about to argue some more, he brought his intense, beautiful hazel gaze to mine. "But for some fucked-up reason, I can't get enough of you. When I'm not with you, I miss you. I've never laughed the way I do when I'm with you. When something awesome happens, you're the first person I want to tell, and when something terrible happens, you make it better. You give me strength to get through the bullshit, Liv, and I want to tell you things I've never told anybody." He exhaled sharply and stepped toward me until he was no more than a foot away. "But mostly, I'm following you because you make me fucking crazy."

He grabbed me behind the neck and pressed his lips on mine. My eyes rolled back, and a small hum escaped me as my entire body weakened from the euphoria that erupted when his tongue entered my mouth. His kiss was a glorious torment, a captivating anguish, a splendid affliction, and I never wanted it to end.

But that powerful poison that drives us to remain permanently locked within the dependable boundaries of our comfort zones wanted nothing to do with this moment. Fucking fear. Fear…of the unknown, of rejection, of another impending loss…is what drove me to break our phenomenal connection.

It took a minute to work up the strength to push him off me, and when I did, his body backed into his car from my shove.

"Stop it. Don't do that again." I pointed at him as I whispered it, my voice quivering. I immediately turned to run back to my car, but his hand grabbed my arm.

"Where are you gonna run to now, Liv? You're in the middle of nowhere. You have no gas in your car."

The fact that he was right infuriated me. It was too late and too far away to call anyone else for help.

"I need to borrow money for gas," I demanded, trying my best to sound strong and unaffected while an enormous lump formed in my throat. "I'll pay you back tomorrow."

His head turned to the side as his eyebrows pulled close together. "No."

"What do you mean 'no'?" I began scanning my brain, figuring out what I would do if he left me here. "You know what? Fine, leave, I'll just sleep in my car. Mel will come and get me in the morning." My lips began to quiver. I told myself it was from the cold winter air, but deep down, I knew it was because this was it. I had pushed him as far as he'd go. *This* was the moment he would leave me.

He watched me carefully as tears started to prick my eyes. He took a step toward me and I backed up, looking everywhere but at him.

"I'm not going to leave you here," he assured me. "Why would you think that? Is that what this is about?" A realization hit him. "You think I'm going to walk away from you, don't you?"

"So you're going to loan me gas money?"

"No, Liv, I'm not."

"What the hell, Logan! You're talking in circles! Are you leaving or not?"

His face was a mixture of confusion and concern. "I'm in love with you, Liv. I didn't follow you all this way just to leave you here…alone and stranded. I would never do that."

It was the second time he said he loved me. "Well then, what are you talking about?"

"You were swerving like crazy on the road. You're tired. You can't drive like that—you'll kill yourself. I saw a motel not far from here. Park your car here. Let's go get some sleep. We'll drive home in the morning."

"A motel room?"

"*Two* rooms if that's what you want. You can even get your own room in your own name. You are eighteen now, you know." He smiled, carefully.

It made sense. My fatigued body couldn't take the ride home. "I'll have to figure out something to tell my mom."

He thought for a moment. "Can you say you're at Mel's?"

"Yeah, I guess so." I hated lying to her, but I couldn't exactly tell her I would be staying at a motel with a boy. Or could I? I was a legal adult now. And she was pretty lenient for the most part, and for some reason, I felt the need to talk to her. I just wanted to hear her voice.

After parking my car in the farthest spot in the lot, I took my phone from the passenger seat and dialed the pub.

"American Pub!" My mother answered. Immediately, I heard the pounding background music and pub patrons. I shouldn't have expected anything different on a Friday night at this time.

"Hi, Mom. I'm not going to be home tonight."

"Hello?"

Oh, you've got to be kidding me. "Mom! It's me!"

"What?"

I sighed and hung up. I'd have to text her.

Chapter Twenty

Even though I had the heat cranked on high on the heating and cooling unit in my motel room, my body shivered under the covers. The smell of burning dust filled the air from the heating coils, but the cool air that seeped through the window above the heater seemed to overpower the warmth. Every once in a while, a loud clunking noise came from it that startled the living daylights out of me.

My mind kept wandering to Logan's kiss. I couldn't stop thinking about it. My fingers moved to my lips from the residual tingling that still lingered on them. He did things to me that I had never felt before. He made me feel alive, even though I had been trying so hard to stay neutral…to everything.

The annoying clunking noise distracted my thoughts yet again. I pulled the pillows over my ears to keep the noise out. It helped a little, but nothing seemed to appease my chilled body. I shifted and squirmed, trying to get comfortable enough to fall asleep, but after hours of trying, I realized my efforts were completely useless.

Overly tired, frustrated, and unable to sleep, I sat up straight in the bed and looked around the empty room. My eyes gravitated to my coat, which hung on a hook on the exit door. Without thought, I stood up and grasped it, sliding my arms into it at the same time my feet slipped into my shoes, and I walked outside into the cold.

I stopped in front of room number three and knocked without hesitation. If I hesitated at all, I might have turned back. The deadbolt unlocked just before the door opened.

"Hey," Logan whispered. His eyes glowed in the moonlight. How is it, that one look from him can completely melt me like that?

"It's freezing in my room," I breathed, suddenly nervous. My heart began to thump hard and fast. "I can't sleep."

Keeping his eyes on me, he opened the door farther, motioning for me to enter his room. I stepped in, and he closed the door behind me. The blue light from the TV danced on the walls, but there was no sound coming from it. I turned to face him. We both quietly stared at each other for several moments.

"I'm sorry I slapped you," I finally confessed.

He nodded, "I'm sorry I stalked you."

As we continued to watch each other, the passionate look of yearning that slowly grew in his eyes began to torture me. What the hell was I doing here?

The simple truth was that I just needed to be with him. I needed to feel his touch. Be wrapped in his embrace, immersed in his acceptance. And *God*, I wanted to taste his lips again. He knew it, too. He knew exactly why I was here, I could tell by the way he was looking at me.

"Liv?" His voice was low and deep.

"Yeah?"

"You need to tell me why you're in my room."

"I'm cold," I responded in a barely audible whisper.

He hesitated. "You're cold. And you want me to help you with that?"

Oh God, now I feel like an idiot.

I sighed. "Yeah, I guess I do."

He walked toward me, stopping only a few inches in front of me. "Are you going to slap me again?"

I shook my head no.

"Are you going to push me away?"

"I don't know," I nervously whispered.

He paused in thought for a moment, then placed his hands on my waist, slowly bringing my body against his. With his kiss from earlier still vivid in my mind, I drew in a sharp breath from the contact.

His eyes, only inches from mine, pleaded, almost as if he were asking for permission to continue. I remained silent because no words could be formed in the jumbled mess within my mind right now. His touch was way too intoxicating. My body was on auto-pilot.

His fingers brushed my cheek and moved my hair behind my ear. Instinctively, as my eyes closed, my hand gently covered his, and my lips kissed the rough flesh of his palm, then moved slowly to his wrist. I hesitated and looked up at him when I realized what I had done. My hand dropped, and I took a step back. The anguish in his eyes when I released him killed me.

I stood frozen, staring into his eyes, unable to move. This was the moment of truth. My heart pounded hard in my throat as I deliberated...as if I had a choice. When it came to Logan Tanner, did I ever have a choice?

"What do you want, Liv? You want to lay in bed with me all night like it doesn't mean anything?"

My eyes stung as tears crept into them. I just wanted him. Forever. The problem was, I couldn't figure out how to make it happen.

"I want to be friends," I breathed, my mind racing. I inwardly cursed myself for saying that out loud...*I* didn't even believe those words anymore. Why was I so stuck on them? Stuck on the thought that we had to stay platonic? Obviously, that ship had already sailed and there was no turning back.

"Bullshit." He moved toward me and grabbed me at the waist, pressing his body on mine. "Friends don't do what we do. Friends don't feel the way we feel. You can't hide it from me, Liv. I know you too damn well. Stop lying to me. Stop lying to *yourself.*"

His face was an inch from mine. My breath became quicker, heavier, as my heart pounded in my ears and my body started to weaken. I wanted his lips. I wanted *him.* He took me behind the neck. "The way you look at me when I touch you..." He tightened his grip on me, his chest heaving up and down, his voice becoming deep and raspy. "...like how you're looking at me right now...I'm not imagining it. I can see it in your eyes. You want me. Don't you. Just as much as I want you."

I couldn't look away from him. Couldn't step back. Couldn't leave. I was exactly where I wanted to be.

"Yeah," I whispered. "I do."

He tilted his head, "What did you say?"

My hand cupped his jaw while my thumb moved slowly across the stubble on his face. He looked into my eyes with a combo of relief and disbelief because finally, I admitted what we both already knew.

My hand slid behind his head and I pulled him to me, pressing my lips gently on his. Our mouths parted open, and as my tongue slid against his, all my fears and anxiety were forgotten. The only thing that mattered, the only thing that existed, was us, right now, in this moment.

"I'm sorry," I rasped between kisses. "Please don't be mad at me. You're right. About everything," I sucked in a breath. "I don't want to hurt you. You mean too much to me." His hot breath heated my neck as he nibbled my earlobe. I let out a sigh as his wet lips slowly made their way down to my collarbone. "I'm just—it's just that—I'm afraid to—"

He exhaled heavily, "You're not going to lose me, Liv. I promise."

Grabbing me fiercely, he removed my coat. My hands slid under his shirt and slowly lifted it up and over his head, revealing his perfect abdomen, which was exquisitely shadowed in the blue flickering light. His eyes darkened as he gazed into mine, but the way he looked at me was more than just lust. He needed me. He needed every part of me. Mind, body, and soul. I knew because not only was it an expression that could not be fabricated, it was a look that matched my deepest inner emotions. We needed each other.

"Tell me," he husked, his mouth and hands exploring. "I need to know this is real. Tell me what you want, Liv."

"You." I breathed without hesitation. His warm breath grazed my earlobe as he exhaled. "You, Logan." He gazed at me with a mixture of shock and hope. "I can't get you out of my mind. All I think about is when I'll see you next. I dream about you." My filter was gone. Any sort of rational thought process became non-existent the moment my lips touched his and my wall came crashing to the ground. Come to think of it, I've never been rational when it came to Logan Tanner. "And yes...I want your touch. More than anything. I want *you*."

His hands cupped my cheeks and as his warm, wet lips consumed every part of my mouth, a whimper escaped my throat. Then, he pulled back and looked into my eyes. "Do you have any idea how long I've waited to hear that?"

I shook my head slightly, causing a slight grin to form on his face. It quickly faded and as the intensity in his expression grew, he studied every part of my face and hair. Savoring me. Appreciating me. Loving me.

He slipped his hands under my shirt and slowly brought it up, as his hands brushed over the bare skin underneath it. I lifted my hands in the air, allowing him to remove it and drop it to the floor. Goosebumps prickled my body from the cool air on my skin. His hands moved down my back and in one smooth motion, he lifted me up as if I weighed no more than an ounce. My legs crossed around his waist and my arms around his neck.

He walked to the bed and slowly, effortlessly, laid me down onto it. He began to kiss my neck and chest, then smoothly unbuttoned my pants, removing them as if he had done it a thousand times before. As I fumbled with his belt, I began to worry about how much more experience he had than I did. I pushed his jeans down as far as I could, then we removed them the rest of the way with our feet.

His warm hand on my stomach slowly moved down under the hem of my underwear, and in an instant, I was no longer cold. My skin was on fire. My heart was coming out of my chest. I needed him, but there was something he needed to know first.

"I've never done this before," I blurted out.

"Never done what?" he absently responded as he continued to kiss me. A second later, he stopped as the realization of the meaning behind my words swept through his expression. He looked at me, confused beyond belief. "Are you serious? But I thought…Really?"

I nodded. "Is that a problem?"

He examined me as if he were seeing me for the first time. His gaze moved from my hair, to my eyes, to my lips, then wandered around the room. "Yeah, it is. We can't. We have to stop."

He began to move off me, but I held him tight. "Why?"

"Look at this place. Your first time can't be in some sleazy motel, Liv. You deserve so much better than that."

"Where it happens doesn't matter to me." I brought my lips to his ear and lightly kissed his earlobe. "Who it's with matters," I whispered against his neck. "And I want you, Logan. I want it to be with you. Right now. Please don't stop."

He strongly exhaled, his control waning, "I don't want you to regret this."

"Look at me," I said. His eyes met mine, searching for any tiny hint of hesitation. I continued, "I will *never* regret a single moment spent with you. Trust me when I tell you that I want this more than anything. Please, Logan, don't make me beg."

His eyes glimmered, mischievously.

I laughed, "Next time. Next time you can make me beg. This time, let's just take it slow."

He nodded and his lips gently pressed against my neck and slowly made their way down to my stomach, teasing, tickling.

"Your skin is freakishly soft," he admitted.

I smiled, "I hope that's a good thing."

He sighed, "It's the *best* thing."

He unclasped and removed my bra, flinging it somewhere, and when he took my breast in his hand, caressing, and gently squeezing, I felt it everywhere. I tugged his boxer briefs down, my need for him intensifying with each kiss, each touch. He removed them the rest of the way, then pressed against me

197

through the thin fabric of my underwear. I panted heavily, waiting for him to remove them, but to my dismay, he stopped.

"Stay here," he commanded.

Where exactly did he think I would go? I watched as he left the bed and walked over to his coat. He removed a small, square packet from the inside pocket just before I heard it rip open. When he finished, he came back to me, and swiftly removed my panties.

I readily waited as he brought his body above mine. I should've been more nervous, more afraid, but with him it was as though all the stars had aligned in the sky, waiting for this moment to happen. All I felt was anticipation. The mixture of love and desire in his piercing eyes, as his face hovered above me, mixed with the feel of his warm body between my thighs made my stomach quiver.

"Are you sure?" he whispered.

I nodded. "Yes." I never wanted anything more.

He studied my eyes, my hair, my lips, savoring every part of this moment. His gaze stayed focused on mine when he gently, cautiously entered me. I took a deep breath in and squeezed my nails into his back from the pain. His eyes flooded with warmth as he leaned down and began kissing my neck.

"Are you okay?" he breathed in a low, husky voice.

"M-hmm," I whispered. "Please don't stop."

As he slowly continued, the pain started to decrease. Then, after a few more moments, it was joined by intense, erogenous pleasure. The mixture of pleasure and pain felt incredible.

A faint moan freed itself from my throat as I began to let go. The more we moved, the heavier my breaths became. Finally relaxed to a point where I no longer felt restrained, I let go of my tight grasp and moved my hands to his hips, instinctively helping to guide the rhythm of our collective motion

"Oh...God...Liv," Logan husked as his thrusts quickened. Sensing my lack of restraint, he pushed himself into me harder, and faster, as his own self-control dissipated. The pain was still there slightly, but I didn't care. The feeling of him finally being this close, outweighed it a million times over.

"I need to see you," he urged. "Open your eyes."

I looked into his exquisite eyes and when I saw their intensity, I could no longer contain myself. "Oh Logan," I breathed as the build-up inside of me finally erupted.

In one last motion, he glided into me and stayed there for a moment, his arms trembling as he let out one last moan. Every muscle in my body relaxed as our movement slowed. Finally, he collapsed on top of me and rested his hot, damp head on my chest. We both breathed quickly and heavily, waiting for our hearts to go back to a normal pace. I wanted him to stay this close forever.

"Holy fuck," he declared. He pulled away and moved himself beside me, looking up at the ceiling. "Holy fuck," he said again, causing me to smile.

"Yeah," I sighed. After several minutes, I continued. "You really do say fuck a lot."

He smiled contently at me as he took my hand and brought it to his lips and gently kissed my fingers. "Yeah, well, I've never felt anything like that before."

Knowing all about his past exploits, I squinted my eyes and asked, "Huh?"

"Nothing like *that*," he repeated. "I'm serious."

After several silent moments, he moved to his side, placing his arm under the pillow that his head was resting on, and he looked at me with serious eyes. "Liv, I've never felt this way before. I've never wanted another human being as much as I want you. And I don't just mean like this. I want to make you happy."

He lifted himself up so that he was resting on his elbow. With his other hand, he traced his fingers down my jawline to my chin, holding my gaze on his. "I don't know what it is, but being with you just feels good. It feels right. It's better than any-fucking-thing I've ever known."

My body turned to the side to face him. "Why are you so nice to me? I've been so mean."

He hesitated. "Because I love you. And you're not mean— don't ever say that. You're fucking amazing."

It was the third time he said those three words. Our eyes locked, and he brought his face to mine, gently grazing my lips with his. I smiled as he rested his head on my pillow and kissed my shoulder.

"Thank you for the birthday present," I said.

"Is that what you call it?"

I laughed. "Presents! I mean all of them. At school. It meant a lot to me."

He smiled. "Can I ask you something?"

"You just did."

He chuckled. "Smart ass. Why did you think I was going to leave you back there at the gas station? You have to know I wouldn't do that."

My smile faded as I shifted onto my back and stared blankly at the ceiling. "I don't know. It was just a feeling, I guess." I wanted to tell him that everyone leaves eventually; it was just a matter of time. I wanted to say that there's no getting around that inevitable fact, no matter how hard we would try to fight it,

200

but I knew he'd brush it off or deny it for my sake. "I just got the feeling your time with me was done."

For some reason, my stomach turned when I said it. I peeked at him before turning back to face him. He glared at me, perplexed. "My time with you will never be done. No matter what happens. I'll never be done with you, Liv," he sighed. "You don't look happy."

"Being with you makes me happy, Logan." I moved so that my head rested on his chest and my arm hugged his middle. "I am happy with you." It was only a half-lie. In truth, being with him made me happier than anything. But it was a bittersweet happiness because from this moment on, it would be overshadowed by the wait and wonder of when and how our relationship would dissolve.

Chapter Twenty-One

The room vibrated. Rattling from the pictures on the walls grabbed me, pulling me out of my dream state. The train felt as though it was directly behind the motel. I didn't remember seeing any train tracks last night, but then again, it was dark and my mind was on other things. As I laid still with my eyes closed, the rumble and roar dissipated until it was gone completely.

Slowly, as I evolved into a state of consciousness, I became aware of the heat radiating from Logan's abdomen onto my back, the arm blanketing my shoulder, and the legs tangled up in mine. His bare skin on mine immersed me in serenity. I breathed in the scent of aftershave, sweat, and Logan as I stretched, and when I exhaled, a small hum came out of my throat. I could get used to this.

I weaved his limp fingers in mine and brought them to my lips. From the dim blue light that came through the cracks on the edges of the closed window drapes, it appeared to be just after dawn.

"Mmm." he moaned as I gently kissed each fingertip.

"Good morning," I whispered.

"Mornin'," he mumbled just before he placed a gentle kiss between my shoulder blades. He kissed my shoulder then rested his head back on his pillow.

I brought his hand to my cheek and gently squeezed his arm to my chest. Being this close to him was better than anything, and I never wanted to let go. My heavy eyes closed, and I drifted back into my dreams. Nothing could ruin this perfect moment.

*

I awoke to Bear Grylls giving survival tips on the TV. Fresh shampoo and steam saturated the air. Fully rested, I opened my eyes and turned over to see Logan sitting on the bed next to me, with wet hair and nothing on but a towel wrapped around his waist. Cracks of bright light came through the drapes, and I looked over at the digital clock on the nightstand which read 9:23 AM.

He leaned down and touched his smooth, warm lips on my forehead. "Morning, sleepyhead."

I smiled, then turned to face the TV. "What's that crazy guy eating this time?"

Logan chuckled. "You don't wanna know."

"You showered."

"I did. I was going to wake you to join me, but you looked so peaceful, I couldn't bring myself to do it."

"Oh." Heat emanated from my cheeks. Why was I embarrassed all of a sudden?

"Do you know how beautiful you are when you're sleeping?"

"You mean silent and docile? Thanks a lot."

"That's not what I meant, and you know it." He looked up in thought. "Actually…come to think of it…"

"Oh please, silent and docile would bore the crap out of you!" I defended.

He laughed. "Yeah, you're right. Your spunk is one of the reasons I love you."

It was the fourth time he told me he loved me. My smile faded. Why couldn't I say it to him?

"It's okay. You don't have to say anything," he assured me as if he read my thoughts. His warm hand slipped under mine, and he brought my hand to his lips, kissing every one of my knuckles as his incredible eyes gazed into my soul.

"I want you to kiss me," I whispered. The corners of his lips turned upward as he brought his face to mine and enclosed his mouth around mine, causing me to take a sharp breath.

"Mmm, you smell good," I breathed. I didn't think I could ever get enough of his intoxicating scent. Suddenly, I stopped kissing him. "And I probably stink. I should get in the shower."

"You smell amazing," he said as he kissed my neck.

Ignoring his comment, I sat up and started to wrap the sheet around me, but he was sitting on it. I gave it a tug as I gave him a smile. "'Scuse me."

"What, this?" he teased, pointing to the sheet. "Nah, you don't need this."

"Yep, I need it."

He grudgingly removed himself from the bed allowing me to wrap the sheet around myself. I felt his eyes on me as I wandered around the room in search of each article of my clothing. Once I found them all, I headed to the bathroom.

"I can help you in there, you know," he announced.

I grinned as I turned to face him. "I think I can manage." My smile faded and my heart skipped a beat when I saw the way he looked at me as he stood with his thumb tucked inside the fold of his towel.

Those eyes.

Any thought I had of being anywhere but in his arms immediately disappeared.

He noticed my hesitation. One corner of his mouth turned up as he slowly walked toward me. I remained frozen until his fingers lifted my chin, and his mouth united with mine, igniting the familiar spark that only he could light.

How does he do that?

With his soft lips moving in perfect harmony with mine, his hands grazed my neck and moved down my shoulders, finally settling on my delicate fingers which were holding my clothes in one hand and the sheet to my body in the other. My clothes dropped to the floor as he took control of the hand which was holding them and moved it to his lower back. My breath intensified in anticipation of what I knew he would do next.

"But you already took a shower," I managed to say.

I felt him smile against my lips, but he didn't say anything in response to my comment. Instead, he took my other hand, causing the sheet to float smoothly to the floor, and he led me to the shower.

*

Saddened by the fact that we had to leave so soon, I slipped my shoes on, then watched Logan as he dressed.

"Can we stay here forever?" I asked.

He smiled. "We can do whatever you want." He put his shirt on then looked around the room. "Can we pick a different place to stay forever, though?" He put his hand up to his mouth as if he were about to tell me a secret. "This place is kinda sleazy."

I laughed. "I don't care where we go. I'll go anywhere with you."

My phone chimed from the end table, indicating a text.

"Will you hand that to me?" I asked. "It's probably my mom."

He picked it up and looked at it before handing it to me. "Who's Tyler?"

Oh shit.

I took my phone from him and looked at the text.

Change of plans, won't be there til 9pm 2nite.

"Liv, who's Tyler?"

My heart sped up. I wasn't going to lie to him. "Promise you won't be mad?"

"Just tell me who it is."

I reminded myself that he loved me and the only way this would work was for us both to be honest with each other. "It's the guy from Rain." He looked at me, confused. "The one you got in a fight with."

His jaw clenched tightly. "How did he get your number?"

Oh shit.

"I gave it to him. I ran into him yesterday morning at the coffee shop by school."

"What does he want?" His brows pulled together.

"You look mad, Logan." I nervously stepped toward him and wrapped my arms around his body. My cheek found a place on his chest. "Please don't be mad at me."

The tension in his muscles relaxed. "I'm not mad, just tell me why he's texting you."

"We have plans tonight. He's just letting me know that the time has changed."

He stepped back and gently pushed me away from him. "Why would you want to make plans with someone who tried to beat the shit out of me?"

I took a deep breath. "Logan, you were the one who jumped him, remember?"

He stared at me as if I were a lunatic.

"It's okay," he said, trying to shake it off. "It's fine. Just tell him you can't make it. Actually, tell him you won't be able to see him. Ever."

The controlling tone in his voice caught me off guard and immediately put me on the defense. "What? Why?"

"Because you're with me now."

"So that means I'm not allowed to have friends?"

"Not boyfriends."

"What about friends that are boys?"

"No way," he said, irritated.

"You can't be serious. What about Matt? Or Isaac?"

"No, Liv! Nobody!"

Now I was getting mad. "Alright, you are being completely irrational here. You can't tell me what to do, Logan. You're acting crazy!"

"Liv, you are not hanging around guys. Guys do not want to be your friend," he said condescendingly. "Guys want to fuck you."

My jaw hit the floor. Completely shocked, I had nothing to give in response to his brutal, insensitive comment, except for the tears that stung my eyes.

Oh my God, it's starting already. Please tell me it's not happening so soon!

Reality set in that this very moment may be the beginning of the end. When he saw my expression, remorse swept through his. "Shit, I didn't mean it like that."

"Yes, you did." I whispered. "Is that what you think of me?" Anger built up inside me as a coping mechanism, sweeping away the sadness, and my voice strengthened. "Is that what I am to you, Logan? A conquest?"

"No, of course not. I'm sorry, I didn't mean…"

"Save your apologies. I don't believe you!" I had enough apologies from my father to last a lifetime. When I was younger, they came frequently, but now it only came once a year in the form of a birthday card. Apologies were nothing more than empty words.

I took my coat and wrapped myself in it just before bolting outside. I ran to my room to get my handbag. Then, I remembered. I had nowhere to run to. Having no reason to chase me since we both knew I needed him to get home, Logan stayed in his room.

"Ugh!" I plopped down onto the bed and stared at the ceiling, taking several deep calming breaths and trying to figure out a way to make this right. As much as I understood the deep rooted cause of his need for control, our relationship would never work if he tried to control me to such a great degree. Regardless of the history with his parents, his requests were outrageous.

Twenty minutes passed as I continued to lay motionless on the bed, when a knock on the door interrupted my thoughts. I gathered my strength and opened the door where Logan stood waiting with tormented eyes.

"I was wrong," he said softly. "You are my best friend. *That's* what you mean to me. I know I can't tell you what to do.

You have to make your own choices. I'm so sorry, Liv. I swear I didn't mean what I said. Please forgive me."

Another train came barreling through behind the motel. The loud thunder from it drowned out all other noise. I was grateful to have the extra moment to think. I stared at him as I contemplated, and he kept his eyes on mine. The more we gazed into each other's eyes, the more the rest of our surroundings deteriorated. Finally, the roar dissolved and only the sound of the interstate and my heartbeat was left.

"The feeling is mutual, you know," I said.

"What do you mean?"

"You make me fucking crazy too." I pulled on his coat and pressed my lips on his, and everything else in the world melted away.

Chapter Twenty-Two

It took three hours to drive home from that middle of nowhere place that will forever be somewhere to me. I had just enough time to stop home and change my clothes before reporting to Frank's. My entire shift had gone by in a daze.

Olivia, can I get some help here?

Standing motionless in the candy isle, my eyes focused on nothing as my mind absorbed every moment of the last two days. I needed to figure out a way to make my relationship with Logan work, but the more I thought about it, the more doubts I had.

"Olivia!" Stacy called, and I immediately turned my head in her direction. A long line of customers trailed behind her register.

"Sorry, Stacy," I replied as I stepped to the second register. "I can help the next person over here."

I unconsciously checked out customer after customer. Lost in my own thoughts, I heard myself sputter out automated remarks to them.

Hi there.

I'm great, how are you?

Would you like a bag for that?

Have a good night.

I snapped out of whatever funk I was in when my favorite chocolate caramel coconut bar was placed on my counter. "These things are amazing. Have you ever had…" I looked up to see a pair of remarkable hazel eyes staring back at me. The smile that crept onto my face could not be contained. "Oh…Hi."

"Someone once told me that these things were like a little piece of heaven on their taste buds," Logan said.

My cheeks burned as I thought about all the heavenly things about him that were so much better than that little chocolate bar. I handed him the bar with his receipt. "Sounds like a smart someone."

"It's for you," he said as he handed it back to me. "Do you get off soon?"

My smile faded. He knew I had plans tonight that I hadn't cancelled. As of yet, anyway. I couldn't help but feel a bit smothered. "Yeah, I'll be done in fifteen minutes."

"Good. I'll wait for you." He smiled a goodbye but something in his eyes struck a nerve in me. It was something that looked a lot like fear. And it was the first time I had ever seen it on him to such a degree.

*

Smoke floated out of the exhaust pipe of Logan's muscle car as it idled in the parking lot, the water vapors contrasting with the freezing winter air. I crossed my arms in front of me as I stepped outside, bracing myself for the cold…and for whatever might happen when I talk to Logan. Bass pounded from one of the passing cars on the strip as I walked to his car.

I dropped into the passenger seat, closing the door quickly. "Brrr! Why does winter have to be so long?"

He only half-smiled. He didn't say anything. And he didn't look at me.

"Logan, are you okay? What's wrong?"

He turned toward me but looked down at the shifter instead of looking at me. "Are you still going out with that guy tonight?"

Oh, it's about that.

"I haven't cancelled yet," I said softly.

He looked at me, pleading, begging, scrutinizing. His expression surprised me. "Are you going to?"

"I don't know, Logan. Not if I'm being forced to. I mean, it's not like a date or anything. He's going with a group of friends and suggested I drop by if I want to. That's it."

"Fine, then I'll go with you."

"Why? So you can babysit me? I just don't understand why you can't trust me."

He stayed silent for a moment, then dropped his head in his hand. "I don't know if I can do this."

My eyes widened. "Do what?"

He shook his head slightly.

"Logan, please tell me what you can't do." I couldn't hide the anxiety in my voice.

"Why haven't you cancelled?" he glared at me. "Why would you want to go out with someone else?"

"I don't want to go out with anyone else. You told me I can't have friends. Honestly, Logan, I'm not willing to stop having friends."

"Boyfriends, Liv. You can't have boyfriends. I think that's fair, don't you?"

"Tyler's not my boyfriend."

He shook his head again, then realization swept through his expression. "You're doing this to prove a point. My God, you're stubborn. Why can't you just cancel the fucking plans? For us."

"Logan, what if I asked you to stop racing? For us," I said, irritated.

"What does racing have to do with anything? Is that what you want me to do? Quit racing?"

Yes! Stop putting yourself in danger!

"No, I would never ask you to do that because I know what it means to you. I need you to trust me. You have to know that I would never do anything to hurt you."

"Just so we're clear, you're going out with another guy tonight so that I'll trust you?"

"Well…yeah…But it doesn't sound right when you say it."

"That's because it's not right! It's not okay!" he said as he ran his fingers through his hair. "Goddammit, I've been thinking about this all day. I just don't know how the fuck to get around it. I don't know if I can."

The shock from his words silenced me. I don't know how long we sat idling quietly. Finally, Logan broke the silence. "I can't." he said as if he had just figured it out. He looked at me. "Liv, I love you. I *love* you, do you understand that? I can't sit by and watch anymore while you go out with other guys. I can't fucking do it," he sighed and brought his trembling fingers to the bridge of his nose. "And I also know that I can't change you. And I shouldn't want to."

Oh my God. Not now. Not already. Not after everything we've been through!

"Logan, please don't do this." I could barely breathe from the enormous rock that formed in my throat. He was giving up on us…on me…before we ever even had a chance. Over what? Jealousy? Control? Fear? Droplets accumulated in my eyes, blurring my vision.

"I thought last night meant you were finally mine," he continued. "I can't believe it took me this long to realize that it's never going to happen. You'll never be mine, will you?" A tear trickled down his left cheek as his broken eyes begged me to stop him.

I've always been yours!

Petrified by fear of losing him, my mind went completely blank as every last atom in my body tried to figure out how to make him stay without giving up my independence. Why couldn't I just give in to him? Maybe it was because I had learned from my mother's mistakes. Maybe I had seen her lose herself in a man one too many times. Seen her change everything about herself to fit their mold of what they wanted her to be, just to have them take those parts of her with them when they eventually abandoned her…abandoned *us.*

Regardless of how much I loved Logan, the thought of doing exactly that made me cringe. There was no getting around the fact that he needed control, and I could never be happy under the control of someone other than myself. Love was one thing. Being in love with Logan was something I was finally ready for. Love was something I knew with all my heart that I could actually give to him. Codependency, on the other hand, was a whole 'nother monster that I was not willing to surrender to.

Because of that, he was going to leave me.

This was all happening way too fast. My entire body began to tremble. Tears welled in my eyes as nausea crept up my throat and a small whimper came out of me.

"Oh fuck, Liv. Please don't cry," he said as he turned away from me. "I'm so sorry. I can't. We can't." He wouldn't look at me. "I'm sorry, but I can't see you anymore. I can't do it. Not like this."

My jaw dropped open. I knew it was coming but that didn't stop the shock of his words from entering my heart.

But you said you love me. You said you'd never be done with me.

Hot tears trickled down my cheeks, but I remained silent. This was the moment I had feared since that first almost-kiss. The moment that I had taken every possible crucial precaution to avoid. The moment which was inevitable, no matter how hard I tried to stop it.

I wanted to touch him. I wanted to kiss him. I wanted him to wrap his warm arms around me and hold me. I wanted to change his mind, but he had made his decision. He didn't want to try. He didn't want me anymore. He didn't want me *enough.*

I studied his perfect face, committing it to memory, devastated that it would be the last time I'd be this close. Then, slowly, it began to kick in. The numb. The un-feeling. The barrier that had deteriorated to barely anything had begun rebuilding itself. I took a deep breath, and finally my body calmed to a functional point and the tears slowed. Thank God it was coming back.

"I understand," I said robotically. It was true. I understood why it could never work. He didn't trust anyone. Not even me. I didn't trust anyone either. Not even him.

After taking one last look at the interior of his car, but not at him—I needed to remain strong and looking at him could easily break me—I opened the door and stepped out.

The moment I closed the car door, his tires squealed as he rushed the car wildly out of the lot and down the strip. I watched until I couldn't see the car anymore. Then, I watched some more. My last glimmer of hope faded as the wall continued to build itself back up around me. He was never coming back.

I didn't realize I was cold until my keys fell out of my fingers. When I tried to pick them up, my frozen fingers refused to grasp them.

"Shit!" I shouted. "Shit!" My foot kicked the front tire of my car. "Goddammit!"

"Olivia, is everything okay?" Stacy called as she stepped out the front door of Frank's, locking it behind her.

Embarrassed, I turned to face her. "Yeah, I'm fine. I dropped my keys, and I can't pick them up. My hands are frozen."

"Oh my God, hon! How long have you been out here?" She took my keys off the ground and handed them to me. When she saw my face up close, a look of concern came over her. "Is everything okay? Have you been crying? What happened?"

"I'm fine, just having a bad night." This was not something I wanted to discuss with my manager.

"Alright, well, you know I'm here for you if you ever need to talk. You've got my cell number, right?"

"Yeah, thanks, Stacy. Really, I'm fine."

"Okay, hon. Warm up! See you tomorrow."

I forced a smile and nodded.

Meeting Tyler tonight was the last thing I wanted to do. In fact, I had lost all interest in Tyler the moment I received the pen with the male exotic dancer on it. Come to think of it, I never had any real interest in Tyler. I'd never had any real interest in anyone. Until Logan.

As I sat in the driver's seat of my car, waiting for my hands to defrost, I realized where I needed to be. After waiting another few moments, just long enough to be sure my fingers could function, I took my phone and began a text.

I need you

My phone buzzed after a moment, and I looked at the text.

I'm here. I'll make time.

Chapter Twenty-Three

With my hands tucked deeply in my coat pockets, I jogged to the front door of *The American Pub*. Two men and a woman stood next to the door, smoking. When I opened the door, I was slammed by an off-key version of "Me and Bobby McGee." Then I remembered that tonight was karaoke night, which always drew in a pretty big crowd.

I peered past the cluster of people at the bar and spotted my mother's wavy blond ponytail behind the bar. She was playing bar dice with one of the patrons. Jeff was there too, taking drink orders and mixing cocktails.

As she laughed at something the customer said, she glanced my way. The moment my eyes caught hers, I let go of everything I was holding in, and the tears started rolling down my cheeks again. Why couldn't I keep myself together? She gave me a comforting smile, then after saying something to Jeff, she walked over to me and wrapped her thin arms around me.

"I'm so sorry, sweetheart," she whispered in my ear.

My only response was to bury my eyes in her shoulder as a sob pushed itself out of me. She held me for a few minutes, rubbing my back while I cried, then pulled her face away.

"Let's go somewhere quiet," she said.

Embarrassed by my outburst, I held my head down as I followed her through the pub and out the back door to a hallway. She led me up the steps to the apartment that she and Jeff slept at once in a while when they had too much to drink to drive home.

I could still hear the muffled karaoke music beneath the floor as she led me through the empty kitchen, to the living room where a single couch rested against one of the walls. It was the only piece of furniture in the room.

"Do you want to tell me what happened?" she asked as we sat down.

"Not really." We both knew I was going to tell her anyway. I took a deep breath in an attempt to stop the tears. "Do you know my friend, Logan?"

"Is he that really cute boy with the car? The one who brought you the chicken soup?"

She had seen him in passing on several occasions. I nodded as more tears pushed themselves out of my eyes from her bittersweet reminder of just how incredible my friendship with him actually is.

Not is...was. He's gone now.

She listened quietly as I told her everything. Except the racing. I told her how we met and the peaceful, yet electric feeling I had when he looked at me. How sparks ignited in my blood when he touched me, and how I had never experienced anything like it. I told her about his history with his family and about my own promise which I made to myself when Adam left, and I told her how a relationship with Logan would never work. I knew she was the only one who would understand, and it was liberating to be so open with her.

She patiently watched me as I told her what had happened in the last few days, including where I spent the night last night and how it ended with him telling me he didn't want to see me anymore.

"How could he just give up like that, Mom? I feel tricked. I feel like he tricked me into falling for him, and now that I did, he doesn't want me anymore."

"It sounds to me like he's confused. It sounds like he's in love. People aren't always rational when they are in love, sweetheart."

"You think?" I said sarcastically. Why was she taking his side? She was supposed to be on *my* side.

She shrugged. "Think about how long you resisted him. Maybe to him, now that you are an actual, tangible thing, he's a little freaked out. It sounds like he's feeling the same way you've felt all along. Scared."

"But he told me he didn't want me. Everything that I thought would happen...happened." I hesitated before saying the next thing. I wasn't sure how she would react. "I don't understand why you keep doing it."

"Keep doing what?"

"Why do you keep letting people in, when you know how it will end. How do you do it, knowing how you will feel when they leave?"

She thought quietly for several moments. "I guess it's because there's always hope that maybe they won't. And if you can let go of worrying about what *might* happen, I promise you something wonderful *will* happen, and nothing can ever compare to the feeling you get when it does. Being in love is worth the risk."

I sighed, "It doesn't even matter anymore. It's too late now. He's gone."

She shook her head and smiled. "Stop thinking so much and do what your heart tells you." I rolled my eyes. She sounded just like Mel. Her hand patted my knee. "Just sleep on it. Things are always much more clear in the morning. But first, we're gonna have a little fun. I hate seeing you sad."

I forced a grin as she took my hand and started to lead me back downstairs. I knew exactly what her intention was, and I was instantly reminded of the daily princess dance parties we had in our living room for several weeks after my dad left. She was a master of distraction. And I loved her for it.

"Mom, I'm not doing karaoke."

She pulled me down the stairs and stopped to talk to the DJ for a moment just before pulling me to the bar. I sat on a stool as she took her place behind the bar.

"Everything okay?" Jeff asked.

I shrugged. "Eh."

My mother looked at me with sympathy. "If you want to sleep here tonight, Livie, you can have a drink or two. But no shots. And no driving."

I smiled. "Okay, Mom, I'm down."

"You're down? Geez, Olivia, I think you're way too cool for me," she teased. "What'll it be?"

"Hey, Gracie, is that your sister?" some guy shouted from a few seats down. "She looks just like you!" I wasn't sure if he was looking at me, or through me, or at his own nose.

My mother grinned from ear to ear as I scowled at him. She turned to me, still smiling. "He thinks we're sisters."

"He's a little inebriated, Mom." I turned to face him. "She's my mother!"

With a confused expression, he looked away, appearing to be deep in thought trying to figure that one out.

"I'll have Southern Comfort on the rocks," I said.

"How about a So Co and sprite." It wasn't a question. She decided it for me. I watched as she expertly poured the drink and set it on the bar in front of me.

The DJ spoke into the microphone. "Next up is a mother-daughter duo. Please give it up for Grace and Olivia!"

"That's us, Sweetie!"

"I told you I'm not doing it!" I shouted as she ran around the bar to get me. My heart began to pound, and my stomach turned. I didn't want to get up in front of these people and sing. She took my hand and tugged, but I remained on my chair, standing my ground.

"Oh, come on! It's our favorite song!" she tried to persuade me.

I sighed and took my drink. If I was going to do this, I needed a little extra courage. My mother frowned at me as I pushed the tiny straw aside, put my lips on the glass, and gulped down the entire thing. I wiped my mouth with the back of my hand and smiled when I was done. "Okay, I'm ready."

"Not funny, Olivia. Not. Funny." She tried to look all motherly, like she was disappointed that I had just chugged the entire drink, but I saw the smile in her eyes. "Your next drink will be a water, my dear."

I inwardly chuckled as we walked up to the stage. My mother stepped in front of the microphone. "Is everyone having a good time tonight?!" Hoots, hollers, and whistles came from the crowd. "Thank you all for being here." She turned to face me but kept her mouth by the microphone. "This is my daughter, Olivia. It's her first time on stage, so let's give her a warm welcome!"

I waved, shyly, as more claps, shouts, and whistles filled the air. I relaxed when the intro to "Girls Just Want to Have Fun"

222

started. The sound took me away from the stage and back to our old living room. It was our staple song in those days.

My mom danced over to me, handed me a microphone, and took my hand to twirl me around. I immediately accepted the fact that the crowd was going to witness an Evans' girls dance party, and I allowed my body move to the music.

Chapter Twenty-Four

I thought I was awake, but I couldn't move my arms or legs. My eyes stayed shut, but there was a brightness in front of them. I turned over to bury my face in...some uncomfortable fabric which could not possibly be my bed sheets. When I finally forced them open, I was blinded by light that shot a rush of pain through my head. They stayed open only long enough to alert me to the fact that I was on the couch in the pub's upstairs apartment.

Was that snoring? I squinted as I took a look around. On the floor next to me rested a glass of water, a bottle of Tylenol, and a cocktail napkin with some scribbles on it. After rubbing my eyes and my temples, I slowly forced myself to a sitting position. My head resisted the action of being upright with a vengeance, and I dropped my head into my hands.

After several motionless minutes, I reached for the glass of water and Tylenol. I washed the pills down with the entire glass, then I went to the kitchen to refill the glass and drank that up too.

My head dropped down as I leaned over with my hands on the counter, waiting for the Tylenol and hydration to take the edge off. Unbeknownst to my mother, a few of the pub patrons had offered me drinks last night, and I had happily accepted them. Now I wish I hadn't.

Suddenly, a snore that could wake the dead came from down the hall, which caused me to snort out a laugh. There was only one person who snored like that. I had no idea how my mother could sleep next to that noise every night. My mind drifted to last night, when I had said goodnight to her and Jeff after bar close, just before they crashed in the bedroom and I crashed on the couch.

What time was it now? I searched my coat pockets for my phone, but I couldn't find it. After searching the couch cushions, I found out that it wasn't there either. I sat back down and stared at the bright, empty room.

I took the napkin from the floor and read the scribbles on it.

Morning clarity: What would you do if fear didn't exist? I mean it. Stop thinking. Listen to your heart.

Love, Mom

(over)

I flipped it around.

P.S. Take a day off from cleaning.
Jeff and I can handle it today.

Resting my head on the backrest of the couch, my headache began to subside, and I started to think about what Logan said last night. *"Why would you want to go out with someone else?"* I mentally kicked myself for being so incredibly stupid. I had been forcing myself to do something I had absolutely no interest in doing, just to prove a worthless point. He was right. I was too stubborn to see that my actions were hurting him. My stomach flipped at the realization that I had made a terrible mistake.

225

I began to think about the excitement I felt when Logan smiled at me. How peaceful it felt to walk with him arm in arm. How easy it was to just be around him without having to force conversation. How comforting it felt when we laid together, his arms wrapped around me while I rested my head in the nook of his shoulder, listening to the pounding of his heartbeat on my ear. His scent. The electricity of his touch and the way he could look into my eyes and see right through to my bare soul.

Being around him brought me a sense of peace and exhilaration at the same time. He was the only one who truly knew me...He had seen my bad side, and he still loved me...until last night.

What had I done? I ruined everything. His love was unconditional, and I had pushed it away. It became difficult to breathe as the boulder in my throat grew. My eyes burned as I tried to hold back the tears. Instead of being so stubborn, I should've tried to compromise. Or, at the very least, I should've communicated to him the reason I was being so stubborn. Maybe we could've worked through it...together.

My gaze wandered back to my mother's note. I was tired of fighting. My eyes closed as I breathed in and made a deliberate choice to let my guard down. It was the only way there would be any possibility of getting Logan back.

Almost immediately, as my eyes shot open, everything changed. Having him back was the only thing I wanted. Having him in my life was the only thing that mattered. It was as though I had finally seen a shining light that had been shielded from me for years. It was a slap in the face, a light bulb going off in my head; someone had shaken some sense into me.

I wanted him. I wanted to be with him, and I had no doubt in my mind that if we could talk through our differences, if we could understand each other and our motives, we *would* make it work. Make *us* work. I never had an epiphany before. It was a strange, foreign feeling to just know...to be so sure of something and not have any doubts. Logan and I have an intense, blissful connection that people search for their entire lives for. I would be an idiot to let that go. To let him go. My only fear was that I realized it too late.

The need to talk to him became unbearable. I needed to touch him and see his face when I told him how I truly felt.

I put my coat on and headed out the door. The only two cars left in the parking lot were mine and my parents'. As I opened my car door, my eye caught my phone laying on the passenger seat, and I reached for it as I closed the door behind me. It read 7:24AM. What in the name of Jesus was I doing up so early? *Ah, yes, the snoring...*

To my complete shock, my phone was flooded with missed calls, texts, and voicemails from Logan. I cried happy tears when I retrieved them. In about a million different ways, he told me he made a mistake. Before this moment, apologies were worthless to me. But Logan was different. We had something special. And I wanted to believe him.

The keys jingled as I turned them in the ignition. His apartment wasn't far. I would make it there in ten minutes. When I arrived, I was elated to see his Mustang parked in the lot. Since the shop was closed on Sundays, the majority of the lot was empty, with only one other car there which was parked next to his.

I opened the trunk of my car to retrieve his birthday present. A day after the dinner with his mother and sister, I had contacted them for an idea I had for his gift. Together, we all sorted through his father's John Wayne memorabilia and created a shadowbox with some of the smaller items we found and placed the picture of him and Logan in the middle.

Walking to the side door of the shop, I could barely contain the exhilaration I felt as I thought about what an incredible weight had been lifted off my shoulders. My finger pushed the annoying buzzing button, and I waited. After a while, I buzzed it again. Finally, the door opened. When Logan's eyes met mine, an expression of confusion and sadness came over him.

"Liv...What are you doing here?" he asked.

"Happy Birthday." I took a few steps forward, letting myself in, then placed his gift on the floor against the hallway wall as he closed the door behind me. I took his hand, pulling him close, then wrapped my arms around his body, placing my head on his chest and held on like I never wanted to let go. His scent brought me a feeling of peace. His touch sparked a light inside my soul. His heart pounded hard on my ear. After a moment, I broke the silence.

"You are my best friend," I confessed as I held him. Then I pulled my head off his chest and brought my palms to his face, looking into those beautiful hazel eyes, with my lips inches from his, and whispered, "I love you, Logan...I am in love with you..." I took a long, deep breath in. "Letting you go would be the biggest regret of my life."

His eyes closed, his head dropped and his shoulders sunk down as if all the air had left his body. He looked up at me with pleading, glazed over eyes. The look of sadness was still there but much more intense.

Why is he sad? He should be happy.

"Liv," he whispered as tears welled in his eyes, and he started looking around. "I'm so sorry...There's something I need to tell you..."

228

It was then that I heard the door to his apartment open at the top of the steps.

"Who is it, baby?" Chloe asked in her usual overly "fake nice" voice.

Logan's eyes squeezed shut while his face crunched up as if he were in actual physical pain. My wide eyes gazed to the top of the steps where she stood with only his t-shirt on, flashing a devilish smirk. Her bleach blond pink hair was all tangled up. I took a step back from Logan who was in only his boxer briefs, with matching messed-up hair. Seeing the terrified, apologetic look in his eyes was all the explanation I needed.

"Oh my God," I whispered as my fingers covered my mouth. Then, after my palm struck his face, I turned around and stormed away.

"Liv, wait!" he pleaded, but I kept going without looking back until his hand grabbed my arm and jerked me around to face him, and I realized he had chased me outside in his boxer briefs. "Where did you go last night?" he asked.

"What the hell difference does that make? You said you loved me! Do you even know what that means?" I screamed. "It sure didn't take you long to move on! You're a liar!"

"I *do* love you! Goddammit! Please, Liv, let me explain…"

"Fuck you, Logan! I hate you!" I cried as I turned around, trying to make another run for it, but his hand grabbed my arm, again stopping me. He turned me around, holding onto both my shoulders so that I couldn't turn away this time, and he looked right into my soul, his eyes becoming deeply determined.

"I couldn't find you, Liv. I realized I made a mistake, and I tried to find you. I called Mel to find out where you went with Tyler, and I went there."

"You did what?" I couldn't quite comprehend that.

"I saw him, and he told me you stood him up. Then I drove everywhere trying to find you. Your house, Mel's, I drove up and down the strip, hoping to spot your car. I must've run every red light. I called everyone I could think of to try to find you, and you wouldn't answer your fucking phone."

"Why were you running red lights? Were you trying to get killed?"

"No! I just wanted to be where you were! I wanted to tell you I made a mistake. When I couldn't find you, I came back and started drinking. I thought you were gone, Liv. I thought I'd never see you again. I was out of my mind...I didn't think you would ever forgive me. I blacked out and woke up with her next to me." A disgusted look came over him. "Fuck, I don't even remember what happened or how she got here. Please, Liv." He tried taking my hand, but I pulled it away.

"Logan, I can't..." I cried as my heart shattered into a million pieces thinking about him waking up next to another girl one single day after he woke up next to me. Revolting thoughts raced through my mind. Did he hold her the way he held me? Did he think of me at all while he was with her?

"No, Liv, we can make this work!"

"How can I trust you?" I looked at him, nauseated at the thought of...her...still on him. "There is a girl in your bed!"

"I don't remember how she got in my fucking bed!"

"Is that supposed to make me feel better? Just let me go!" I bolted for my car.

"Stop running away from me, Goddammit!" His voice was deep. Authoritative. Then, it softened. "For once. Stop running."

His words struck a chord with me and as my hand slipped under the door handle of my car, I hesitated. He was right. I always ran. And I had made a decision this morning to change.

I turned to face him. His arms were crossed in front of him with his hands tucked underneath them, his jaw was tightly clenched, and goose bumps covered his body. White fog came out of his nose as he breathed heavily.

I glanced past him, to the building. "I'm not going in there."

Relief washed over him. "Can I come in your car?"

"You should get dressed first."

He shook his head. "No way. I'm not walking away from you."

I made sure not to look at him as I deliberated. One look from him would melt me. "Fine. Get in."

He jogged to the passenger side as I sat down in the driver's seat. After slamming his door shut, he began cupping his hands together and blowing into them. He had no idea how much I wanted to take his hands in mine and warm them up the way he had done for me so many times. But everything was different now. He had betrayed me in an unforgivable way. Those hands had been on *her*.

"What do you want to say, Logan?" I asked as I turned the key in the ignition, resisting the unyielding urge to break down.

"I'm sorry."

That's it?

"What exactly are you sorry for? Breaking my heart last night? Or completely destroying it this morning? Or are you just sorry you got caught?" I finally looked at him as tears fell out of my eyes. "Why didn't you listen to me? I told you this would happen. Why couldn't you just stay my friend?" I buried my head in my hands as a sob forced its way out of me. "Now it's over."

"Please don't say that. Please don't say it's over," he whispered as he placed his hand on my shoulder.

I shoved his hand off me as I looked up at him, pissed and confused by his comment. How could it not be over? "Do you think this sort of thing is acceptable in a relationship, Logan? Because it's not."

His demeanor changed in an instant. "Do you think it's acceptable to go out with other guys when you're in a relationship, Liv? Because it's not."

My mouth fell open. He was mimicking me. "I didn't!"

"No, you just made me think you were going to."

Had I entered some sort of alternate reality? I allowed him in my car for *this*? "Are you telling me *I'm* the reason you slept with someone else?" At first I was hurt by his comments, but then I realized that it just reinforced the fact that we were incompatible. I sighed. "Just go Logan. Get out."

His hands grabbed his hair. "No! I'm not going anywhere until we figure this out." His fist pounded hard on the dashboard, startling me. "Fuck!"

"Stop swearing!" I cried out, involuntarily.

"I'm sorry. I'm so sorry Liv, I've fucked it all up. I'm saying all the wrong things. All I know is that I love you. I'm better when I'm with you. I need you," he sighed, defeated. "Any way you want. I'll start over. I'll respect whatever you want and if that means being only friends, I'll find a way to live with that. I'll deal with it, Liv. Whatever you want, I promise I'll give to you, just…don't walk away from us."

My mind filled with nothing but visions of Logan and Chloe. Together. Did he touch her the way he touched me?

Was she better than me? Was she on top, or was he? Did he smile at her the way he smiled at me? Did she make him laugh?

Did he *ever* really love me?

I felt like I was going to be sick.

"Logan, you were in bed with another girl." Just saying it pushed tears out of my eyes. "How would you feel in my shoes? Some lines just can't be crossed."

His shoulders slumped, and his eyes closed as he bowed his head down and shook it softly. He knew. He knew what it was like to be in my shoes. He knew exactly how I felt.

He ran his fingers through his hair, leaned his head against the headrest, and closed his eyes. With his elbow on the window ledge, he dropped his forehead into his hand, covering his eyes. His chest lifted up and down with each heavy breath as he stayed silent. Minutes passed, and he said nothing.

"It's too late to be friends. There is no more us. It's too late." I was thinking out loud, completely baffled at how it could've come to this.

His fingers rubbed his eyes, and a sniff came from his nose. As angry as I was, and as hurt as I felt, I hated seeing him like this. But I couldn't help how I felt. And I felt betrayed. Still, no matter what happened, the connection between us would never go away. I could barely resist the urge to comfort him, and I wanted him to comfort me.

I watched him as he remained silent, blanketed in devastation. Without thought, I took his hand from his thigh and laced my fingers in his. He turned to me with those deep, beautiful, hazel, tearful eyes, and we stared at each other for a moment before he pulled me close and wrapped his arms around my body, resting his forehead on my neck.

Our time was done. It was time for goodbye.

We held each other quietly for several minutes, and then he looked up into my eyes as he brought his hand to my face, slowly brushing my cheek with his thumb.

"Please say it's not over. It can't be over," he breathed.

I wanted to tell him what he wanted to hear. I wanted to kiss him and hold him forever, but he had just been with that girl who was still in his apartment. He placed his forehead on mine and brought his hand behind my neck, evoking my tears which escaped even though I was trying so desperately to hold them back. Then I forced myself to pull away, causing an expression of anguish in his beautiful face.

"We need some time," I whispered. I kissed his forehead, savoring the feeling of his warm skin on my lips for a moment. Then with all the strength I had, I let go. I took one last look into his broken eyes, then turned to face the dashboard and put both hands on the steering wheel.

"Goodbye, Logan." I stared straight ahead, forcing every resistant muscle in my body to remain still.

"Liv, no. Don't leave it like this." He reached out and placed his hand on my arm. I tightened my grip on the steering wheel.

"Please don't touch me," I whispered as I closed my eyes. More tears fell quietly down my cheeks. It was taking all my strength not to break down completely.

I felt his eyes on me, but I didn't flinch. My eyelids remained shut as I waited. Several moments passed.

"You told me you love me," he said as if he had just realized it. "You finally said it."

I do love you.

"Love isn't enough," I took a breath for strength. "Please get out of my car."

"I'm so sorry, Liv. You need to know that I love you. Nothing will ever change that."

He waited for a reaction, but I was too wounded and stubborn to give one. How could I ever get past him and Chloe being in the same bed together when he was supposed to love *me*? None of this made sense to me.

Finally, he opened the door and stepped out. I watched through the rearview mirror as he headed toward the building. Once he reached the door, he turned around, facing my car. After a moment, he opened the door and disappeared into the building.

I left the parking lot and drove for several blocks until my heart began to pound so hard in my throat that I thought it would explode. Despite the cold, I felt as though I were having a hot flash. I couldn't catch my breath as the dread for what would happen next flooded my thoughts.

I parked the car by the curb trying to prepare myself for the feeling that had been waiting for years to consume me again. I put the car in park and waited, knowing it was about to happen at any moment.

Finally, it struck.

I watched my hands bang on the steering wheel and heard my voice cry out. It became even more difficult to breathe as the sobbing started and my face became drenched in tears. I thought about how incredible it felt, sleeping in his arms…less than twenty-four hours ago, and I became overwhelmed by the loss of him. It's funny how life can completely change in an instant. It was over. I would never get to have that feeling again. My best friend…the one true love of my life…was gone.

Chapter Twenty-Five

Just when I thought I had been able to hold myself together long enough to get home, I thought about the look on Logan's face when Chloe came out, and another wave of agony crashed into me at full force. I had to pull the car over again. With my hands covering my face, I released the cries that begged to escape. Then, I thought about the look in his eyes the first time he told me he loved me, and the grief that had already consumed me became even more unbearable.

My hand reached to the glove compartment, and my fingers pulled it open. Melody always left an extra stash of cigarettes in my car, just in case. I grasped the package, taking a lighter and one slim white roll out of it.

I hated smoking. I had never done it and never wanted to do it. The thought of it disgusted me thoroughly. But I needed to do something to get rid of this stabbing pain in my heart. And in this moment of collapse, my mind could not come up with a better idea than to divert the pain to my lungs.

With conviction, I placed the filter in my mouth and lit the other end. My chest constricted the moment I inhaled, and I immediately hacked out several long, raspy coughs.

That was a horrible idea.

I opened my window and threw the lit cigarette out of it. Then I proceeded to snatch the rest of the cigarettes out of the package, opened my door, and crushed them to tiny little pieces onto the road. I wheezed in and out, still trying to catch my breath. I was terrified I would never breath normally again, and my mouth tasted like an ashtray.

Good, I'm thinking about something else.

Moving the gear to the 'drive' position, I pulled out onto the road and finished my ride home. It was a short drive, but by the time I arrived in my driveway, my body was drowning in exhaustion. All I wanted to do was sleep.

My keys jingled as I unlocked the front door. Once inside, I headed straight to my room with the intention of dropping onto my bed, but just before I did, my eyes caught a pink stamped envelope on top of the comforter. I took it in my hands and looked at the return address.

Dad's annual apology.

I already knew what it said. The cards had been getting less and less personal every year, yet the dollar amount of the check inside kept increasing. By this time, the message inside probably said something along the lines of *"Hope you have a good birthday"* or something equally generic. The last three cards included some form of *"Sorry I didn't get a chance to see you this year. Love, Your Father."*

He didn't even call himself "Dad." I didn't care about his stupid card or his stupid check. I let out one sarcastic chuckle before ripping the card in two and throwing it across my room. I didn't even know the man. The thought of accepting his apology or his money repulsed me.

Letting my coat drop to the floor, I kicked off my shoes and collapsed onto my bed, immediately falling into a state of unconsciousness

Chapter Twenty-Six

"Piece. Of. Shit-car!" I yelled as my palms slammed on the steering wheel. I tried turning the key again for the fifth time and got nothing. I'd have to deal with my car later; I needed to get to school. Reaching into my coat pocket, I grasped my phone and dialed Melody's number.

"What's up girl?" she answered.

"Hey, my car won't start. Can I catch a ride to school with you?"

"Yeah, I'm actually leaving now. I can be there in a few minutes."

Thank God for Melody. She was always there for me. As promised, she arrived in less than five minutes.

Our morning ride to school was a quiet one. In fact, I hadn't said much of anything to anyone in the last week. I barely remembered if the last few days even happened. The time felt almost robotic. I forced myself to go through the motions, but it was as though I were outside my body, controlling it from another place. Sleep felt good, and my dreams were peaceful... Mostly, they were of me and Logan, together...happy. I wished I could sleep forever.

"C'mon, Liv. You've got to snap out of it, girl," Melody said as she parked her car in the lot at school. "You've been walking around like a zombie all week. It's getting old."

"I'm fine, Mel. Really, it's no big deal." She rolled her eyes and gave me a *"yeah, right"* glance so I tried to change the subject as I stepped out of the car. "What are your plans with Nate tonight?" Today was their anniversary, and there was no doubt they would be spending it together.

"Not sure. He's going to surprise me." She smiled at the thought, and I was happy for her. They were good together...good to each other. Logan and I used to be good to each other too. A surge of pressure swept through my heart at the thought of just how good Logan and I used to be.

*

The first half of the day dragged. No matter how much I tried to focus on my teachers, school, or anything else for that matter, my mind kept wandering to that morning.

The last I heard from Logan was the text he sent to me the day I left him.

Thank you for the gift. It means everything to me.

I hadn't received a call or text from him since then. I didn't expect to, but at the same time, I found myself constantly wondering why I hadn't. Despite the betrayal I felt, there was a small part of me that wanted to hear from him. Come to think of it, there was a huge part of me that wanted to. I missed him terribly. I had never felt so empty before. Never.

We hadn't been apart for this long since we met. Maybe he had finally given up on me. Maybe he finally heard what I had been saying all along and decided there was no use in trying. It was what I had been pushing him to do. It was what he *should* do. It was what I should do. The thought of it, however, caused a wave of sadness to pass through my entire body.

His persistence had given me hope. Regardless of what I saw that morning, I wanted to believe that I was wrong. He told me he didn't remember anything. A little voice in the far depths of my mind kept telling me that maybe nothing actually happened. I wanted to believe he didn't throw away what we had together. I wanted to believe in *him.*

A clicking noise distracted me, and my focus centered on Mel's fingers snapping in front of my face.

"Are you here, hon?" she asked from across the lunch table. The school cafeteria had begun to clear out as everyone headed to their next class.

"Huh? Yeah. What?"

"Have you heard anything that I've said at all?"

"I'm sorry, Mel." Tears began to prick my eyes. *Crap, here it comes again.* Ever since I let my guard down that fateful morning, I've been a hot mess. Yesterday, I started crying in Spanish class, and the day before, it happened in Psych. I've never been so freaking fragile in my life. "I don't know what's wrong with me."

She looked at me with compassion. "Has he called yet?"

I shook my head. The fact that he hasn't called yet could only mean one thing. I had been right about what I saw.

"He will. There's something off about the whole thing with Chloe. That boy loves you, Liv."

The sound of her name made me cringe. Unable to speak, I nodded and pressed my lips together into a forced smile, as I kept the tears at bay. I took a deep breath in through my nose as I stood up and looked at my tray full of uneaten food. My appetite had become almost non-existent in the last week.

Mel had no doubt been talking about her Christmas break plans during lunch. Her parents were taking her and her brother to Costa Rica. They were even letting her bring Nate, but he had to pay his own way. As we walked out the cafeteria doors and into the hallway lined with lockers and other kids, it occurred to me how thoughtless it was that I had been ignoring her. "I'm sorry, Mel. I really want to hear all about it. Did you say you're going to swim with dolphins?"

She smiled and began telling me her itinerary. I listened intently, as any good friend would, until my phone buzzed just as we reached our lockers.

"Why is Gavin calling me?" I interrupted her.

She shrugged, annoyed.

I put my phone to my ear. "Gavin?"

"Hey. Um. Shit. I don't know how to tell you this."

"How about you just say it," I replied, irritated and a little amused.

"He'll probably be pissed at me for telling you, but of all people, you should know."

"Gavin?"

"Yeah?"

"Tell me why you're calling."

I heard him sigh into the phone. "Logan's locked up."

My eyes widened as my mouth dropped open.

Mel looked at me concerned. "What's wrong?"

I shook my head and began to get frantic. "What happened? Where is he?"

"He got busted at a race last night...Well, this morning. Early. Or late if you consider it last night. I don't know—I just woke up. What time is it, anyway?"

"Gavin, just tell me what happened!"

"He should've just gotten the hell out of there. They never would've caught him if he would've tried."

241

"Gavin! Start from the beginning."

"The spotters didn't see the cops in time. Those bastards snuck up on us quick. They came out of nowhere just after the race started, and they chased Logan right away. He pulled right over. Didn't even try to get away. Dumbass."

"Why is he in jail? Why didn't they just give him a reckless driving ticket or something?"

"I don't know. I didn't stick around to find out."

"That's shitty, Gavin! You're supposed to be his friend!"

"Hey, Logan's one of my best friends, but I'm not getting busted for him."

I let out a single sarcastic laugh. *Unbelievable.* "Where is he?"

"Downtown Police Department. That's what I would guess anyway. He hasn't called at all, so I'm thinking he's probably still there."

"Meet me there in twenty minutes," I demanded.

"No way. I'm not going there. They know me too, Liv. Who knows what bullshit they'll say to lock me up. This is the Midwest, Liv. There aren't any laws around here that could've gotten him arrested for anything he did. Reckless driving and speeding aren't arrest-worthy. They must've pulled something out of their asses."

Shit! "Okay. I'll figure it out." I took a calming breath. "Hey, Gavin?"

"Yeah."

"Thanks for telling me."

"Yeah. Of course. Keep me posted."

I took the phone away from my ear and looked at Mel. "Logan's in jail. I need to borrow your car."

242

I rushed through the front doors of the police station and straight down the wide hallway to the unoccupied reception window. It was quiet. Two police officers in uniform sat at desks towards the back of the area, laughing and talking. I looked around the desk for a bell to ring but found nothing.

"Excuse me," I called out.

Neither of them noticed me.

"Excuse me!" I raised my voice louder that time, and they both turned. They looked at each other to figure out who was going to deal with me, then one of them finally came to the window.

He didn't say anything. He just stared at me and waited.

"I...uh...found out my friend is here. What do I need to do to get him out?" I asked.

The officer looked at the computer in front of him, bored. "Name."

"Logan Tanner."

He typed the name onto the keyboard while I anxiously waited. "Here he is. Oh. He was released this morning."

Oh, thank God.

"Why was he arrested?" I asked.

He did more typing. "Huh." He looked at me and squinted his eyes. "And who are you?"

"Olivia Evans. I'm a friend."

He nodded, then looked back at the monitor. "We got him for second offense reckless driving, endangering persons or property, and unpaid motor-vehicle citations. Tell your friend to be more careful."

"Okay, thank you." I turned away, walked back down the long hallway and out the exit door.

When I reached Mel's car, I took my phone out and dialed Logan's number. It rang twice.

When he answered, he hesitated before saying anything. "Liv…"

Hearing his voice made me miss him even more. I had to take a breath to hold myself together. "Gavin told me what happened," I said quietly. "Are you okay?"

He sighed. "Yeah, I'm fine."

I could tell by his tone that he wasn't fine at all. He sounded completely defeated. He needed help. "Logan, where are you?"

He paused. "Liv, I don't need any help, okay?" he said as if he read my mind. He had a funny way of doing that. "I'm fine. Really. You need to forget about me."

He had to know that would never happen.

"Just tell me where you are," I coaxed.

I waited patiently as the phone stayed silent for several moment. Finally, he spoke. "I'm at the shop."

"I can be there in ten minutes."

"Aren't you at school?"

"No, I'm at the police department. Gavin told me you were still here. I came to try to help…"

"What did they tell you?" he nearly shouted, suddenly anxious.

"They told me you were arrested for reckless driving and that you were released this morning."

He sighed. "Shit. Liv, I'm sorry, it's not a good idea for us to meet right now. Just go back to school. You can't keep cutting classes."

Why? And then it hit me...stabbed me, actually...right in the inner cavity of my chest. He didn't want to see me.

"Oh. Okay," I said, trying to keep my cool, but failing miserably. "I guess I'll see you around then."

Just as I was about to hang up, he said my name.

"Yeah?" I replied.

"Why do you even care? After what I did..."

"What *did* you do, Logan?"

After several seconds, he sighed. "All I know is I fucking miss you." His voice cracked as he said it.

It's astonishing how a simple phrase can thoroughly break you. I had absolutely no control over the tears that began to fall down my cheeks the second after he said it.

"I miss you, too."

*

Mel let me back into the school through a side door between fifth and sixth period.

"Did you get him out?" she asked as we walked to our lockers.

"He's already out. I went there for nothing," I blankly replied as I placed her car keys in her palm. I felt like a complete idiot, running off and trying to 'save' him like that. Like he actually needed me.

"Are you fucking serious?" She leaned up against her locker as I opened mine. "You're probably going to get a detention for it too."

"I don't really care, Mel." I grabbed my books and slammed my locker shut. "We're late for class. I'll see you later. Thanks for letting me use your car." From her expression,

245

I could tell she was worried about me. I pulled her into a hug. "I'm lucky to have you."

She stepped back as I released her. "You know I've got your back, right?"

I contrived a smile. "I know you do." Then I turned away and began jogging down the hall to my next class.

Chapter Twenty-Seven

Even though the day was almost over, the rest of it took an eternity. I practically jumped out of my seat when the final bell rang. I went to Mel's locker and found her making out with Nate while holding a pink teddy bear, which I assumed was the first part of his anniversary surprise. How did he get in here anyway? He wasn't even in high school, let alone *this* school. They really needed to up the security.

"I'll wait in the car," I mumbled, but I wasn't sure if she heard me. As happy as I was for her, I didn't need to see that right now.

"Liv, I'm coming!" she replied. She broke away from Nate and ran towards me. "Hey," she continued, "I'm here for you. Don't forget that, okay?"

I nodded. The last thing I wanted to do was talk about it. I wanted to stop thinking about it. I just wanted to forget.

"Okay, enough of this no talking and one-word answer crap!" she stopped me in the hall and faced me. "You love him. He loves you. What's the problem?"

"The problem is he told me he loved me and then slept with another girl!" Was she delirious? Had she not remembered what happened? I gave her a disgusted look and started walking quickly.

"Bullshit!" Melody argued as she caught up with me. "The problem is you're scared and you're making excuses. You said he didn't even remember it, right? You know how twisted that

247

girl is…maybe it never even happened. Maybe she's just *saying* it happened. You know he doesn't care about her anyway."

"I don't know, Mel, I can't seem to get past it." I said as we walked out the front doors of the school. "Besides, whose side are you on anyway?"

"I'm on your side, Liv. I want you to be happy. Stop torturing yourself for things that you have no control over and let yourself be happy."

"You can't possibly think what he did was okay."

"No. Of course not. If he did what you think he did, it would absolutely *not* be okay. But if there's any possibility that he *didn't* do it, wouldn't you want to find out? You believe that he doesn't remember, right? Why assume the worst?"

I didn't answer her right away. Because I didn't have an answer. Part of me was still too angry to give it a chance, while the other part begged to hear him out at the very least. Ever since meeting this extraordinary boy several months ago, my heart and my brain have been doing nothing but attacking each other. And I had no idea how to get a freaking grip. If this is what love was like, I wanted nothing to do with it.

I stopped instantly when I saw Logan with his backside and palms against the hood of his Mustang, parked in the no parking zone. His head was bowed down as if he were deep in thought. A single red rose hung between the fingers of his right hand.

"I forgot something in my locker," Mel announced as she caught glimpse of him. Next thing I knew she was scurrying away.

A wave of emotions hit me all at once. I took a deep breath, forcing the lump in my throat to cease. I would be strong. I would *not* falter like I did earlier today. This would not faze me. A rush of pain pulsed in my heart as he looked up at me.

God, I've missed those eyes.

His face brightened when he saw me, but there was an underlying sadness behind it. He smiled, but there were dark circles around his eyes as if he hadn't slept in days. I walked to him, stopped two feet in front of him, and waited.

"This is for you." He handed me the rose. "I wanted to give you...something special."

"Thank you." We stood silent for a moment, with our eyes locked. Why did I have to feel so at peace...so at home when I looked in his eyes? I told myself, again, to stay strong. It took all the willpower I had not to jump into his arms. After a few moments, the silence became awkward.

"Okay. Well. I guess I'll see you around," I said, and I turned to walk away, confused as hell.

"Liv, wait!"

I turned to face him.

"Can I give you a ride home?" he asked. "I know about your car."

"How?"

"Mel texted me right after you called her for a ride this morning. It said something along the lines of *'score some groveling points a-hole, step up and fix it.'*"

Of course she did.

"You didn't listen to her did you?" I asked, growing more and more frustrated with her meddling. "I'm not really your problem anymore."

He looked like I had just punched him in the gut, "You were *never* my problem. You were my fucking answer."

I hated that he said that. I hated that he said it in past tense even more so. If I was his "answer" then why did he do what he did? Why did he ruin everything?

"Yeah, your car is good to go," he continued, noticing my discomfort from his words. "Alternator was bad. Easy fix."

I squinted at him, "When exactly did you get out of the slammer?"

A hint of a smile crinkled his eyes, "I don't know. Four. Maybe five this morning."

I sighed, "You might want to give Gavin a call. He still thinks you're locked up."

He nodded, "I will. But first, will you let me drive you home? Please?"

I looked around, fidgeting with my backpack, trying to come up with an excuse not to go with him, but nothing came to me.

"Sure," I nodded.

With a glimmer of hope in his eyes, he opened the door for me, and I took a seat. My backpack found a place on the floorboard between my feet while my eyes stayed glued to Logan as he rounded the front of the car and slid into the driver's seat.

What the hell was I doing?

The ride to my house was a silent one. As I sat in the passenger seat, the scent of Armor All mixed with leather and…Logan…instantly reminded me of everything I had been missing so terribly. I stared out the window, watching the snow-covered trees and houses pass. Feeling him so close to me, with nothing but the shifter between us, but knowing I couldn't reach over and take his hand, only increased my torment. Tears stung my eyes as I thought about how things between us would never be the way it used to be.

As we rolled into my driveway, and he put the car in park, my cheeks began to burn. I tried to force the tears back so

Logan wouldn't see me cry, but ever since my floodgates opened, I've had trouble getting my wall back up. Being near him was more difficult that I thought it would be.

Why is he making this harder?

I stared blankly at my house, trying to pull myself together. "Logan, what do you want?"

He sighed, "Do you still love me?"

Taken aback by the forwardness of his question, I stayed silent. Of course I still loved him. It's not something you can just turn off. Love wasn't the issue. Bad things happen when you love someone too much. I had already made the mistake of letting my guard down once. I had no intention of doing it again. The only problem was, my guard was already gone.

The longer his questions went unanswered, the more tense the air between us felt. "Liv, please, I need to know."

I sighed. "What do you want me to say, Logan? It doesn't matter."

"Yes, it matters!" he banged his hands on the steering wheel. The outburst caused me to jump in my seat. "It's the *only* fucking thing that matters." Resting his elbow on his window, he pinched the bridge of his nose and took a calming breath. "Shit. I'm sorry. Please, I just need to know."

"I don't...I can't..." I couldn't get it out. Telling him that I didn't love him would be a lie. I had to be honest, but I couldn't seem to do that either. All the heartbreak in my life came from love. Everyone I loved had either left me or fallen out of my life somehow, leaving an empty void. I knew if we were together, he would do the same eventually, intentionally or not. Wouldn't it be better to cut the ties now than to wait until he was intertwined so deeply in my life that I would have no way of recovering? I couldn't even bear the thought of having to get over him now. How would I manage it if I fell deeper in love with him?

What if he hurts me again?

I turned to face him but still, no words came out. The hopefulness in his eyes gradually turned to anguish. He had taken my silence for rejection. His head bowed down. His voice was nothing but a whisper when he said, "Did you ever love me?"

"Logan, I'm sorry..." Finally, my vocal chords were cooperating, but I still couldn't say what I needed to. My mind was on overdrive and all the answers were scrambled. Nothing was clear anymore, and I didn't have an answer to give him.

He wiped his eye with the meaty part of his palm, then faced me. "I'm leaving for a while, Liv."

My mouth fell open.

"I tried so hard not to fall in love with you. Not to want you...or even care. But the more I'm around you, the harder I fucking fall for you. You're everywhere I look. Everything reminds me of you. And asking you to forgive me would be an even bigger dick move than what I did. I will never forgive myself and I don't expect you to forgive me either. I just need to leave town until I can figure out how to function here without you. There's a pretty big racing scene in Miami. They're organized there, not like here. I made plans to leave in the morning. I just thought maybe..."

"So it's true? You—and Chloe—you guys—"

He sighed, "I still don't remember. But she says we did, and I have no way of proving we didn't."

Tears welled in my eyes, and this time I couldn't hold them back. A sob escaped me.

"Oh shit, Liv. Please don't cry." He reacted to my expression by reaching over to me, pulling me to him, where he held me tight. He smelled so good. A mixture of leather and aftershave…and him. The thought of never being in his arms like this again destroyed me. He held on to me for several minutes. "This will be the best thing for you. You may not love me like I love you, but I *know* our friendship was important to you. I can honestly say that I will *never* move on from you, Liv, but I can't expect you not to. You deserve to be happy, and my leaving will make it easier for you to move on."

His words cut me deep and made sense all at the same time. I knew he was right. Why did it feel so wrong?

As he slowly released me, he took my chin, forcing me to look into his crushed eyes, and wiped away the tears on my cheeks with his thumb. His touch ignited the familiar electrical current that I had been longing for this past week.

"I couldn't leave without giving this one last chance," he explained. "I would regret it if I didn't try. At least now I know." He brought his lips to my forehead where they lingered. Then, he looked into my eyes, forcing a sullen smile.

After several moments, he sighed and abruptly pulled away, placing both hands on the steering wheel while looking straight ahead. It was my cue to get out of the car. This was it. I was never going to see him again. Silent tears streamed down my cheeks as I took a final look at him. His cheeks were flushed, his jaw clenched, and his knuckles white. I waited for any further acknowledgement from him, but he wouldn't look at me.

Devastated, I opened the door and exited the car. He waited, idling in the driveway until I was safely in the house. I watched through the living room window as his car slowly

253

backed out to the road and rolled away down the street. My ears strained until I could no longer hear the rumble.

My body collapsed like dead weight onto the couch. I thought about the feeling I had when I was with him. Happiness. The way he looked into my soul like nobody else ever could. His strong arms around me. His laugh. Our intimate moments together. How could I let that go?

I felt myself creep into a mental state of despair that was more brutal than the misery I felt after my dad, Kevin, and Adam. Suddenly I realized that I didn't have a say with *them*. I never had the opportunity to fight for what I wanted before, like I do now. And my only chance was slipping away.

He still didn't remember what happened with Chloe. It wasn't a definite *"yes, I had sex with her."* And I believed him with every part of my mind, heart, and soul.

My body shot up to a sitting position. In an instant, I realized that the only thing that would prevent this hurt was being with Logan. I no longer cared about Chloe. I knew deep in my heart that she was nothing more than a mistake to him. To me, she was just an excuse I was using to prevent the inevitable abandonment. He didn't love her; he loved me. But the inevitable was happening anyway. And it was all my fault.

The fear of what *might* happen vanished. All I wanted was to be with him. Even if it was brief, even if it ended tomorrow, I wanted to be with him as long as I possibly could. The only thing that scared me was losing him now. Maybe I could forgive him. The least I could do was try. I would regret it forever if I let him go like this, without even telling him how I really felt.

I'm such an idiot!

I had put him through so much already, I hoped it wasn't too late. I hoped he would forgive me. Without another thought,

I jumped up and impulsively ran out the door, grabbing my phone and car keys out of my coat pocket on the way out the door. As I reached my car, with my fingers under the door handle, I stopped abruptly, as my heart stopped beating.

My ears perked up to the sound of a low distant rumble. A rumble that grew louder and deeper with every passing second. My head turned to face the road in anticipation. A moment later, a canary yellow 1969 Ford Mustang pulled into my driveway. A half-laugh, half-sob came out of me as Logan stepped out of it.

"I still love you!" I cried as he ran toward me. "I've always loved you and I'm never going to stop loving you! Please stay!"

I thought he was going to pull me into a tight embrace, but instead, his strong hands clutched my neck, eagerly pulling me close, and he linked his lips firmly to mine, parting them a second later, deepening the kiss.

Absolute euphoria erupted throughout every part of my body. My skin burned and my heart pounded hard in my chest. The fight in me was gone. The cold winter air was replaced by the fire radiating from our skin. Everything else in the world washed away, with each passing moment becoming more intense than the last.

I slid my hands up his back and pulled him to me, although it still didn't seem like I could ever get close enough. He let out a muffled moan as I tried desperately to bring him closer. He lifted me so that I had to wrap my legs around him, and I buried my eyes into his neck, squeezing them shut to stop the tears, as I clutched onto him. He simply held me that way for several minutes.

"You came back." I mumbled, keeping my face buried. "Why did you come back?"

255

He lowered me back to the ground. With an expression that could only be described as tortured, he stared intently at me. "I can't leave you," he admitted as though he couldn't understand it. "All I could think about was how wrong it felt. I couldn't physically fucking do it because I'm scared to death of not having you in my life. Not being around you in some capacity would be my own personal living hell. I know I fucked up. And there's nothing I can do to change what happened. I'm so, so sorry. I wish you could forgive me, and I know you shouldn't, but I can't fucking leave you."

His eyes filled with tears as his face crunched up in disgust at the thought of what he had done. "Tell me what you need, Liv. I promised you that I would do whatever I need to do to make you happy, and that will never change. No matter what...Regardless of how you feel about me...I am always going to love you."

His profound, heartfelt words brought tears and laughter out of me at the same time. "Just tell me you'll always be here. With me," I pleaded, letting go of any trace of my stupid pride. I pulled him tight to me and rested my head on his chest. "Please don't ever leave."

He breathed a sigh of relief and held me close. "Never. I promise, Liv. I'll never leave you."

"You won't go to Miami?"

"Fuck no." He looked at me and gently brushed my hair behind my ear, as his bewildered gaze collided with my desperate one. "Not without you."

Relief overcame me. He wanted to be with me. But as much as I wanted everything to be okay, I needed answers before I could completely turn a blind eye to the devastating incident that took place with Chloe a week ago. I needed to be sure it would never happen again.

"My parents aren't home...Do you want to come in for a while? We should probably talk about everything." I asked.

He nodded, "Yeah."

Logan followed me into the house and watched me closely as I removed my coat and rested it on one of the kitchen chairs.

"Do you want something to drink?" I asked as I reached into the cupboard for a glass.

"No, I'm good," he replied as I filled my glass with tap water.

"You can take your coat off if you want," I said.

I peeked at him through the corner of my eye as I took a gulp of water. His eyes were still on me. I continued to drink as I watched him take off his coat. His eyes didn't leave mine once, not even when he hung it on the chair, on top of my coat. He looked incredible, as usual, despite the dark circles around his eyes. Before I knew it, my entire glass of water was gone, and I placed the empty glass on the countertop.

He continued to watch me intensely, then followed me as I walked to the living room. He sat down on the couch as I turned on the stereo. After picking a good station, one that played blues music, I sat down on the opposite end of the couch. If I was going to ask the tough questions, I needed to keep my bearings, which meant keeping some amount of distance between us.

"Let's get the hard part over with," I said. "I want you to tell me exactly what happened. And please don't sugar-coat anything. I need you to tell me the truth."

He nodded, then stayed quiet as he looked down. After a moment of thought, he said, "I don't fucking know what happened."

257

"What do you remember? Logan, please. You have no idea how much I want to work this out with you, but I need you to tell me what happened."

His eyes were filled with remorse and longing as he stared at me. "I don't want you to hate me."

I couldn't bear the way he was looking at me. He seemed so sad. I instinctively slid across the couch, gently took his hand in mine, and rested my head on his shoulder. "Please, just tell me what you remember."

He tightened his grip on my hand as he exhaled. "I was so pissed off at myself for what I said to you that night, Liv. I was stupid to say I didn't want to see you anymore because nothing could've been further from the truth. I wanted...I *want* to see you every minute of every day. I wasn't thinking straight, and I thought that if I gave you an ultimatum, you would choose *me*."

"Logan, you didn't give me a chance..."

"I know!" He pulled me closed and kissed my forehead. "I know that now. And I know I was being a control freak. And I know when someone tells you to do something, you do the opposite. I was just so damn jealous, I wasn't thinking straight."

I pulled away slightly, causing the look of remorse in his eyes to intensify. He took a deep breath and continued. "When I couldn't find you, I went back to my apartment, but I couldn't stop thinking about how I had royally fucked everything up. I was pretty damn sure you would never forgive me for letting you go like that. I don't know what happened to you, Liv, but it doesn't take a genius to figure out that you don't let people in. I knew I blew my chance with you. And I hated myself for it. I grabbed a bottle of Jack, took it to my room, stripped down to my boxers and started drinking. It didn't take long to pass out after that."

"You didn't call Chloe?"

"Not that I remember."

"Well then, why was she there?"

"Fuck if I know."

"Logan! Stop being so vague. You have to remember something."

"I remember going to bed. I *know* I didn't wake up until morning. I mean, I've blacked out before, but I'd never forget fucking someone." I tried to remain calm as he looked at me with remorse, trying to gauge my reaction. "After you left that morning, I asked her how she got in and she told me the door was unlocked. She let herself in, Liv."

His words placed hope in my heart. I remembered him saying that he had called everyone that night to try to find me…maybe Chloe heard about our falling-out and used it as an opportunity. But regret still remained fastened in Logan's eyes. There was more to hear. "What happened when you woke up?"

He sighed, then rubbed his forehead. Whatever he was thinking was causing him some serious stress.

"Please tell me," I whispered.

When he looked at me, I knew it wasn't going to be good.

"I thought she was you," he said.

Oh no.

His brows pulled together. "I woke up hung-over, and I didn't open my eyes right away. Her back was on my chest and my arm was around her. I thought you had come back to me. I said 'I love you' thinking it was you, and then you…she…turned around and kissed me."

I completely pulled away from him this time. I didn't want to hear anymore, but I had to know. "How far did you go?" I couldn't hide the hurt in my voice.

259

"Not far, I swear. I knew something wasn't right the second I woke up. She didn't feel good like you do. She didn't smell like you. She didn't taste like you. Fuck, I wanted it to be you so bad, Liv, that I didn't realize right away that it wasn't. I'm so sorry."

The thought of him *tasting* her nauseated me. But I was intent on staying strong. "All you did was kiss her. And you thought it was me."

With a disgusted look on his face, he thought for a moment. "Not according to her."

"Oh." My heart sank deep into my stomach. "Well, what happened according to you?"

He urgently took my hand. "Nothing. Even though I don't remember anything, I know nothing happened because drunk or not, I know I would never do anything like that to you. I love you too much. You're the only one I want. Hurting you in that way would kill me. But I have no idea how she got into my bed, or why she's saying what she's saying, and I have no way to prove to you that nothing happened."

He stared at me with hope. He was asking me to trust him. Even though I didn't know if I could trust him, there was a possibility that nothing happened with Chloe. And the strong bond that we have was too important to me to throw away, over something that may not have even happened. He wanted me to trust that he wouldn't have thrown it away either.

I released his hand and stood up as I tried to sort the jumbled mess of thoughts in my mind. I rubbed my forehead. "I don't know what to think, Logan."

He rested his elbow on the arm of the couch and rested the temple of his head on his knuckle. "I don't blame you. You have every right to feel that way."

His somber eyes made me want to tell him everything would be okay. But trust didn't come natural to me. And I didn't know if I could give him my trust after everything that had happened.

"I just don't know how to make this work," I said, frustrated. Needing a minute alone to think, I turned to walk toward the bathroom. Just before I entered the hallway, the familiar B.B. King song came on the stereo, stopping me immediately. It was the same song used for his ringtone on my phone. The one that played in his car the first night I fell asleep in his apartment and I was instantly taken back to that very time and place. That was the night I realized that he wasn't like other boys. The night he became the exception.

Something clicked inside of me. I needed to follow my heart. And my heart was sitting on the couch, miserable for something that didn't happen.

Nothing happened.

I didn't need any proof; I just knew. Without a doubt, I was sure of it.

Another epiphany.

I turned around to face him. With a mixture of confusion and hope, he lifted his head off his knuckle and cocked his head to the side. I smiled as the weight on my shoulders disappeared. His eyes widened slightly as one corner of his mouth turned up.

"This song reminds me of you," I said.

"Yeah," he said with optimistic eyes. "It reminds me of you, too. It makes me think of the night we first kissed."

"I fell in love with you that night," I divulged.

His eyes widened, "You knew *then*?"

I walked back to him, "I didn't realize it then, but looking back, I know now that night was the game-changer. Why…when did you know?"

"That I loved you?"

"Yeah."

He stood from the couch and lifted my chin with his fingers, "The second I met you."

His soft lips melted into mine, destroying any coherent thought I may have had. To my dismay, he stopped, and kissed my forehead as he took my lower back and gently pulled me closer. With one hand on his back, and the other hand holding his, I rested my head on his chest. Our song still played, and as we held each other, we swayed to the music.

His heartbeat pounded hard in my ear. I had missed his touch, his beautiful scent. My entire body relaxed as he tightened his hold on me. His arms were home. Nothing felt better than his strong, comforting arms around me. We slowly stepped back and forth, continuing to hold each other through the end of the song. Then through the next song. Then the next one.

"I believe you," I whispered.

He pulled his head back slightly. "What did you say?"

I looked into his perfect eyes. "I said I believe you. I believe that you love me. I believe that you wouldn't hurt me like that. I trust you, Logan."

He looked at me like I was crazy, then his face turned into pure warmth. "You are amazing, you know that? I don't deserve you."

His fingers reached behind my ear and through my hair, while his thumb rested on my cheek. The intensity in his eyes made my heart skip. I knew the look he was giving me. It was the look that said he needed me. All of me. His chest heaved up and down as his face slowly came closer to mine. When our lips gently touched, the wave of heat from it weakened me, causing my eyes to close. I needed him too. All of him.

"Let's make a deal," I breathed through kisses.

"Anything," he responded in a low, sexy voice.

I stepped back and held both his hands in mine as I stared up at him. "No more running when we get freaked out."

He grinned. "I can handle that."

"And we talk things out…no matter hard it is. We stay open and honest. We can't have anymore misunderstandings."

"Hell yeah to that."

"And we go upstairs to my room—right now—to show each other exactly how much we mean to each other," I wiggled my brows.

For the first time in over a week, I heard the captivating sound of his laugh, "Oh I'll show you alright. I'll show you until you crash from exhaustion."

"Is that a threat?" I grinned.

He shook his head, "Nope. It's a promise."

"Well then I guess I'll have to hold you to it." I took his hand and led him up the stairs to my bedroom. I sat down on my bed as he closed the door behind us. With his hand still on the door knob, he gazed at me for a moment with disbelief before he came over to me and kneeled down, so that his face was only slightly below mine. With his eyes on mine, he grabbed me behind the knees and pulled hard, forcing my knees apart, and his body against mine. It took my breath away.

His soft lips on my neck sent a surge through me. My hands savored every ridge and muscle of his abdomen as they slid under his shirt and slowly lifted it up and over his head.

He cupped his hand on to the left side of my face, his eyes exploring my face and hair as if he was seeing me for the first time. "You're so beautiful, Liv."

I instinctively rolled my eyes which only intensified his gaze. He took my face with both hands, forcing me to look directly at him. "You. Are. Beautiful. You're an angel."

A smile formed on my face from his words. I didn't feel like an angel, but I knew he was being honest in how he felt. He seemed pleased at my reaction. The corners of his mouth turned up as he brought his face towards me and surrounded my mouth with his. My hands rose above my head, and our lips unlocked as he removed my shirt.

With one hand behind my neck, he brought me back to him, and he unclasped my bra with the other hand. His warm hands moving firmly on my bare skin gave me a chill. He responded to my sudden shiver by pressing his heated chest on mine and laying me down under him, pulling the comforter over us.

The urgency had dissolved into a need to relish in every passing second. He was taking his time now, as his warm wet lips slowly, deliberately, trailed a path of kisses starting from my neck down to my stomach. I savored every sweet moment of it. His tongue entered my navel, provoking a giggle to escape from my throat from the tickle of it.

He reacted by looking up at me with the comforter on top of his head and an amused grin on his face with one eyebrow cocked up. It was enough to make me crazy. I had no freaking idea why this beautiful man loved me so much. But he did. And I would never let him go again.

No longer able to resist, I pulled him back up to me, firmly kissing him. I reached for his belt buckle and quickly opened it, then unbuttoned his pants. A moan escaped him as I slid my hand under the waistline of his boxer briefs. Then, he froze.

"Shit. Liv, I don't have…I didn't think this would happen. I don't have any condoms."

"It's okay, I'm on the pill," I whispered. "I've been on it since I was fifteen to help regulate…um…you know…my period. It's fine. We're good."

He breathed out as he let go of my wrist and dropped his head in relief. "Thank Christ. I promise you I'm clean."

"I believe you Logan," I continued to push his boxer briefs down with his pants, then his feet removed them the rest of the way.

I readily waited as he unbuttoned my pants and moved himself, with the rest of my clothing, to the end of the bed. Holding my bare right ankle in his hand, he began to slowly kiss his way up my leg, stopping at the inside of my thigh, causing my breathing to become heavier, my heart rate to speed up, and the depths of my stomach to quiver. From there, he moved to my left leg, repeating the process, each warm kiss significantly intensifying my need for him.

He kissed his way up to my stomach, then my neck. Each touch, each caress, increased my feeling of bliss. With his face above mine, he gazed into my eyes. And I gazed into his. Without looking away, he slowly slid into me, causing me to inhale sharply and close my eyes. When I opened them, his darkened eyes were still on me, studying my every reaction to him.

"I love you, Logan," I breathed, without thought, as our bodies continued to slowly move.

Overwhelmed by my words, his eyes closed as his forehead dropped onto mine. "I love you, too." He breathed, simply.

We moved in perfect harmony with heat, passion, and true love surrounding us. This moment felt so perfect...so right...and we slowly indulged in every moment of it. His lips firmly kissed mine as the intensity between us increased.

"You feel amazing," he whispered, deeply.

His words mimicked my thoughts. My palms explored him, moving from his shoulders, down his chest and abdomen, then around to his back as he gently pressed into me over and over again. The feel of his bare skin on me was incredible. I didn't know it until this moment, but being this close to him, having all of him—mind, body, and soul—was all I had ever wanted. I had never felt so content in my life.

The passion between us increased until I could no longer handle it. My breathing increased. "Logan, please." I needed him to finish this.

He moaned as our bodies moved faster and with more intensity.

"Oh my God," I heard myself say as my body pulsed.

With my hands on his back, as I stared into his darkened eyes, I pulled him into me one final time. A moan escaped him as his eyes closed.

He brought his face to me and kissed behind my ear one last time before his body fell beside me, with his head resting on my pillow. His hand continued to caress me as we laid there, silently.

I had never prayed before. But in this moment, as I stared at the ceiling, I prayed that we would last. That nothing would ever tear us apart. That I could be with him forever.

"Liv, I promise you, the bullshit stops here," he said, as if he read my mind. "You're too damn important. I'm not going to fuck up again."

"Okay." I moved to my side so that I could face him. "But you know we're going to mess up once in a while, right?"

He shook his head with a serious expression. "Uh-uh. No way. If you had any idea how much you mean to me…there's no way I'm ever going to lose you again."

I brought my face to his and gently closed my mouth around his bottom lip. He smoothly kissed me back. "Let's just promise we'll always work through the bullshit," I whispered between kisses. "Even if it's hard."

He pulled away from me, studying me while his fingers brushed my hair behind my ear. "That sounds perfect." His intense eyes gazed into my soul…like they do. "I promise I will try not to fuck up. Which means I promise not to freak out over stupid shit. And I promise to always work through the bullshit with you. I swear I will do everything in my power to make this work. I want to make you happy, Liv."

I believed him. For the first time, I believed our relationship could actually succeed. "I'm done running, Logan."

He smiled, then looked to the side as if he had a thought. "So what does this mean? For us."

I smiled at the realization that he wanted to put a label on us. "I guess it means we officially *do* relationships."

He breathed in, deeply, and brought his soft lips to my forehead. "One relationship. This one. You and me."

Moving towards him, I gently pushed him back and lifted his arm up so that I could place my head on his chest. The sound of his heartbeat on my ear was a serenade. His scent—a thousand times better than fresh lilacs on a spring day. His touch—heaven. I could lay like this forever.

Chapter Twenty-Eight

I knew they were waiting for him, but I didn't care. His lips tasted too good. His hand on my cheek was soothingly warm. I wanted to keep him with me.

Logan's car idled in the parking lot of an industrial building as we leaned over the stick shift, kissing each other softly. Tonight would be different than the usual "free for all" of races. It was an organized tournament with the top five racers in the area. And the winner would leave ten grand richer.

In addition to tonight's payout, all the men competing were itching to take Logan's status as number one racer. It wasn't just for vanity, although that was part of it. In addition, they all knew that the higher their rank, the more races they'd get offered, which meant more winnings they could bring home.

With a snowstorm predicted for later tonight, this would most likely be the last race of the winter. Logan had assured me a number of times that he would never race on wet or icy roads. Until now, the weather had been easy on us with just one snowfall on Christmas night, which quickly melted from the streets two weeks later.

With a pound on the driver's side window, a muffled Gavin shouted through the glass, "C'mon, man, you want a fuckin' payday, or you gonna make out with your girl all night?!"

Unfazed, Logan continued to move his lips against mine. My eyes cracked open to see Logan respond to him by slowly lifting his arm with the middle finger extended from his hand. Gavin pounded on the glass one more time before walking away. I thought I heard him mumble, "Dumbass," but I wasn't sure.

"I think they're waiting for you," I smiled, pulling away.

"Let them wait," he replied, closing in on me again.

Keeping my distance, I laughed. "Okay, then, let's just go home. I hate standing out in the cold anyway."

His expression became concerned. "You don't want to be here?"

"No. It's not that. It's just…Do I have to flag all the races, or just yours?"

"You don't have to do anything. I thought you liked doing it." His face morphed into confusion.

I grinned. The last thing he needed before a race was to be concerned about anything other than driving. "I do. Trust me. I have fun with it. I guess I'm just worried. Did they check the roads for ice patches?"

"Yeah, Gavin and I scouted the street earlier today."

I nodded. "We've been to this spot a few times in the last month alone, and you've already been busted once. Aren't you worried about police?"

"Nah, Gavin knows a guy." He pointed to the computer screen on the dash. "He's hacked into their system. If they get a lead that we're here, we'll be long gone before they get anywhere near us. Plus, we've got more spotters out than usual. Trust me, we're good."

My eyes got wide. "Hacked into the police department's system? Logan, are you crazy?"

"No…I'm being safe."

I immediately felt apprehension. We stared at each other momentarily. It seemed to me like he was getting in way too deep. There was plenty I wanted to say, but the timing was less than ideal. He needed a clear mind for the races. We'd have to talk about it later.

I took a deep breath and gave him a comforting smile. "Okay. I trust you."

Taking my hand, he relaxed. "Good. You have no reason not to. I promise."

We stepped out of the car and approached Gavin and a group of several other men. Five men would be in the tournament, including Logan, each of them putting in a two thousand dollar bet. As Gavin collected the cash from the participants, I vaguely noticed a figure approach. Before I knew what was happening, Logan was thrusted forward by the man.

"Oh, sorry dude, didn't see you there," a glossy-eyed Derrick chuckled. A black knit hat covered his shaved head. I had only seen him one other time...at my very first race. And tonight he looked a million times more loaded than that night.

"Watch your step, asshole," Logan challenged.

Derrick ignored the comment and stumbled his way into the circle, waving a wad of cash around in the air. "How come none of you motherfuckers told me about this tonight? Ain't my money good enough for y'all?" He handed his cash to Gavin. "Well, I'm here now assholes. Count me in."

Logan stepped in and placed his hand on Derrick's shoulder. "Relax, Derrick."

In an instant, Derrick pivoted around and grasped Logan's coat with both hands, bringing his face within an inch of Logan's. "Did you just fucking touch me?"

Logan's expression turned furious. "You better back up right now, Derrick." He stood tall, challenging Derrick. "Back. The fuck. Up."

After a moment of deliberation, Derrick let go and chuckled as he brushed off Logan's coat. "Hey, man, all I want to do is race." He glanced around at the men in the circle. "Ain't nobody got a problem with that, right?"

Nobody said anything at first. They all glanced at one another, gauging the situation. Then, one of the men spoke up. "Sorry, man, you gotta have a clear head to race. You know the rules."

Derrick let out one long, humorless laugh. "Oh no, you've gotta be shitting me. You think I'm fucked up?" He shook his head then stood with both feet together and his hands extended out. "Watch this." He closed his eyes and touched his index fingers to his nose. First the left one, then the right. "Does that look fucked up to you? Look." He found a line on the road and proceeded to balance on it as he walked forward, one foot directly in front of the other. "See. Straight as an arrow."

Logan pointed to Gavin. "Give him his money back. I'm not racing him."

Derrick stomped over to Logan with rage building in his expression. "Fuck that! Are you scared, little man?" he said, face to face with Logan. "Oh yeah. That's it, isn't it? You know you can easily take these fuckers, but you can't beat me. I'll *smoke* you."

"You wish, douchebag," Logan replied.

Derrick's drug use had become well known in the racing circles, and there were very few competitors who were reckless enough to race against a ticking time bomb like him. Most had girlfriends, wives, or families at home, and although they could never give up the thrill of racing that was in their blood, they were level-headed enough to be as safe as possible...considering the circumstances.

271

Derrick was here to prove himself.   But was failing miserably.

Tommy, a frequent racer, approached Derrick from behind. "Dude, you're a liability.   Get your shit together, then maybe we'll talk.   But it ain't happening tonight, man.   Go home."

Tommy placed his hand on Derrick's shoulder, and before anyone knew what was happening, Derrick flung himself around, pulling a handgun out from somewhere and pointed it at him. "Get your hands off me, Tommy!"

Our circle backed up, spreading out, with a few of us putting our hands in the air while others shouted a mixture of "Whoa!" "Hey now!" and "Shit!"

Gavin slowly stepped toward Derrick with his hands up. "Look, man, we're all friends here.   There's no need for that. Put that shit away."

With the gun shaking nervously in his hand, Derrick pointed it from person to person.   "I came here to race!"   His voice cracked and his face became tainted in a combination of anger and fear.   He pointed the gun frantically at every one of us. "And that's what I'm gonna do!"

Suddenly determined, he turned to me, pointing the gun directly at my face. My eyes widened, and my breathing stopped completely.

"What would happen if you didn't have your precious flag-girl, little man?" Derrick mocked.   "What if your little good-luck-charm, here, didn't exist?"

"If you hurt her, I'll kill you," Logan fumed.   "I promise you that."

Derrick's eyes narrowed.   He turned to face Logan while his gun clicked with the cock of the hammer.

I gasped.   "NO!"

"I've been racing since long before you came around," Derrick said to Logan, waving the gun in his face. "You don't make the fucking rules. I make the rules."

"*Stop!*" I shouted. I instinctively lunged forward but was held back by a strong arm wrapped around my torso from behind. I struggled to get it off me. I saw Gavin dive into Derrick from the side. The arm around my front jerked me backwards, causing me to fall back onto the ground. At the same time, an ear piercing popping sound vibrated in my ears. The man holding me cushioned my fall. "*No!*" I cried as my cheeks lined with tears. "*NO!!!*"

I heard metal scraping the sidewalk, and I knew it was the gun sliding across it. I escaped the grasp that was holding me and sat up to see Logan on top of Derrick, bashing his fist into Derrick's face over and over and over again while Gavin and Tommy tried unsuccessfully to pull him off. The left side of Logan's face and neck were covered in blood.

Derrick laid motionless on the ground while Logan continued to pound him.

"LOGAN, STOP!" I cried as I brought myself to a standing position.

With his fist raised, ready for another blow, Logan paused and immediately lifted his head to meet my gaze. His murderous expression instantly transformed into panic. He looked down at the face he had just mangled, then brought his bloody hands in front of him, focusing on them as if the sight of them had brought the reality of the act he had just been performing to life. He looked at me again, then removed himself from Derrick, and hurried toward me. His hands grasped my shoulders, pulling me into a tight embrace.

"Oh my God, Liv, are you okay?" He gently pushed me off him and began examining my face and body for any sign of injury. "I'm sorry. I'm so sorry."

My eyes focused on the side of his head where blood was pouring out of his earlobe. "Shit, you're bleeding!"

Logan turned his head, focusing his attention on something else. That's when I heard the faint sound of sirens in the distance.

"Someone called in the shot!" Gavin shouted. "We gotta get outta here!"

Logan tugged on my arm, "C'mon, we've gotta go."

"Wait!" I yanked my arm out of his grasp. "What about Derrick? Is he okay?"

I ran to where Derrick laid on the ground and gasped at the sight of his face, swollen and covered in blood. He moaned and turned himself to the side, spitting out teeth and blood. My hand covered my mouth as I stared at him, shocked and appalled.

Thank God. He's alive.

Tires screeched as our group drove off in their cars, making a run for it. The sirens grew louder, and I could see flashing red and blue lights reflect off the commercial warehouses in the distance. Logan gently took my shoulders and looked into my eyes, calming me with just one look the way only he could. "He'll be fine," he said, struggling to make his voice sound calm. "We can't say here. We have to go. Now."

I nodded. "Okay."

He took my hand and we dashed to his car. The moment our doors slammed shut, Logan started the engine and floored it.

"Put your seatbelt on!" Logan shouted once we were on the road.

I did as he said and not a second later, he pushed the little blue button on the steering wheel. My head whipped back, slamming into the headrest as we thrusted forward at unthinkable speeds. The engine screamed. My panic increased when a dead end closed in on us, but Logan spun the wheel just in time, stomping on the brakes while recklessly whirling to the right, onto another road. The car fishtailed wildly, and I grabbed at anything that would keep me steady. My hands settled on the dashboard and passenger door. Logan pressed on the gas and expertly steadied the vehicle back into his control.

I looked back, out the rear window, but all I saw was white smoke. No flashing lights. No sirens could be heard over the roar of the engine. No sign of police.

The car slowed just before we arrived at a busy city street. I breathed a sigh of relief as we blended with the moving traffic. We were safe. Still in a state of shock, my focus directed to the car beside me. A woman in her late twenties sat behind the wheel with a smile on her face as she looked into her rear-view mirror. Two young children in the backseat, a boy and a girl, both in booster seats, appeared to be singing a song.

I wondered about the woman. Had someone like her, who looked so well put together and *normal*, ever experienced anything like what I just had? Had her loved ones ever left her, either by choice, or death, or fate? Or did she come from a traditional suburban home with two loving parents? Did things like this ever happen to people like her?

As the car slowed to a stop in front of a red light, my attention turned to the hands that tightly gripped the steering wheel. The blood on them had already begun to dry, turning a crusty blackened red. My eyes traveled up to Logan's bloodstained face which was turned in my direction. His chest billowed with each breath, his worried eyes searching mine.

"Are you okay?" he asked.

There were no words to be said. Because in that moment, as Logan's eyes flooded with love and concern, I realized that "normal" was a concept that was open for interpretation. What happened tonight was a mistake. An anomaly. A break from our norm. And despite the circumstances, I was *still* exactly where I wanted to be. I gave him a reassuring smile and nodded.

"Are you hurt?" he continued.

"No, I'm fine," I replied. *Just completely freaked out.*

We arrived at his shop a few minutes later. At this late hour, it was closed. All the mechanics had left hours earlier, and we were thankful for that. The last thing we needed were questions. Once in the apartment, Logan threw his coat on the couch then went directly to the bathroom to wash his hands. I followed him in.

Looking down at his hands, he scrubbed vigorously, turning the lather a bright red. When he held them under the running water, the blood splashed against the white porcelain of the sink just before washing away, down the drain. His hands were clean now. Except for the few crimson scrapes and cuts that lined his knuckles.

My eyes focused on his ear at the same time that he finally took a look at himself in the mirror. Blood continued to trickle from the lobe. He turned his face to the side to get a better look.

"Ah, shit," he said under his breath.

"Do you have gauze?" I asked.

"Yeah, it's in there," he replied as he pointed to the linen closet behind us.

276

I took the package out and placed it on the sink. "Let me see," I said as I brought my hand to his cheek. A closer look revealed that the very tip of his earlobe was gone. "Oh my God, Logan, you need stitches!" I quickly ripped open the gauze packaging and pressed a piece of it on his ear, causing him to flinch and swipe the white cloth from me.

He examined the injury in the mirror. "Nah. It's fine."

"That's from the bullet, isn't it? He shot you. He could've shot you in the head!"

He didn't say anything. He just watched me, hesitantly, holding the gauze to his ear.

"He had a gun pointed at you, Logan. You could be dead right now." I dove into him, wrapping my arms around his waist. "Why did he do that? What's wrong with him?"

"I have no idea. He's a fucking psychopath." He sighed, "God, I'm so sorry. I damn near lost it when he pointed the gun at you. I was glad when he turned to me. If anything happened to you, Liv, I'd lose my mind. I came pretty damn close to losing it tonight."

"Well, I can't lose you either! And I'm tired of being scared that I might."

He pushed himself off me and took my shoulders, looking directly into my eyes. "I know. Which is why I'm done. After tonight—after seeing the look in your face—I'm not going to put either of us at risk anymore. I'm done racing. There are too many variables that come with it."

"But you love racing."

"No. I love you. Nothing else even comes close."

We stared at each other momentarily. Deep down, I knew he was only acting on impulse. There was no way he could quit something that was in his blood. He'd change his mind. I would

277

have to prepare myself for that. "I don't think you should decide that right now," I said, stepping toward the door. "You should get cleaned up. Take a long, hot shower. Sleep on it." I walked out of the bathroom.

"Liv," he said. I stopped and faced him. "Are you leaving?"

My heart sunk from the torment in his voice. He thought I was running again. I shook my head no. "Of course not. I'll be here when you're done."

He nodded. "Okay."

I collapsed on the couch a moment later, letting my head fall on the armrest. My attention diverted to the sound of water running through the pipes in the wall from the shower turning on. I closed my eyes only to see visions of Derrick being beaten to a bloody pulp.

Startled by the image, I tried to think of something else. I had no interest in watching TV or listening to music. I took the *Hot Rod* magazine off the coffee table and sifted through it. Before I knew it, I had paged through the entire thing without recalling anything from the pages.

I couldn't sit still, so I went to the kitchen. After searching the refrigerator and cupboards for something to eat, then realizing that I had no interest in eating either, I found myself eventually walking back to the bathroom.

I knocked gently on the door then cracked it open. "Can I come in?"

"Yeah," Logan replied from the other side of the shower curtain.

I leaned back on the countertop and crossed my arms. "Are they going to come after you?"

"Who?"

"The police. What if Derrick presses charges?"

He paused. "He won't."

"How can you be sure?"

"Because he'd be an idiot to do that."

"You said he's a psychopath. Psychopaths are unpredictable."

The water turned off. I took the towel that hung on the rack above the toilet and handed it to Logan just as he opened the shower curtain. He dried his face and hair, then wrapped the towel around his waist. His eyes looked me up and down. "You're still wearing your coat."

My eyes narrowed. "Why are you worried about my coat?" My eyes gravitated to the crimson that still trickled out of his ear. I sighed as I took my coat off and hung it on the door handle. "C'mere. You're still bleeding."

I took another gauze package and ripped it open. I felt his concerned eyes on me as I gently placed the dressing on his ear.

His hand brushed the side of my face. His fingers combed my hair behind my ear. "Liv, look at me."

Slightly irritated, I did as he said and met his magnetic eyes.

"I promise you everything will be okay," he continued. "Nothing bad is going to happen."

It was what I needed to hear. The compassionate way he said it instantly calmed me down. I believed in him. Trusted him. I pressed my lips together in a tight smile. "Okay."

"I'm done, Liv. I don't need to sleep on it. I don't need to think about anything. And I don't need to race. But I do need you." He lifted me and sat me down on the countertop. "And I need you to understand that *you* are what makes me feel alive. Not cars. Not betting. Not racing."

"I just don't want you to give up anything for me."

He looked at me like I was a lunatic. "I'd give up everything for you."

Chapter Twenty-Nine

Life returned to normal considerably quicker than I had expected. Logan wanted me to stay that night, but I had a curfew to abide by, even though I had been eighteen for over a month. When I woke up alone in my bed the following morning, I almost believed I had dreamed-up the entire incident with Derrick. I even questioned whether or not it had really happened.

The only reminders of that night were Logan's injuries on his ear and knuckles, and the fact that he had been turning down races for the last two weeks. The injuries had healed substantially, but I still had a sinking feeling that he would resent me for the choice he made to stop racing.

Just as Logan promised, we hadn't heard a word from Derrick, and I was beginning to feel that we never would.

I sat at my kitchen table, viewing my various social media sites on my phone while my mother fixed breakfast and Jeff read the Sunday paper. Today would be a day of work. First cleaning the bar, then Frank's.

My phone chimed. It was a text from Logan.

Wanna grab breakfast before cleaning the pub? I have something to tell you.

I met him a half hour later at a small family diner on the strip. My mouth watered from the smell of bacon and pancakes as I walked through the door. He was already waiting at a window booth when I arrived. I took a seat across from him and grinned at the goofy smile on his face.

"Oh, so this must be good news," I teased as I removed my coat and set it beside me. "You had me worried for a second there."

"I think you worry too much." His eyes gleamed as he pointed to a mug on the table in front of me. "I got you some coffee. Black."

"Thank you."

We looked at our menus silently, but it only took us a minute to decide. We had been here a few times before and already knew our favorites. A middle-aged waitress approached and took our orders. An omelet for Logan and a blueberry waffle for me.

"Will that be all?" she asked with her full attention on Logan.

He looked at me, silently asking if I needed anything. I shook my head no.

His eyes fell on her nametag a split second before meeting her gaze with a smile. "We're good, Katie. Thank you."

Her face flushed a faint rose color before she nodded and scampered off to the kitchen.

I know the feeling, Katie.

With the bright morning sun shining through the window, his eyes practically glowed. Sometimes it was hard to see the amber in the middle of his iris, but today, it sparkled. I raised my coffee to my lips as I contemplated the colors beaming back at me.

"I love it when you stare at me like that." He smiled, leaning forward with this arms crossed on the table.

A half-cough, half-snort came out of me as I tried to swallow my coffee instead of spitting it out from laughing. I loved how he still flustered me. "I wasn't staring. Cut to the chase, Tanner," I teased, "What do you want to tell me anyway."

He laughed as he leaned back in his seat. "Oh, I'm Tanner to you now? I don't think you've ever called me that before. Come to think of it, no girl has ever called me that."

Grinning like a fool, I shrugged.

After a moment, his face became more serious. "I've been thinking a lot for the last two weeks. Ever since that night. I know that you have reservations about me giving up racing. And I know it's because, for some crazy reason, you think I'll resent you for it." He took my hand. "Which would never happen in a million years. I have no doubt that I could live without it if I needed to."

"But you don't need to. Especially not for me."

He hesitated. "The thing is, you're right. I do get a thrill from racing. I don't need it, but I enjoy it. And I also like rebuilding cars." He paused for a moment gauging my reaction.

My heart dropped to the pit of my stomach. "I know you do."

Something about the look in his eye made me feel strangely at ease, despite the words he had just spoken.

He squeezed my hand. "Just hear me out, okay?"

I nodded.

"I want to open an auto refurbishing business. I'm going to rebuild cars and sell them at auction. There are people who have no clue how to rebuild old cars who will pay a lot of money just to store one in their garage and drive it occasionally. I already spoke to my uncle about it, and he's on board. He's actually

283

thinking of moving the shop away from basic maintenance and into a full blown refurbishing operation."

"Logan, that's a great idea! It's perfect!"

"There's a legally-sanctioned drag-way about an hour from here. It'll be the perfect place to network for the business and race safely when I get the urge. It's completely legal. And safe."

A smile spread across my face. "Really?"

"Really." A look of pride came over him in reaction to my expression.

Still grinning, I scooted out of my seat and into his. My arms found their way around his middle, while my head rested on his shoulder. "That sounds perfect. Thank you."

He kissed the top of my head. "Working through the bullshit isn't that hard, is it?"

Chapter Thirty

Logan sat in the passenger seat of my car as we followed the U-Haul through a residential subdivision to his family's new home. My backseat and trunk were loaded with boxes. With all the renovations his mother and stepfather had done to Logan's childhood home, it didn't take long for them to get a good offer, even with the current real-estate market being less than ideal, and they had their eye on this new home before even putting theirs on the market. Everything fell into place for them perfectly.

I looked over at Logan, who had an annoyed expression on his face. He had helped his stepfather lift the heavy items into the U-Haul this morning, while I helped his mother and Lanie with the smaller boxes. He had been quiet the entire morning and was being a bit of a buzz-kill. As his elbow rested on the window, he leaned his head on his fist.

I reached for his free hand. "I'm proud of you, you know."

Unfazed, he continued to stare out the windshield. "You are, huh?"

I squeezed his hand. "Yes. I am. I know this isn't easy for you. You're doing the right thing, Logan. It means so much to them that you're helping today."

He huffed. "It still doesn't feel right."

"I know it doesn't."

"I don't think I ever told you this, but you know that week that we were apart?"

It had been two months since that week, but I would never forget it. "You mean the week from hell?"

He smiled. *Finally, a smile.* "Yeah, that week. I talked to my mom that week. She told me that nothing happened between her and Robert until months after my dad passed. She said what I saw was nothing more than a friend consoling a friend."

"Do you believe her?"

"I mean, they weren't making out or anything. But what I saw...the way they were holding onto each other...it didn't look very friendly. At all. Then, she married him so quickly. It was kinda hard to believe I guess." He paused for several moments, then turned his face toward me. "But then, when you said that you trusted me, despite what *you* saw...it made me reconsider."

"Oh, well, glad to be of service."

He laughed. "The thing is, I know I need to let it go. He's an okay guy, I guess. He's good to Lanie. I just can't seem to let it go."

I gave him a reassuring smile. "You'll get there, babe. Some things just take time."

His one eyebrow lifted up. "You know I love it when you call me that." He brought his face to my neck and started tickling me behind my ear with his tongue.

"Hey! I'm driving!" I giggled. "Stop it!"

I slammed on my brakes, noticing a little too late that the U-Haul had slowed down in front of me. Luckily, I didn't hit it.

"Geez, Liv, you're a crazy driver. You shoulda let me drive," Logan said with a smirk, knowing full well that it was his distraction that caused the near-collision. I responded to his comment with an eye-roll.

We waited in the middle of the road as the U-Haul backed into the driveway of the new home. It was a bit smaller than

Logan's old home but looked extremely well kept from the outside. I pulled into the driveway just as Jen, Robert, and Lanie stepped out of the U-Haul. They immediately went to the back of the truck to start unloading.

I turned the ignition off and reached for my door handle when I felt a tug on my right elbow.

"Hey," Logan said.

I turned to him, meeting his eyes, immediately melting. I hoped his looks would always have this effect on me. "Hey."

"Thank you."

Having no idea why he was thanking me, I looked at him like he was crazy. "For what?"

"For being here today. You make everything better."

I smiled from his words. "There's nowhere I'd rather be."

Our lips gently touched just before knocking on the window distracted us.

"Get a room, you guys!" Lanie said as she opened Logan's door. "Seriously!" She grabbed him by the hand and tugged, trying to get him out of the car. "You have got to see this! You're not going to believe it!"

Logan looked at me, confused, and shrugged.

"C'mon, Liv!" Lanie shouted.

We stepped out of the car and began walking down the driveway to the back of the U-Haul. Lanie quickly pulled Logan ahead while I trailed behind them. As the garage came into view from behind the truck, I noticed the overhead door was open, and Robert and Jen stood with their backs to us, with their arms around each other, staring at something inside.

As we approached, a sniffle came from Jen. *Was she crying?* Robert turned to her and kissed her forehead. Logan stopped next to his mother, and as the sight of whatever it was overtook him, he pulled Lanie close to him, wrapping his arm around her shoulder. His mother wrapped her arm around Logan's waist.

I walked up and stopped next to Lanie and finally saw what all the commotion was about. In the back of the garage, hanging on the wall between two studs, hung the same John Wayne movie poster that hung above the desk at Logan's shop. This one, however, was older, faded, and it looked like it had been here for years.

Logan turned to his mother. "Did you put that there?"

She faced him and shook her head to say no.

Logan looked back at the poster. "Holy shit."

Out of the corner of my eye, I noticed Lanie turn to me. Her hand took mine, pulling me close, then she wrapped her arm around my waist, as I put my arm around her shoulder. The five of us stood side by side, holding each other, taking in the scope of what that old, beat-up poster, actually represented. Logan turned to me, shocked.

No words needed to be said. I knew that for Logan, this was the validation he needed to move on. To let go of the resentment he had been holding on to for so long. It was a sign. Literally. His father was giving his blessing. Finally, Logan would have some peace.

I'm not sure how long we stood there before Lanie finally broke the silence. "Those boxes aren't going to carry themselves inside, you know."

Logan chuckled and messed up her hair. "I guess we better get to work then, boss."

Chapter Thirty-One

It had been raining for days. Most of the snow banks were melted down from the spring showers but a few still remained. Today was the first day in a while that the sun had peeked out, and I had been stuck inside Frank's, admiring the shining light from through the front glass doors. It was dark when my shift ended.

"See you tomorrow, Olivia." Stacy waved just before she opened her car door and slid into the driver's seat of her car.

"Bye, Stace." I waved and watched her drive out of the parking lot and into the flow of traffic.

I opened my car door and threw my purse on the passenger seat when I heard footsteps quickly approach and felt something hard jabbing my side.

"Close the door," a deep, unfamiliar voice husked before I had a chance to turn around to see who it was.

Was this some kind of joke? Confused, my head turned to see my assailant.

My breathing stopped. All the muscles in my body stiffened. Except for my heart, which banged wildly against my ribs. "Derrick."

A dark grey hood covered his head, shadowing his eyes. Looking down to see what was poking my side, my eyes widened. A hand-gun. "What are you doing? What do you want?"

He dug the gun further into my side. "Close the damn door and get in through the passenger side."

I did as he said, looking everywhere on my way to the other side of the car. Could I scream? Would he shoot me if I did? Would anyone even hear me? The parking lot was dimly lit, making it difficult for passersby to witness anything from the road. I slid into the passenger seat then scooted over to the driver's side as Derrick slipped in behind me.

We both buckled our seatbelts just before I started the car. I placed both hands on the steering wheel and glanced over at Derrick who still had the gun pointed at me. "What is this about? What do you want?"

With the phone in his other hand, he clicked a picture of me. "Drive. I'll tell you where to go."

"Did you just take my picture? Derrick, tell me what you want."

His initial response was only a look. It was a look I had never seen on anyone before. Ever. It was a wide-eyed mixture of fury and psycho. He pressed the gun into my side so hard that it would definitely leave a bruise. In an overly calm, yet wicked voice, he responded, "I. Want. You. To. Drive."

I suddenly became incredibly aware of what was happening. The look in his eye had spooked me even more so than the gun, if that was even possible. My breathing became shallow as my body tensed. Every nerve ending in my body went on high alert.

I followed his direction and drove onto the road. As I continued to drive, following his orders to turn here and turn there, I noticed him tapping on his phone. My eyes moved from the road, down to the gun, and up to Derrick's unsympathetic eyes.

"Eyes on the road," he instructed.

With my eyes wide, I did as he said and kept them on the traffic. What was he going to do with me?

"You're little boyfriend should be opening up a text with your picture as we speak. I'm calling that little fucker out. He's not gonna say no this time."

After what seemed like forever, we arrived at an empty industrial park that I had never been to before. Warehouses surrounded us. Derrick had me park next to another car in a parking lot of one of the buildings.

The same woman who had been with him at my very first race, stepped out of the parked car and waited. She appeared nervous and worried. The ends of her brown straggly hair met the tops of her shoulders.

"Get out," Derrick ordered me, then followed me out the driver's side door. He faced the woman. "Is the car ready?"

"Yeah, baby," she said as she approached us. "Camcorder too. Everyone's gonna see what you can do."

"Damn right, they are." Then he turned to me and started shaking the gun at me as if he were using it as a pointer finger. "The only reason your little boyfriend won't race me is cuz he knows I'll win and he don't wanna pay-up. Well, he's gonna pay up today when I win, fair and square."

All I could think about was the gun going off. What if he shook it so hard he accidentally pulled the trigger? I could see his eyes now under the halogen light attached to the industrial building where our cars were parked. They were glossy. Bloodshot. Was he high? Or just crazy?

Nobody had heard from Derrick in months. He probably had no idea that Logan was out of the street racing circles.

"Logan doesn't race *anyone* anymore," I blurted out, instantly regretting it.

291

Derrick looked at me with hatred. "Do you think I'm an idiot?"

My mouth snapped shut. I shook my head no, vigorously. There was no room for tears. Too much adrenaline coursed through my system for tears. Instead, I was acutely aware of everything. The drip of water falling off the roof of the building beside us and onto the puddle below. The hum of the light on the concrete wall. The constant sniff from Derrick's nose. The mist of our breaths in the cool air. But mostly, my attention focused on the darkness of the barrel of the gun pointed at me.

Then, a rumble.

"He's here," Derrick said, handing the gun to the woman. "You know what to do."

The gun shook in the woman's hand as she trembled, and he looked at her with concern. He stood behind her and surrounded her hand with his, helping her point the gun at me.

"Like this," he said firmly, visibly calming her nerves. "Like we practiced. You're a natural born shooter, Amber, don't you forget it." He placed his other hand on her stomach. "We're not doing this for just us, remember? How are we gonna support a baby if I can't race?"

I wanted to say something smart and clever, like they do in the movies, to get myself out of this situation. Something like, *you don't have to do this, it's not too late*. Or *you've got so many other options*. But nothing came out. What if I said the wrong thing? What if they simply didn't like what I had to say?

Amber nodded, recovering her confidence. "You're right, babe. Our baby girl deserves the best. And everyone deserves to know that *you're* the best."

She turned her head to the side to face him, but he grabbed her head with both hands, forcing her to face me. "Don't you ever take your fucking eyes off her, you understand me?"

She nodded eagerly. "Yeah, baby. You can count on me, I promise. I won't make that mistake again."

"If anything goes wrong. You shoot. Do NOT hesitate. Don't think. Just act. Do you understand?"

"Yeah, baby."

"Good. Now follow me to the edge of the building and wait for my signal."

The rumble got louder as Logan's car approached, but I couldn't see him because the building was in the way. Derrick darted in front of us and turned the corner while we waited behind the wall at the edge of the building. The growl of Logan's engine silenced as he turned off the car.

I heard a car door open and slam shut.

"Where is she?!" I heard Logan shout.

"You'll get her after the race, you little fuck," Derrick replied. I heard some shuffling and what sounded like a body being slammed against a metal door or a metal car hood. "Whoa, take it easy, son," Derrick continued. "You wouldn't want anything to happen to your precious flag girl." There was a silent moment. "Yeah, that's what I thought. Get in your car. Your little good luck charm will flag the race so everyone can see it's fair. Yeah, that's right. We all know you can't do shit without her flagging."

The gun pushed harder into my back as a car door opened and closed again.

"Bring her out!" Derrick called.

Amber nudged me with the gun as she kept a tight grasp on my shoulder. "Move. Now."

We turned the corner, and my heart jumped at the sight of the Mustang. It was parked next to Derrick's car in the middle of the road. Seeing Logan's car, and knowing he was here for me, set off a chain of reactions in my body, like I could release what I had been holding back. My eyes began to swell, my cheeks burned, and I began to breathe heavily. Something about him being here was giving my body permission to break down.

But I couldn't let myself fall apart now. I had to be strong. Brave. I needed make smart choices, and even though my heart pounded hard in my chest, choosing to break down right now would be the worst possible decision.

We stayed close to the building, and I wondered why Amber hadn't walked me directly to the cars. Then, she stopped me. "I can't go any further, baby. The camera will see me!"

Derrick stood in between the two cars. "Good. Turn the laser on."

I heard some clicking behind me. "It's on, baby!" Amber shouted.

He nodded. "Now walk over here…*Sweetheart*."

She shoved me forward. "That means you, bitch."

I did as they said and started toward Derrick. Walking between the cars from behind, I saw that Logan's car window was wide open. Absolute fury seeped out of every pore of his body. His face was a dark shade of red. I had never seen him so angry before. Our eyes met as I walked past him, and his expression became more determined.

"Get over here, lover-girl. You've got a job to do," Derrick commanded.

He took me and turned me around so that I faced the cars, while his hand stayed firmly on my shoulders as he stood behind me.

"Look down, sweetheart," he whispered in my ear. His breath smelled like death and cigarettes. I followed his order and looked down at the ground, but a bright red dot of light on my shirt immediately caught my attention. "That's our insurance policy that you—and your boyfriend here—aren't going to try anything stupid." He spoke louder now, so that Logan could hear. "My girl's been instructed to shoot if either of you make any wrong moves. You got it?"

My eyes locked with Logan's. We both nodded.

"Good," he continued. "There's a camera here." He pointed to the sidewalk, a few yards in front of the cars. "And another one at the finish line. Everyone's gonna see that the only reason you won't race me is cuz you know I'll win and ruin your precious reputation." He pointed at Logan. "Now start your fucking engine."

Logan immediately brought his car to life. The loud roar sent a surge of thrill through me. Derrick removed his hands from me and out of the corner of my eye, I saw him walk to his car. A second later, he started his own engine.

Logan mouthed, *"Are you okay?"*

I didn't know what I was. I had been doing everything I could to stay calm. So I guess I was calm. Calm is what I needed to be. I nodded in response. His gaze left mine and moved to my chest: to the red dot. His jaw clenched and a pained expression came over him just before his eyes returned to mine.

My face began to crunch up slightly as the enormous rock in my throat pushed against all my senses, trying to force out a sob. My entire body trembled. I closed my eyes and took a calming breath, pulling myself together. I needed to stay calm.

When I opened them, I looked to Derrick on my right. His evil face nodded that he was ready. I turned my head to Logan's beautiful, determined gaze on my left. He gave a nod as well, but included a small reassuring smile. His gesture showed me that he, too, was ready. And that everything would be okay.

Engines revved as I lifted my hands above my head. I closed my eyes and breathed deep. Then forced my hands down.

The high pitched roars of both cars vibrated in my chest, and the smell of exhaust was released in the air. I quickly turned around and opened my eyes to watch. I couldn't tell who was winning for sure, but it looked like Logan. Almost simultaneously, both cars boosted forward from the nitrous.

Suddenly, the blue Honda Civic started fishtailing and screeching. The back end moved side to side, only slightly at first, but each swing became more erratic until it was completely out of control. The back end of the Civic whirled to the side. The front of it jetted forward, directly into the back side of Logan's Mustang.

I stopped breathing. All the hairs on my body stood on end.

The Civic did a full circle turn. Flying wildly, the passenger side of it smashed into a light pole. The pole acted as a severing mechanism, completely breaking Derrick's car in two, just before crashing to the ground.

Holy shit!

The Mustang screeched as it swung to the side then began to roll over. Glass shattered. It rolled over again. Metal crunched. And again, it rolled. The cars were far away now, but the noise of the crashing seemed to be right in front of me, like nails on a chalkboard.

"No!" My mind screamed it, but the word came out in only a whisper. My hand covered my mouth as the Mustang rolled one more time, then tipped on its side slightly, before it bounced back on its wheels. "Oh my God."

I was running now. All was silent except for the panting of my breath and my feet stomping on the pavement. The cold air blew into my wide eyes as I ran, pricking them, causing tears to flow out the far edges of them.

I vaguely noticed the screaming cries of terror from Amber behind me, but it was constant. I continued to push forward, but everything was happening in slow motion now, and I wasn't getting close enough, fast enough. My blurry eyes didn't leave the flattened version of Logan's car for a second. And there was no movement coming from the inside of it.

Please come out. Please come out. Please be okay.

I was closer now, almost there. Were those footsteps behind me?

A gunshot sounded just before I was stung by something sharp on my left bicep. I stumbled but couldn't keep on my feet. I tried to put my arms out to catch my fall but only one of them worked. Something snapped in my fingers when they hit the concrete, just before my face followed.

I remembered Derrick's last words to Amber. *Don't think. Just act.* She had followed his orders and my arm now had a bullet in it as a result.

In a state of shock, I laid with my forehead on the pavement for several moments, as the burning in my bicep increased to a level beyond tolerance. My fingers throbbed and my head pounded. Something warm and wet was flowing out of my nose and my arm. Somehow, I managed to push myself onto my side, on the arm that didn't burn, but I couldn't lift my head off the pavement.

I looked at Logan's car again, searching for any possible tiny movement, but there was none. I waited, never taking my eyes off it. Then, I waited some more.

"Please come out," I whispered, trying to move my body to get to Logan. But it wouldn't move. *"Please*, Logan, come out."

You can't leave me. You promised.

My breathing shallowed. The pain became too much to bear. The edges of my vision started to blacken, closing in to the center of my focal point—Logan's car. As much as I tried to fight it, the darkness slowly overtook my vision until it was completely black.

Chapter Thirty-Two

A white flashlight shined into my pulled-open eye, causing me to squint. The other lid was propped open next, with the light shining into my pupil. As the bed I laid in bumped upward, I heard the shuffling of supplies in the cabinet walls all around me.

"What's your name, dear?" a woman asked from behind me. She seemed so far away. I continued to squint as I pried my eyes open a slit. Everything was blurry, and my head spun. I kept them open just long enough to realize I was in a moving ambulance. A man in uniform sat on the bench next to me and propped me to my side just before putting his hands on my exposed arm. He applied pressure to the back and front of it and laid me back down, keeping his hands on the wounds. The pain from his touch nauseated me.

"It's a through and through GSW. She's lost a lot of blood," the man's voice said.

I squinted my eyes open again. The man hung a bag of clear liquid on the hook above me. It was too bright in here. My head couldn't take the light, so I gave up trying to see what was happening and decided to keep my eyes closed. Something poked the vein in my arm, on the inside bend.

I couldn't shake the dizziness. My entire body began to quiver. Why was it so cold in here?

Where's Logan? I tried to say it, but it came out as nothing more than a weak groan. I tried again, but nothing came out.

The woman pressed a bandage on my head. Then, I felt myself slipping away.

"Try to stay awake, hon," the woman's voice echoed in the distance. But I was tired. Everything hurt. I needed to sleep.

Chapter Thirty-Three

"They think one of the cars hit black ice," I heard a man mumble. It sounded like Jeff. "The other driver is dead."

It felt like a vice grip was squeezing my head. I laid motionless, unable to open my eyes right away.

"Oh my God, if I had any idea she was involved in…" My mother didn't finish. Instead, she began to weep. I imagined Jeff holding her. Consoling her.

The room smelled sterile, like hospitals do. When I finally opened my eyes, a whimper came out of my throat. My tongue felt swollen from the dryness of it. I smacked it against the roof of my mouth a few times trying to moisten it.

"Livie?" My mother immediately rushed to my side and took my hand. "Livie? It's Mommy. Are you awake?"

Mommy?…Really?

My voice came out as a whisper. "I'm not a five-year-old, Mother."

A relieved half-laugh, half-sob, came out of her. She sniffed. "I know that, sweetie."

My head pounded, and it was itchy. I moved my right hand toward my forehead but something pulled from the inside of my arm.

"Be careful, Livie. You don't want to pull that IV out," Jeff warned.

My hand rested back down on the bed, beside my thigh. It was then that I realized the middle and ring fingers of my right hand were taped together in a finger cast. I looked to my left arm which had also been taped up, and held in a sling.

"Do you remember what happened, sweetheart?" my mother asked. "You've been out all day."

I remembered waking up briefly as I was wheeled into the ER and the chaos of people talking and prodding at me, just before I lost consciousness. I remembered the ambulance. I remembered the pavement digging into my forehead as I watched for any sign of…

Logan!

"Where's Logan, Mom?" My voice was stronger now but still not at a solid decibel. "Is he okay? Where is he?"

"Shhh, you need to worry about you right now, Livie." She gently rubbed my good arm.

With all my strength, I slowly forced my body to a more upright position. My movement was sloppy, and it gave me a massive head rush. I didn't care. If she wouldn't tell me, I'd find out for myself.

"Olivia, stop it right now. You are not getting out of this bed."

"Then tell me where he is." My voice quivered as the tears began to flow. I was too weak to try to hold them back. A million thoughts of what could've happened to him ran through my mind, and most of them scared the living hell out of me.

She and Jeff exchanged a concerned glance. Jeff nodded to her, and she sighed. "He's in the ICU, sweetie. He banged his head really badly, and they had to operate to relieve the pressure. And he's got some cracked ribs. He lost a lot of blood…just like you." Her eyes moistened, and her face distorted as if she were about to break down.

302

Jeff stepped in for her. "He's been unconscious. At first, they kept him sedated, but he's been weaned off the sedation since the swelling went down. They just have to wait to see if…I mean, when…he'll wake up. You two were out there a long time before that girl called anybody…"

"Who are those *people*?" my mother interrupted. "What are you involved in?"

Jeff placed his hand on her shoulder. "Grace, not now. Now's not the time."

My mother and Jeff exchanged a few words, but I have no idea what they were saying. All I could think about was Logan's broken body.

He must be in so much pain.

"Mom, I'm going to ask for your help right now." I interrupted the two of them, and they both turned their heads to face me. "And I need you to say yes, no matter how much you want to say no."

She met my eyes and nodded.

"I need to see him."

Her lips pressed together in a compassionate smile, but her eyes were pure worry. She hesitated for several long seconds before saying anything. "Alright, sweetheart."

"I'll go get a wheelchair." Jeff squeezed my mother's shoulder and walked out of the room.

*

The elevator bell chimed as the door opened. My mother pushed me through it and onto the carpeted hallway, towards the ICU. Jeff had persuaded my nurse to cap my IV until I returned to my room. After a check of my vitals, she agreed. Satisfied that he had been able to help, he decided to stay behind, saying he had errands to run.

We approached a waiting area where we saw Robert sitting in one of the chairs, reading a magazine.

"Mom, that's Logan's stepdad," I said.

She wheeled me to where he was sitting. He lifted his head as we approached. "Liv." His eyes moved to my mother behind me, and he stood to greet her. "Grace. Good to see you."

"Hello, Robert," my mother replied.

"You know each other?" I asked.

My mother put her hand on my good shoulder. "We met last night in the ER. When the police questioned us about…what happened."

"How is he?" I asked Robert. "Can I see him?"

Robert nodded. "Jen is in there with him now. He hasn't woken up yet. I'll show you which room he's in."

We followed him all the way down the hall, stopping at near the nurse's station. Robert knocked on the door.

"Only two visitors in the room at a time," a nurse said from behind the desk.

"Yes," Robert replied, irritated. "We're aware of your rules."

"It's for the good of the patient, sir."

The door opened with Jen behind it. When she looked down at me, she attempted a smile. "Liv, I'm so glad you're okay. I'll help you in."

Jen began to walk around me to push me in, but I didn't want Logan to see me like this. Helpless.

"Wait!" I said. "I can walk in. I want…"

"Not a chance, Olivia," my mother interrupted.

"Mom, my legs are fine. I'm walking in there. I'm sorry, but you'll just have to deal with it."

After a few more argumentative comments and some exaggerated sighs, she agreed. With the help of Jen and my mother, I slowly forced myself to a standing position, trying intently to hide my dizziness from them. Jen held my good arm by the elbow and walked in with me.

It took everything I had not to completely break down at the sight of him. But it wasn't because his face was completely swollen or bruised, as I had expected. And it wasn't because he was being kept alive by a ventilator tube coming out of his throat.

In fact, I almost broke down because, in contrast to my fears, none of those things were there. Actually, except for the gauze wrapped around his head, he kind of looked okay. Like he was sleeping.

But he wasn't asleep.

With one hand still on my arm, Jen pulled a chair close to the bed and motioned for me to sit down.

"He had a subdural hematoma," she informed me. "They did a burr hole procedure to drain the blood. His swelling went down pretty quickly, so they took him off sedation around lunch time today." She looked at him, concerned. "He should be waking up. I don't know why he's not waking up."

"How long will it take?"

"They can't say. Brain injuries are unpredictable. All we can do is wait." She paused for a moment and looked at her son. "You can hold his hand. But his ribs are cracked, so be careful by his chest."

I nodded. "Okay."

She looked at me with as much compassion as she could give under the circumstances. "The neurosurgeon said it's good to talk to him. There's a chance he can hear you...even if he can't respond." Her voice cracked with those last words, but she quickly pulled herself together. "He'll wake up. He has to." She looked at him, then back at me. "If you think you'll be okay in here alone, I'll give you two sometime together."

I nodded. "Thank you so much, Jen."

She pulled the nurse call button from the end table and rested it next to Logan's hand. "If anything happens, or if you need anything, push this button. I'll be back in a few minutes."

With that, she left the room, closing the door gently behind her.

I stared at him for several long moments, not knowing exactly what to say or do. Normally, if he were in bed sleeping, I would crawl up next to him, wrapping my legs around his and squeezing my arms around his body. With his current condition, however, doing something like that would hurt him.

I tried to take his hand but fumbled when my finger cast got in the way. I settled on placing my palm over his hand and locking my thumb with his. His chest rose up and down with each breath. The look of peace on his face mesmerized me, and I couldn't stop watching him, hoping for any hint that he might actually know that I'm here with him.

"I'm here, babe," I said gently. "I'm okay. They didn't hurt me."

No reaction. Nothing.

My eyes began to sting as I continued to wait for the slightest twitch or movement. Suddenly, the undesirable idea that he may *never* respond came to the forefront of my mind. I quickly shoved that thought away. Losing him was not an option I was willing to entertain.

After several minutes of analyzing his motionless face, I finally spoke. "You changed my life, do you know that?"

I waited, but still, nothing.

Please wake up.

"I had no idea that unconditional love actually existed until I met you, Logan. I never believed that any two people could actually be *meant* for each other…" I hesitated for a second, unsuccessfully trying to hold myself together as I finished, "…like we are."

I removed my hand from his to wipe my eyes, and I inhaled deeply to settle my nerves. I took another look at his still, spiritless face. I needed to be closer to him. Grabbing the bedrail, I pulled myself to a standing position and closed my eyes, waiting for the dizziness to cease. Finally, it did, even though my head continued to pound.

Leaning with my hip on the bedrail, I brought my hand to his face and caressed his cheek with my thumb. "You woke me up, babe. When I was so numb to everything, you woke me up. You make me feel things…wonderful things that I never knew existed. You made me believe that love can withstand anything, and that we can have a future together. You made me believe in us. You're always calling me an angel, but you're the angel, not me. It's always been you."

Still, no reaction.

Frustration crept into my system. Even though it was irrational to feel that way, I was mad that he wasn't reacting to me.

"So you can't leave me now. It's too late. You have no choice. You're stuck with me. You made a promise to me,

Logan. You said you'd never leave me, so you need to be strong now." My voice cracked. "Because I can't picture my future without you in it anymore. When I try, it's just…it's..." I tried to stay in control, but tears leaked out of my eyes. "I just can't picture it, okay? I don't want to. Keep your promise to me. You have to, babe, there's no other option. Please."

When his face continued to remain motionless, and my head began to pound so hard that I thought I might pass out, I sat back down and locked thumbs with him. My head found a place on the bed, beside our hands, where it rested until I felt myself slipping into my dreams. Dreams of us. Together. Happy.

Jen woke me after a while and persuaded me to return to my room. I only agreed to leave Logan's side when Jen told me that Lanie wanted to see him, and even then, I only stayed away for a half hour. When I returned to my room for that brief amount of time, a police officer was waiting to question me. With nothing to hide, I gave him all the details of what had happened.

According to the rules of the ICU, only family members could stay overnight, which meant I was forced out of his room and into mine for the night. Jen promised I would be the first to know if there were any changes. Even though I wanted to stay awake to hear any news about Logan, sleep took me over the minute my head laid on the pillow of my hospital bed.

I awoke at dawn, to an empty room, feeling ten times better than the day before. The nausea and dizziness was still there but barely. I slowly rose to a sitting position and tied the back of my gown while my head rush dissipated. Regardless of how long it would take me to walk myself to Logan's room, I was intent on doing so. The halls were empty for the most part, and I stayed to the side, by the wooden wall rail.

When I reached his room, I knocked quietly. After listening for an answer, I opened the door and peeked in. Except for Logan, the room was empty. Jen must've needed a break. I walked to his bed and watched him for several minutes. Nothing in his face had changed since yesterday. It was still blank. I already missed his smile. His eyes.

I leaned down and pressed my lips gently on his forehead, letting them linger for a moment.

"I love you so much, Logan," I whispered. "Please wake up."

When he didn't respond, I sat down in the chair beside the bed and took his hand. I lifted it, gently kissing each fingertip.

"Mmm," he moaned.

He made a noise!

I lifted my head and searched his face, which was still blank. "Logan?"

His eyebrows moved slightly.

My eyes widened, and I stood to get a better look at him. "Logan? It's morning, baby. Time to get up."

He tried to breathe in deeply but stopped half-way through the breath, pulling his brows together. "Ow," he whispered.

A half-laugh, half-sob came out of me. "Careful, babe, your ribs are a little cracked."

It took a few moments for him to open his eyes. When he did, his head turned to face me. "You're okay."

The corners of my mouth turned up. "I am now."

Chapter Thirty-Four

Screams from the rides and the low pound of music thudding in the distance brought on a feeling of déjà vu. A smile formed on my face from the thought of being right here, exactly one year ago. I locked my arm around Logan's as we walked through the grass to the lively festival.

Logan had almost fully recovered, except for a slight delay in reflex, which only he and I noticed. According to the doctor, there was a possibility that it would go away in time.

By law, he hadn't been able to drive since his head injury. Since he hadn't had any seizures, however, he could re-apply for his driver's license next month.

We were lucky. Something changes when you defy death. Life looks different. Brighter. You appreciate every passing moment, and you stop worrying about the future. *"What if"* had officially been wiped from my vocabulary.

We had decided to move in together right after I graduated high school. Aside from the few growing pains of getting used to living with a man, our relationship was stronger than ever. I could deal with soaked, dirty dish rags left in the sink and greasy fingerprints on the door jambs, as long as I had him.

Hand in hand, we approached the beer tent, where Mel, Nat, Isaac, and Jess waited for us.

"Isn't this the same band that played last year?" I asked.

"You remember them, huh?" Logan replied.

"I remember everything about that night."

"All I remember from that night was your smile. I knew I was in trouble the second you looked at me," he grinned.

"Trouble? *I'm* trouble?"

He laughed. "Maybe we're both trouble. But together, we work."

The bouncer was someone I had never seen, but apparently, he knew Logan. They exchanged head nods as we passed him and entered the tent.

I spotted our friends on the dance floor and began to pull Logan towards them when he tugged me back. Confused, I turned to face him.

"I'll meet you out there," he shouted over the music.

"Okay."

We parted and I headed to the dance area. When Mel saw me, she grabbed my hand and pulled me into their circle where we rocked out to the music.

When the song ended, the lead singer of the band spoke into the microphone. "We don't normally do anything like this, but we've got a special guest here tonight."

Someone in the crowd whistled.

The singer continued, "Liv Evans, will you come to the stage, please?"

My heart stopped. *What did he say?* Shocked and a little confused, I turned to Mel to see if she heard what I heard.

She nodded and pointed to the stage. "Go!"

My heart restarted and began pounding viciously in my chest cavity. I sternly shook my head at Mel. "No!"

A familiar voice came over the speakers. "C'mon, babe. I promise I won't make you sing."

My head slowly turned to the stage where Logan stood with a sly grin, holding the microphone in his hand.

I still couldn't move. Hands on my back pushed me forward until my legs started to work on their own. Once I reached the stage, Logan reached down and took my hand, helping me up. Shocked and confused, my eyes scanned the crowd, where they found Melody smiling from ear to ear. Then I focused my gaze at Logan. He looked nervous. His hand stayed gripped to mine, while his other hand held the microphone.

Then, he spoke. "Liv, we met right here in this tent exactly one year ago today. I knew the moment I saw you that my life would change, but at the time, I had no idea how much it would, or why. All I knew then was that I needed to get to know the person behind that magnetic smile. And what I found was a strong, intelligent woman who makes me feel more alive than I've ever felt in my life."

He let go of my hand and reached into his front jean pocket. What he did next completely blew me away.

Taking a little black box out of his pocket, he kneeled on the stage. Gasps and whistles sounded from the audience, along with a few "Woo-hoo!" exclamations. He opened the box, revealing a ring which sparkled in heavenly ways against the stage lights. My hand trembled on its way up to cover my open mouth.

"I love you, Olivia Evans. I love the way you make me better. I love your strength, your spunk, your weird humor. I love the way your voice gets twangy when you sing along to country songs, and how it gets all ghetto when you try to rap. I love your smile, and I promise to make you smile every day. Forever. If you will let me. Liv, will you..."

"Yes!" I shouted as I crouched down and wrapped my arms around his neck, causing him to drop the microphone. "Yes! Yes!"

I vaguely noticed the crowd applauding as I kissed Logan repeatedly on the cheek and neck.

"You didn't even hear what I was going to ask," he whispered in my ear. "I was gonna say, will you get me a beer because I'm getting pretty thirsty up here."

I laughed through my sobs. "Shut up, you dork."

He chuckled and moved his face in front of mine. "Just so we're on the same page here, will you make me the happiest man in the world and marry me?"

My smile took over my face. "Yes, Logan. Nothing would make me happier. I love you too."

Dear Reader,

Thank you for reading The Fine Line! If you enjoyed it, please consider telling your friends about it, and/or leaving a short review on Goodreads, Amazon, Barnes and Noble, or anywhere else you'd like. Word of mouth is an author's best friend!

Thank you!
Alicia Kobishop

Feel like some questions were left unanswered from The Fine Line? In The Fragile Line, it'll all be laid out in detail from the one person who knows exactly what happened "that night." But that's only a small part of this story...

Available on Amazon:
http://www.amazon.com/gp/product/B01BA1H474

Add it to your Goodreads TBR here:
https://www.goodreads.com/book/show/26593982-the-fragile-line

Acknowledgements

To my inspiration, my muse, my source of constant encouragement. To the person who took care of the kids and the house even after a hard day's work so that I could have the time to create a fictional world. To the man who has loved me, unconditionally, since the day we met. Don, your infinite love and support mean the world to me. Thank you for being my very first reader and for loving my writing even when I thought it was less than ideal. I could not have completed this book without you.

To my children. Thank you for your patience when Mommy started writing and didn't have so much time to have the kind of fun you like to have with me. I promise that no matter what, you will always be my first priority, and I will never stop being a fun Mom.

To my mother Linda for being my first female reader, for giving me your honest feedback, and for reminding me how much I loved to write even way back in the fifth grade.

To my father Don for helping however, wherever, and whenever needed, and for loving my book even though contemporary romance is not exactly your "cup of tea."

To my brother Mike for your enthusiasm and for promoting me as an author long before this book was ever completed.

To my first readers. Linda Hirthe, Penny Diehn, Andi Larson, and Arlene Katka. Your thoughts and enthusiasm made be believe that maybe I could live out this crazy dream of writing a real novel.

To Angela Barber Farley, my editor and friend. Your expertise and guidance brought life to my "attempt" at a novel. Your feedback was invaluable.

To the self-published authors who came before me. Thank you for clearing the road for the rest of us.

To Officer Rodney Nelson for cluing me in on street racing and reckless driving laws & penalties in our neck of the woods.

To Michele Nickels, ND. The opportunities you gave me, and your belief in my ability to overcome certain challenges, have helped to shape me into the person I am today. I honestly do not think I would have the confidence to follow my dreams without my experiences at IFWC. Thank you for a remarkable five years.

To Jen McCommons, PA, for your medical expertise.

To Jon Russell for your mechanical expertise.

To Tenley Pipp for taking beautiful photos.

To Pop for giving us your blessing.

To the people who reminded me of the important things in life: John Crippen, Jr., Bryon Beatka, Kim Saxe, and Erin Ziemendorf. You will each have a special place in my heart. Always.

To all the book bloggers, reviewers, and supporters. You are the reason people other than my family have read this book. THANK YOU!

To all my family and friends who have helped to promote and support my dream of becoming an author. I am incredibly blessed to have you all in my life!

About the Author
Alicia Kobishop

Alicia Kobishop is a contemporary romance writer who lives in Milwaukee, WI, USA with her husband and two children. Before trying her hand in writing, she worked her way up in the field of administrative healthcare with experiences ranging from working within a large local healthcare organization, to smaller independent physician practices.
In early 2013 her life took a change of course when she re-evaluated her passions in life, and sought out to try many new things. She reclaimed her childhood passion for reading, and after reading tons of fictional novels in a short amount of time, and loving every moment of it, she became absorbed with the idea of taking her experience with books to the next level, and decided to write one. Nine months later, her debut novel, The Fine Line was published.

Alicia loves connecting with readers. Feel free to reach out to her through email or social media.

Get writing updates, news about upcoming releases, and sign up to follow her blog here:

<u>Website/Blog</u>
http://aliciakobishop.com/

Find out which books Alicia is reading here:

<u>Goodreads</u>
https://www.goodreads.com/author/show/7353109.Alicia_Kobis
hop

Connect with Alicia on social media:

<u>Facebook</u>
https://www.facebook.com/AuthorAliciaKobishop

<u>Twitter</u>
https://twitter.com/aliciakobishop

<u>Instagram</u>
https://www.instagram.com/aliciakobishop/

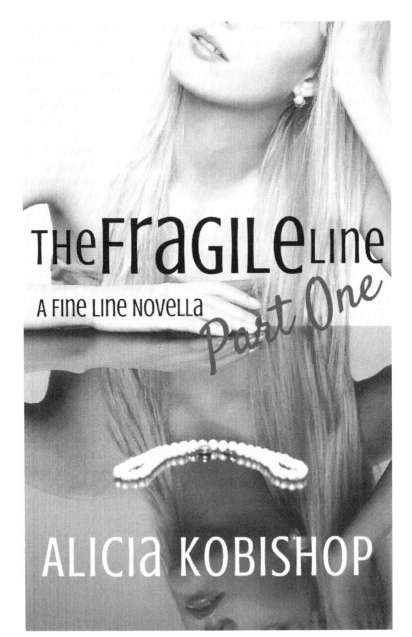

THE FRAGILE LINE

A FINE LINE NOVELLA

Part One

ALICIA KOBISHOP

The Fragile Line: Part One

Chloe McCarthy thought she had found the perfect guy. Someone just as detached as she was when it came to love and commitment. Someone who never pressured her for more than just sex. But when she gets a little too comfortable with their arrangement, and he rejects her for someone else, it triggers heartbreaking memories that leave her questioning her resolve for a commitment-free life. In a moment of self-pity, she calls on the one person who she knows will make her smile.

Matt Langston lives a drama-free life, and he wants to keep it that way. Chloe McCarthy? *All* drama. Which is why he needs to stay away from her. A mechanic by day and bouncer by night, he tries to focus on work, but the more he tries, the more she creeps into his thoughts and his dreams, until he realizes that he needs to get her out of his system once and for all.

The Fragile Line is a spin-off to *The Fine Line*, told in an addicting three-part romance novella series, with each part building on the last. The series may be read alone, however, reading *The Fine Line* first will provide a further introduction to the characters which may enhance the overall reading experience.